The Crusader's Chronicle

A

Commissaire Pierre Rousseau

Mystery

Graham Bishop

The Vidocq Press

This print edition published 2017

by

The Vidocq Press

By the same author

Joker in the Pack

Le Mystère de Gornac
(in French)

Commissaire Pierre Rousseau Mysteries

Achilles' Helmet

The Athenian Connection

Return to the Parthenon

The Walking Man

The main Characters

Commissaire Pierre Rousseau – now based in Bordeaux and on attachment to the O.C.B.C.*

Detective Inspector Patrick Bruni - his junior partner.

Katja Kokoschka – architect, art expert living in Bordeaux

Marcel Bouvier - director of the architectural partnership in Bordeaux where Kokoschka works

Jean-Louis Deveau – second-hand book dealer and fence for illegally obtained manuscripts

Isabella Marquessa – gallery owner and former jewel thief; out for revenge on Giovanni Lucca

Detective Chief Inspector Antonia Antoniarchis - former academic and television presenter, joined the Greek art fraud squad to help protect Greece's heritage from illegal smuggling

Her junior is **Detective Inspector Eleni Tsikas**

Chief Superintendent Ioànnis Lýtras – Chief of Police in Athens

Kóstas Chatzidákis – restaurant owner: former resistance fighter against the rule of the Colonels

Giovanni Lucca - former leader of an Italian gang of tomb robbers *(tombaroli)*. Now deals in illegal export of works of artefacts with help of **Marco Platini**

George and **Mira Leontarakis** - Greek-Americans. Art dealers and collectors

Capitano Gino Frisoni - Chief of Police on Sardinia and attached to the CTPC**

Sir Geoffroi de Vinsauf – Crusader knight in Richard the Lionheart's forces taking part in the Third Crusade

   ***O.C.B.C. –** Office centrale de lutte contre les trafics des biens culturels – the French Art Fraud Squad

   ****CTPC** Carabinieri Tutela Patrimonio Culturale – the Italian Art Fraud Squad

Acknowledgement

The extract from Sir Geoffroi de Vinsauf's eyewitness account of the Third Crusade is reprinted from:

Chronicles of the Crusades, Bell and Dandy, London 1865

Cover photograph from same edition

Prologue

In the year of Our Lord 1192 King Richard, he of the Lion's Heart, summoned the knights and barons of Outremer to a Grand Council in the Great Hall of the castle in Acre. News of the treachery of King Philippe August of France and of his own brother Jean Sans Terre had reached him and Richard knew he must return to England and Normandy forthwith to defend his lands and save his throne. But he was required to perform one last task before he left the Holy Land.

In the vast chamber the company fell silent as King Richard rose to his feet. For a few moments he stood looking down at the assembled lords and knights.

"My Lords of Outremer, our work here is not done. In his wisdom Our Lord recalled to his bosom our dear cousin the Emperor Frederick, he known as Barbarossa, as he led his army on the arduous journey overland to join with us. Without him his forces could not complete the voyage and we were deprived of their valour and strength. Sadly, Jerusalem remains in the hands of the Infidel and lost to Christendom."

At King Richard's words a murmur of anger rose in the chamber followed by an uneasy silence as they waited for him to continue.

Although Jerusalem was still in Saracen hands, those present in the Great Hall could not fail to be conscious of the compassion shown by Salah al-Din when he retook the Holy City after the battle of Hattin only five years before.

Almost all those of Christian faith were allowed to leave the city unharmed.

Such generosity contrasted with the frenzied massacre of the Muslims and Jews which the leaders of the First Crusade inflicted on the hapless inhabitants of Jerusalem when the city first fell into Christian hands nearly a century before.

More recently, horrific scenes of the slaughter of thousands of Saracen prisoners together with their women and children on the orders of King Richard himself were seared in their memories from just two years before when the city of Acre had been recaptured from the Saracens.

Despite this, Salah al-Din had again shown compassion and generosity in the truce he concluded with Richard. The Christian lands of Outremer along the coast were to remain free from attack and Christian pilgrims would have access to the Holy Places in Jerusalem. Acre would be their new capital.

Now the lords and knights of Outremer looked to Richard to settle a long running dispute between them before he departed for England. Guy de Lusignan, King of Jerusalem, had led his forces to the disastrous defeat at Hattin and was captured by Salah al-Din. Jerusalem fell soon after. Later, Salah al-Din released him on condition he took no further part in the fighting, an oath he immediately broke. Now the barons of Outremer wanted rid of him and proposed one of their own number for the throne of the Kingdom of Jerusalem.

Richard broke into their thoughts and began speaking again.

"But now you know I must depart from this place to defend the lands and the rights granted to me by my ancestors. I am betrayed by my own brother Jean Sans Terre and by our erstwhile companion King Philippe Auguste of France."

Once more a growl of anger at such treachery spread through the chamber, which Richard quelled with a raise of his hand.

"But I require of you, My Lords, to safeguard what remains of our Christian Kingdom in this place.

"Salah al-Din has granted us right of access to our Holy City and freedom from attack. But there is a weakness here which must cease forthwith if the Kingdom of Jerusalem is to survive. You are divided in your loyalty to your king, Guy de Lusignan.

"Conrad de Montferrat, valiant defender of the city of Tyre, disputes the throne. Marriage to the Princess Isabella, daughter of our dearly missed cousin King Almaric, has given him claim and title."

Richard paused and looked slowly round at the assembled company. Every man felt the power of his gaze.

"This dispute between you must be settled without delay."

The lords nodded their agreement and again waited for him to continue.

"Thus, My Lords, I grant you one hour to decide which of Guy de Lusignan and Conrad de Montferrat will be your king."

A stunned silence greeted his words and the noble company watched as Richard turned abruptly on his heel and withdrew from the Great Hall.

In the ante-chamber Richard sat down heavily and accepted the draft of wine a squire offered him. He settled back into his chair and seemed to drift into a reverie, but his eyes opened again suddenly and alighted on one of the knights waiting in attendance.

"Sir Geoffroi de Vinsauf. Come before us."

The knight approached and knelt before his sovereign. Richard stretched out his hands to help him to his feet.

"Valiant Sir Geoffroi, I charge you with the task of assisting the lords and knights of the Kingdom of Jerusalem to reach their decision. But remember they have just one hour."

Sir Geoffroi bowed and left the ante-chamber. On the stroke of the hour Sir Geoffroi returned from the Great Hall.

"So Sir Geoffroi, what is the decision of the Lords of Outremer?"

"It is the wish of the noble company that Conrad de Montferrat be their king, Sire."

Wearily Richard rose from his seat and signalled to the heralds to announce his presence in the Great Hall. As he entered the noisesome discussions in the Hall ceased abruptly and the lords and knights turned to face him.

"I am informed of your decision, My Lords. Acclaim your sovereign Conrad de Montferrat."

The roar from the hall left no doubt as to their will.

"The mind of the company is clear. Guy de Lusignan, you must leave this place and accompany us as we leave for England. I grant you sovereignty over the island of Cyprus and charge you never to return to the Kingdom of Jerusalem on pain of death."

With that Richard left the hall with Guy de Lusignan at his side to prepare his own departure first to Cyprus and thence to England. In the ante-chamber again he called Sir Geoffroi de Vinsauf to his side.

"As you are aware we lost many of our ships on our way to this blessed land from the Kingdom of Sicily, Sir Geoffroi. Now I must leave in haste and cannot take all our faithful companions with us. Guy de Lusignan will accompany us to Cyprus from whence we must make all haste to England."

Richard reached out and placed his hand on the knight's shoulder.

"I charge you, my brave companion in arms, to lead the return home overland of those of our army able and willing to make the journey. I wish you Godspeed and a safe passage."

Richard turned away from him and was quickly surrounded by his closest advisors as he gave orders for their immediate departure.

Sir Geoffroi de Vinsauf felt the loneliness of leadership descend upon him.

Chapter 1

The car screeched round the corner out of the cathedral square into the pedestrianised *rue des Remparts* in Bordeaux. There were still a few people about at that early hour of the morning and a young couple strolling home arm in arm were forced to jump aside in fright as the car passed within inches of them and came to an abrupt halt, skidding slightly, in front of the entrance to the building.

The driver sprang out, leaving the car door hanging open, charged into the building and took the stairs two at a time up to the second landing. She paused, looking for flat number 7. Spotting it immediately, she strode across the landing and hammered on the door with both fists, shouting furiously.

"Come out, you bastard. I know you're in there. Open the door or I'll kick it in."

Her voice carried down into the street and a small crowd quickly gathered outside growing more excited as the shouting continued. They could hear raised voices coming from inside as the residents of the other flats tried to restrain the woman and drag her away from the door.

Somebody called the police and soon a patrol car arrived, lights flashing and siren going. Two patrol men stepped slowly out of the car, in no hurry to become involved in a domestic or a lovers' quarrel. They started up the stairway, but were nearly knocked off balance as the woman flew down the stairs forcing her way past them and out of the building before they realised what was happening.

The crowd outside scattered in haste as she gunned her car and wheeled it round in a tight circle. The door slammed shut in the violence of the turn and with squealing tyres the car sped down the street and out of sight round the far side of the cathedral. The two patrol men recovered quickly, ran for their car and executed the same screeching manoeuvre as they set off in pursuit in a puff of rear wheel smoke.

The crowd hesitated for a moment craning their necks to stare down the street at the retreating police car. As it disappeared they realised the spectacle was over. Couples came together again and strolled away animatedly discussing the unexpected early morning's entertainment.

At the wheel Katja Kokoschka turned down the *rue du Maréchal Joffre*, clipped the wing of a van parked half on the pavement and went through a red light before twisting and turning through the side streets to reach the embankment and the ring road out towards the François Mitterrand bridge.

In her rear view mirror she could see the flashing lights of the patrol car not far behind. Soon there would be others on her tail, maybe even a road block. She swung into the ring road in front of a lorry, forcing it to brake sharply and the driver to pump furiously on the horn.

Weaving across the lanes through the traffic she fishtailed back to the inside lane, nearly causing another lorry to jack-knife, and took the exit road to the motorway to Toulouse. As she entered the motorway proper, she realised the police car was catching up and would soon be alongside. As it did so, the patrol man signalled to her to pull over. The only exit before the toll booths, where she would be forced to stop, appeared suddenly on her right. At the very last moment she swung the wheel and nearly lost control as she entered the slip-road and left the motorway. The patrol car shot on past, too late to turn.

*

Pierre stretched out his free arm and his fingers scrabbled in the dark across the bed-side table for the phone. After knocking over the lamp his hand closed on the receiver and he listened to the voice on the other end. Swinging his legs over onto the floor and gently pulling his other arm out from under her, he grunted a reply:

«D'accord. Donne-moi vingt minutes. J'arrive.»

Detective Chief Inspector Antonia Antoniarchis of the Greek art fraud squad opened her eyes and looked at him.

"Go back to sleep – it's only two o'clock. Something's come up. That was Patrick. I've got to go."

"I'll make some coffee, while you dress," she replied, getting up and pulling a robe round her. "What's happened?"

"They've found a body in a flat on the *rue des Remparts*. That's all I know for now."

He entered the kitchen a few minutes later and gratefully accepted the coffee she poured out for him. He downed it in one gulp and headed for the door pulling on his jacket. He turned and for a second their eyes met.

"I know, you don't know when you'll be back! Don't worry, I'm going back to bed ..."

Commissaire Pierre Rousseau of the Bordeaux police headed into the city and made for the *place Pey-Berland*. The main arteries into the city were mostly free of traffic at that hour and he made good time. He stopped in front of the Hôtel de Ville at the top of the square opposite the west door of the imposing *Cathédrale St. André*. By the light of the moon the newly cleaned towers gleamed against the dark sky as he finished the journey on foot, turning into the narrow *rue des Remparts*.

The police cordon was already in place and an officer raised the tape to let him through. He climbed the stairs to the second floor and entered the flat. The forensic team was busy searching the rooms. Detective Inspector Patrick Bruni was standing by the pathologist who was kneeling by the body. He looked up as Pierre came in.

"*Bonjour, Commissaire*. White male, about 55-60, no obvious signs of foul play. There is evidence of an old bump on the head, but that's not what killed him. I'll know more after the autopsy, but he's been dead some time – perhaps five or six hours. The name in his wallet is Jean-Louis Deveau. He's a second-hand book dealer with a shop down near the *place du Vieux Parlement.*"

Patrick held Pierre's eyes for a second.

"How was the body found?"

"That's the odd thing. About an hour ago the neighbours heard a woman banging on his door and screaming his name. He didn't answer, but she kept on hammering on the door. The neighbours on this floor came out and argued with her, but she wouldn't stop, so one of them called us. Two patrol men arrived, but before they reached this landing the woman had already made a dash for the stairs. She rushed passed them as they were coming up, ran outside and took off in her car."

The pathologist paused and stood up to let the photographer take more pictures before turning the body over and continuing his examination.

Pierre looked at the face and nodded to Patrick. He turned towards the senior officer in charge.

"The patrol men gave chase, Commissaire, but she drove like a maniac and refused to pull over. She did 150 on the ring road, lost them for a while by taking the first slip road before the toll booths on the A62, but another car picked her up on the road to La Brède. Loud hailer warnings made no difference and finally she stopped of her own accord in front of her house in Saucats. She got out of the car and calmly waited for the officers to approach her

"So, do we have a name?"

"Katja Kokoschka. She's 32. An architect working here in Bordeaux but originally from Paris."

"Did she say what she was doing visiting Deveau in the middle of the night?"

"She refused to say. She wasn't drunk. Her papers are in order and her driving licence is clean – so far."

"So she had no idea Deveau was dead?"

"Apparently not."

"So where is she now?"

"At home. Uniform just charged her with various road traffic offences and let her go."

Turning to one of the policemen on the door of the flat, he said:

"Bring her in and see she makes a proper statement. *Mais tout de suite! Allez! Allez!*"

The officer saluted and headed off to his car.

"Let me know as soon as you have anything, Serge," he said turning to the pathologist.

"In a hurry as usual, Pierre! I need some breakfast before I work on this," he replied, sighing and looking at his watch.

Pierre walked towards the door and went out onto the landing with Patrick following close behind, after exchanging a complicit glance with the pathologist.

The doors of several apartments stood open. The occupants were standing in the doorways and on the stairs from the floor above watching all the commotion and grumbling loudly about the scandalous noise at this hour of the morning. None of them however showed any inclination to leave their vantage points, nor any shock over the death of their neighbour. Pierre walked on ignoring the requests for information and Patrick was about to accompany him.

"No, stay here. See what you can find out from this lot," he said loud enough for them to hear and glaring round to include them in his disapproval, upon which they all fell silent.

"They've already been interviewed by the uniforms," Patrick replied hopefully.

"I know, but I want you to interview them yourself. None of them seem very concerned about Deveau. Find out who knew him best and when they last saw him."

"What about the girl?" asked Patrick.

"I want to know what exactly she was shouting and whether she called out a name. And I want to know what the connection is between her and Deveau. Do what you can."

Relenting somewhat he added: "Come over to the house when you've finished – I'll have the coffee waiting."

He started down the stairs and smiled to himself as he heard the residents protesting when Patrick ordered them all to remain available for interview.

*

It was light by the time Patrick arrived and Pierre had already drunk all the coffee. Chided by Antonia, who had just entered the kitchen, he set up the coffee machine again, while she invited Patrick to sit at the kitchen table and help himself to croissants. Joining him, she looked carefully at him, a worried look on her face.

"How are you Patrick? Eleni said you were tired and needed a break. Is Pierre driving you too hard?"

"I've hardly started," said Pierre grimly coming over with the coffee pot. He helped himself to a croissant and sat opposite Patrick.

"OK, Patrick, what have you got?"

"Nothing new about Deveau. No-one seemed to have much contact with him and they added nothing to what we already know about him."

Patrick looked at Antonia.

"We have had an eye on Deveau for some time, but we have nothing solid against him."

"True … what *do* we know?"

Pierre answered his own question mostly for Antonia's benefit.

"Firstly, he's a second-hand book dealer suspected of money laundering. Secondly, he's dead. What we don't know is the connection between him and a woman who hammered on his door in the middle of the night when he had already been dead for several hours."

"We also know," added Patrick, "that an antiquarian bookshop can hide a lot of sins. Old manuscripts, contacts with collectors, contacts with auction houses, book fairs in Frankfurt, New York and so on. Not forgetting the excuse to travel around the country visiting anyone who wants to sell their libraries privately – and anything else they happen to have …"

"…which is the perfect cover for looking over items which might do well on the private art market," said Antonia.

"Exactly," said Patrick. "There was a recent case of a clock made for Louis XVI which was stolen from a château in the Indre. A dealer had been there a few weeks before to look at some paintings the owner wanted to sell, but had clearly looked around him for other items.

"The O.C.B.C., our art fraud squad," he explained, "traced the route followed by the clock to a fence based in Belgium, through to a Dutch dealer, then a German dealer and finally to a genuine buyer in England."

"Well, now Deveau's dead, we can do what we wanted to do before. I want his shop gone over with a fine tooth comb. We should have done it years ago. Talk to the O.C.B.C. – it's their field. We need everything catalogued and accounted for."

"That's some task. There are thousands of books."

"The books are not our first priority – leave them for the moment. I want all the prints and pictures looked at carefully and catalogued – they are more valuable. We also need to know who he has had dealings with recently."

"Will do, Commissaire," said Patrick reaching into his pocket for his phone and going outside for a signal.

"You think his death may be connected with a deal gone wrong?" asked Antonia.

"It's possible, but there's the girl who banged on his door. She may have had a grievance, but I think it's just a coincidence."

"I thought we didn't believe in coincidences after the cases we've worked on recently."

"I know, but perhaps for once …"

Patrick came back into the kitchen snapping his phone shut.

"They're on to it," he announced.

"So now to the driver of the car. What more did you find out from the neighbours?"

"Nobody had seen her before. She definitely wasn't a regular visitor. Nothing of that sort. They couldn't add anything to what they told the uniforms and she didn't say anything other than the reported 'Come out you bastard, I know you're in there.'"

"Did you read the patrol men's report?"

"Yes. The mystery is how calm she was when she finally gave herself up. She denied nothing; had no excuses for leading the police away on the car chase and didn't seem to be the slightest bit embarrassed by her behaviour."

He picked up the folder on the table in front of him and opened it at the first page where the photographs of the young woman stared back at him.

"She claims to be Katja Kokoschka, 32, an architect working in offices on the *cours de l'Intendance*. She owns a house in Saucats in the Landes, but also has a flat in the *rue du Palais-Gallien*. Her parents were Czech; fled from Prague before the Second World War. Now deceased. She was born in Paris and did her training there. Nothing on her record."

"It all sounds too perfect to me," said Antonia. "That's a well constructed background. Probably impossible to trace where her parents came from or to find any relatives. Or is that just a detective's suspicious mind?"

"Maybe not. OK, Patrick, follow all this up and ring Paris to check out her story. We'll interview her later when we've filled in more of her background."

Patrick drained his coffee and stood up.

"Take time to go home first – you look as if you need to restart the day in your usual way! Is Eleni still with you?"

Patrick breathed a sigh of relief – it had been a rough start. Not naturally an early riser, it was only now his normal breakfast time and he felt he had already done a full day's work.

"No, she's gone back to Athens," said Antonia for him. "Something has come up and I had to send her back. I'll have to leave myself today."

Pierre nodded and signalled with his eyes for Patrick to go. Turning to Antonia he asked:

"What's happened? Why must you go?"

"There's been a kidnap. Lýtras wants me to take charge of the investigation. Leave is over I'm afraid."

Chapter 2

The morning after, Katja Kokoschka left the small flat she had bought on the *rue du Palais Gallien* to be convenient for her work and walked down street towards the Jardin Public. She entered via the imposing gates in the tall wrought-iron fence which surrounded the park and started her warm-up routine of stretches and bends, before settling onto a steady run to do her regular laps of the park.

She passed several other joggers as she ran and nodded to those she recognised. We are like a silent band of secret agents, she mused as she weaved her way through a line of young mothers pushing buggies. We recognise each other, but never stop to talk and don't know each others' names or where we come from. We are all strangers, yet we understand each other on one level.

She knew none of the runners if questioned about her would be able to reveal anything other than a rough physical description and confirmation she ran most days in the morning in the park.

Anyone wanting to know more would find records of her qualifications as an architect – which were genuine – at her place of work here in Bordeaux. She had been lucky to find the job at a time when she needed to distance herself from her previous spell working for a private gallery in Paris, where she had researched the provenance of works of art and manuscripts.

She had got on well with the owner, Isabella Marquessa, but there had been times when she knew the gallery was sailing close to the wind and that the suspicious origin of some items had been covered up. At a time when many famous museums and public galleries were not asking too many questions and paying good money for their acquisitions the temptation not to delve too deeply was irresistible.

The gallery had even been investigated by the O.C.B.C. fraud squad, but nothing was proven in the end. After the dryness of the years of training to be a architect that small brush with danger and adventure had been the perfect antidote. And, even better, she had been sent on assignments abroad for the gallery. She had visited places she could not have afforded to go to otherwise and seen so much of Europe's architectural heritage at first hand. That had proved to be an advantage in her present work in Bordeaux.

But she was cross she had drawn attention to herself, because of Deveau and his dodgy book deals. How weird, she thought as she passed another familiar face in the park and nodded a greeting, that as I banged on his door, he was lying dead on the other side. Why hasn't it been reported yet in the papers? I wouldn't have known myself if the interviewer hadn't told me when he took my statement at the police station.

She stopped and paused for a moment to steady her breathing before doing ten press-ups by the side of the path. Her shoulder was still giving her trouble. She had torn a tendon lifting a heavy statue in the gallery, but it was slowly getting stronger and she could manage ten much more easily than even a week before. The tear had taken several months to heal, but she was lucky not to have lost the strength in her arm completely. Now she had to get the muscles working properly.

Thanks to computers she could still continue to design without too much physical strain and her new employer had been very understanding, after she had explained her injury by saying it was caused by a car crash in Paris.

Katja rested for a minute on a nearby bench to massage her shoulder and watched the other strollers and joggers in the park pass by. The early flowers were beginning to come out and the mild maritime climate of Bordeaux was kicking in. So different from the cold starts in the morning in Paris. Spring begins much earlier here she thought gratefully. Perhaps having a house out in the Landes as well was going to turn out to be a good idea after all. At first she had hesitated when the estate agent suggested it, but she was beginning to see how good it would be as the days became warmer. Her office was quite happy for their employees to work at home – all part of the green image the architectural practice wanted to project to their clients.

It would also be a good base for her to start dealing again on the side. Working on the fringes of legality at the gallery in Paris had whetted her appetite and she missed the buzz. She got up from the bench and resumed her run. One more lap, she said to herself, and then back to the flat.

Passing the small lake for the fourth time her thoughts turned once more to the book dealer. But what had happened to him? How had he died? She wondered again why there was nothing yet in the papers about his death. The police would have gone over his flat in fine detail by now. It was unlikely they would have found any evidence there to show he was involved in selling stolen manuscripts, he was too clever for that. But it would come out in the end if they searched his shop.

Then the police would want to know more about her connection with Deveau especially if they connected her with the gallery in Paris. Her first statement would not be enough. They would soon be back with further questions. Because of her stupidity, charging off like that, she knew she would have a hard task to convince the police she was no more than a client who had been ripped off by Deveau.

On the other hand if she acted quickly, she might be able to break into his bookshop and retrieve the book he had cheated her over. More importantly she needed to find the file on the deal Deveau had set up with the Italian collector before the police did. It must be in the shop. She was sure he would not have kept it in his flat. There were so many more ways to hide the file amongst the rows of books in the shop. She had to find out if there was any connection between the deal and why he died. If there was a link then she might be in danger herself.

Leaving the park she jogged back lost in thought, hardly noticing her surroundings and feeling pleased at having decided on a plan of action. She turned into the bottom of the *rue du Palais Gallien* passed the ruins of the old Roman amphitheatre and ran up the street towards her flat. It was only then that she saw the flashing lights and the police car.

The officer who had been leaning against his car watching her approach stepped out in front of her.

"Mademoiselle Kokoschka? We would like to ask you some further questions. Will you please come with us to the Hôtel de Police ."

It was a statement, not a question.

"Of course, Monsieur. May I take a shower and change first?"

She indicated her tracksuit and ran her hand across her forehead.

"A policewoman will accompany you in that case, mademoiselle."

He signalled to his partner, who stepped out of the car and introduced herself.

"Inspecteur Leanne Despagne, Mademoiselle."

The two of them went up the steps to Katja's flat on the third floor.

"Don't mind him, Mademoiselle. At least he does everything by the book. It's just a routine follow up to your previous statement."

They entered her flat and Katja went into the bedroom and then the bathroom to take a shower. The policewoman began to take a professional look around the living room. It was sparsely furnished, but everything was of good quality; two armchairs, a handmade rocking chair, a coffee table, a writing desk and chair, fashionable lighting and vases of flowers, some on the floor. Though clearly used as an office too, the room had a relaxed and welcoming feel to it.

The shelf unit contained a few books on antiques and paintings, the history of art and some catalogues from the world's museums, but mostly a huge collection of books about architects – Le Corbusier, Mies van de Rohe, Frank Lloyd Wright, Norman Foster, James Stirling, Pie and other names she didn't recognise.

There were a few photographs of holidays on a beach, perhaps in Greece, showed bronzed smiling faces of friends, but they meant nothing to Despagne. There were a couple of sketchbooks on the coffee table showing pen and ink drawings of architectural details from buildings in Bordeaux and designs for modern houses and chalets.

Katja returned from the shower dressed in trainers, jeans and a shirt. Her hair was swept back and held in place by a hair band. She wore no make-up and just a simple bracelet and watch. Her shoulder bag was zipped shut and revealed nothing of its contents. This time she felt better prepared to face her interview.

"Nice flat," remarked DS Despagne. Katja did not reply and followed the policewoman down to the car. She sat in the back and said nothing during the short journey to the police station. In the interview room they offered her a cup of coffee, which she declined. Then they left her alone. Fifteen minutes later Pierre entered the room carrying her original statement.

"Commissaire Pierre Rousseau," he said, shaking her hand as she stood up. "Please take a seat, Mademoiselle."

He waited until she was seated before pulling up a chair and sitting himself. He fingered a packet of cigarettes in his pocket, sighed inwardly and began:

"Now, Mademoiselle, tell me what this is all about. First you create a disturbance in the early morning shouting and banging on the door of Monsieur Deveau and then you involve my officers in a highly dangerous car chase. What is your connection with Monsieur Deveau?"

"He owes me money, Commissaire. I took him a quantity of books which he agreed to look at and to let me know their value. When I returned to collect them he told me the value and I accepted his offer to buy them. A few days later I saw one of my books for sale on his web site for ten times what he paid me for the whole lot. I went to demand more money off him – he swindled me."

"If you agreed to the price, Mademoiselle, he did not swindle you."

Pierre appeared to consult the statement on the table in front of him. Katja remained silent, aware of the technique.

"Are you sure that is your only connection with Monsieur Deveau?"

"What are you suggesting, Commissaire?"

"I am not suggesting anything, Mademoiselle. But tell me why you waited until two in the morning to go and visit him at his home. Why did you not simply go back to his bookshop and make your demands there at a more normal hour?"

"I had only just found out what he had done that evening when I was looking at his web site and I was so angry I just charged out of the house."

"How did you know where he lived? Had you been to his flat before?"

Katja glowered at him and replied:

"I had his business card from the shop on which he gave both his home address and the address of the shop."

"Are you sure you hadn't been there before? It's unusual thing to go to visit someone, however angry you are, at two in the morning."

Katja pushed her chair back and rose to her feet in one movement.

"I know what you are trying to suggest, Commissaire. No, I did not have any other relationship with him – I did not sleep with him. He's a swindler and he tricked me – I just wanted what he owed me. He virtually stole those books off me, the bastard."

Pierre sat back calmly and looked up at her.

"Sit down, Mademoiselle! I was not suggesting anything of the sort. I see you have a short temper – unusual for a professional."

Katja slowly sat down trying to regain her composure.

"Tell me more about your work here in Bordeaux."

"You know already I'm an architect. I often browse around second-hand bookshops on the look out for old books on design and architecture. I had been to Monsieur Deveau's shop many times before and bought several books from him."

"That does not answer my question, Mademoiselle."

Katja shrugged her shoulders.

"Could I have a glass of water? I am thirsty after my run."

Pierre nodded to the officer by the door. They sat in silence until the officer returned and set the glass down on the table. Katja nodded her thanks and took a long draft.

'So, go on, Mademoiselle"

"We work in teams in the design office. At present we are working on the plans for a new holiday complex near Arcachon. I also do designs for vineyards – extensions for bottling plants, wine presses and warehouses – that sort of thing."

"So you visit the châteaux in the area and have access to their properties?"

"Of course. They are clients. What are you implying?"

"Again nothing, Mademoiselle. I am just trying to form a picture of what it is you do."

Pierre glanced down at her statement on the table in front of him, although he knew it already off by heart.

"You do know Monsieur Deveau was lying dead inside the flat when you arrived?"

"I do now; your officers told me. But of course I didn't know when I knocked on his door. How could I have done? I just went there to confront him about the book, as I told you."

"So, why did you rush off when my officers arrived instead of staying and explaining what you were doing there?"

"I really don't know. Just panic, I suppose. I thought they would arrest me for causing a disturbance."

"And when you finally stopped outside your house?"

"I'd calmed down and realised I'd been stupid."

Pierre stared hard at her and she held his gaze.

"Are you still sure you have nothing further to tell me, Mademoiselle?"

Katja remained silent and shook her head.

"In that case, an officer will take a further statement from you and then you are free to go. Do not leave Bordeaux – we may need to ask you further questions."

Chapter 3

In the early hours of the morning after the interview with Rousseau, Katja took a deep breath, threw off her duvet and slid reluctantly out of bed. The cold air on her body made her shiver as she reached for her bath robe and wrapped it tightly around her. In the distance she heard three chimes coming from one of the many churches in the city – a sound you didn't notice during the day, drowned as it was by the noise of the traffic and the buzz of the population going about its business. She flipped the switch on the coffee machine which she had set up before going to bed and headed for the bathroom.

The smell of coffee revived her as she came out dressed in a dark track suit. It was not far to the bookshop from her flat, but there was always the danger of being spotted by a roving police car at that hour and being questioned, so she had dressed as she would for a jog in the park, remembering to pull on gloves against the cold.

Making sure her ID papers were in her pocket, she set off at an easy pace up to the *place Gambetta* and down the *cours de l'Intendance*. She moved lightly on her feet as she easily covered the distance. At the *place du Grand Théâtre* she turned into the *rue Ste Cathérine* and down into the smaller side streets leading to the oldest part of the city around the *place du Vieux Parlement*. Just before the entrance to the square she stopped a few metres from an antiquarian bookshop. Standing back in the recesses of a doorway opposite she checked the street carefully for any witnesses, watched a cat rummaging in a split plastic bin bag for a moment and then crossed over to the shop.

It took her only a few seconds to slip the lock and open the door. She stepped quietly inside and stood for a moment to let her heartbeat slow to normal, before getting out her torch and advancing further into the building. Behind the desk a door led into the office proper. To her relief it was not locked.

Inside everything was neat and tidy. She had expected this, based on what she had seen in Deveau's flat on her previous visits. On the one hand it would make finding the right files easier, on the down side she would have to be careful to put everything back exactly in its place.

Firstly, she wanted to find out how much Deveau had sold her books for. That much of what she had told Rousseau had been true. Deveau had taken advantage of her, knowing she did not know the value of one of the books she had brought him.

Flicking through the files she quickly found the one relating to the sales. Most of the books had been sold on at a normal profit margin, so what was so special about the one book he was advertising at ten times the sum he had paid her? And where was it? She wanted it back while there was still a chance.

The safe was shut, but it was an old iron one operated by a key. After a brief search she found the key taped to the back of one of the filing cabinet drawers. The safe door opened easily and inside the book she was looking for was the only item locked away. She took it out, flicked the pages quickly and put it carefully into the small backpack she had brought with her, relocked the safe and replaced the key.

Standing with her hands on her hips she looked about her. So what else had Deveau been up to? Where would he have hidden the paperwork on his illegal deals in stolen manuscripts and early books?

After he had found out from Isabella Marquessa in the gallery in Paris that Katja was an expert in investigating provenances, he had as good as admitted to her the shop was a cover for other dealings. He said he would pay well for her expertise from time to time tracing provenances of manuscripts he acquired. So why did he screw her over the value of the book? Just habit, she supposed.

Only a couple of weeks before he had mentioned an Italian business associate who was looking for a manuscript for him. When it was found he wanted her to check it was genuine. It was her first commission from him. Since he was meticulous to the point of obsession about keeping records, she knew there would be evidence somewhere of his contacts with this man Lucca, the so-called business associate.

She sat down in the chair behind the desk and fiddled idly with the pencil lying beside the phone, trying to get into his mind. Where would be the obvious place no-one would think of looking? In a file marked Lucca perhaps? Too easy, she thought, but on checking the filing cabinet, she froze. There, tucked in at the back, was indeed a file marked Lucca. She quickly pulled it out, only to find it empty.

So, where had he put the contents of the file? Then she remembered Lucca was also the name of a town. She returned to the main part of the shop where she knew the books were arranged in clearly labelled categories on the shelves, having spent so much time there browsing in the past. It really says something about the old bastard's character she said to herself.

Running her gloved fingers along the Travel shelves she quickly located Italy and then Lucca. She began pulling out the books, looking behind each one for a hidden file. Nothing. Looking up, she could see several large format books lying on their side on the top shelf. She found a step ladder and reached up. One book had not gathered as much dust as the others. She took it down and opened it. Neatly disguised as a repository, it had been hollowed out and was full of papers.

She glanced quickly through them and then stuffed them inside her track suit top. She replaced the book carefully and blew some dust from the other shelves onto it. Returning the ladder she went back into the office. The papers went into her backpack and with a rapid glance around to check that nothing was out of place, she went towards a door at the back of the office which led into a small courtyard with a narrow passageway out to the street behind. She slipped out and resumed her jog, turning down towards the river.

She had parked her car the evening before near the *place des Quinconces* a few hundred metres along the embankment. After stowing her backpack and gloves in the boot, she jogged back to her flat in the *rue du Palais Gallien*. This time there was no police car waiting for her.

*

Later that day, Pierre sat in his office reviewing the case with Patrick.

"So, all we have so far is that a well known crooked book dealer is found dead in his flat. No signs of a break-in and no indication of how he died as yet. We know he used the business for money laundering and as a cover for gathering information about what private collectors were in the market for, but we've never been able to establish firm proof."

Pierre sat back for a moment and fiddled with the cigarette pack lying on the desk, before tapping it in resigned renunciation and reaching for a strip of gum instead. Patrick watched him struggle, hardly able to suppress the grin gathering momentum behind his outwardly impassive face.

"Then we have a young woman banging on the door of the flat and leaving in a hurry when the patrol car arrives. She denies all knowledge Deveau was dead when she called. Anyway the fact he had died several hours before speaks for itself. Her papers are in order and she has a professional job in the area. So far her identity checks out. Deveau cheated her over the sale of some books and she claims she only wanted to make him pay her a fair price."

"We have no evidence of any other link between her and Deveau, so perhaps there is no other connection," said Patrick.

He got up, went over to the coffee machine and poured himself a cup, and, after a nod from Pierre, poured another. Still standing and handing him the second cup, he continued:

"Which leaves us exactly where?"

"With no crime having been committed – at least until we know the cause of death."

"So, we can leave it to the uniforms? No case as far as we are concerned?"

The phone sounded and after picking up the receiver and listening for a few seconds, Pierre handed it to Patrick. Still standing, Patrick listened and turned to Pierre to report:

"I sent a forensics team over to the bookshop to do a search as you wanted, but it seems someone was there before us. They found a book which had been hollowed out as a hiding place, but someone had recently pulled it out and presumably taken whatever documents were inside. There was an attempt to cover up the removal by scattering some dust off the shelves onto the book."

"It could have been Deveau himself."

"It's possible, but the office had been searched too and the safe opened."

"Perhaps there is more to this than meets the eye after all," Pierre said getting up. "Come on! Let's go and look for ourselves – tell the team to wait till we arrive."

Patrick spoke to the caller and put back the receiver.

Pierre dropped the anti-nicotine gum into the waste paper bin as he gathered his hat and led the way out to the car, lighting up a cigarette as he went, which he promptly stubbed out as Patrick got behind the wheel.

They entered the bookshop and were greeted by the officer in charge of the team.

"We haven't found anything else since I called, Commissaire, but one of my team is sure it was a woman who was last in here – she recognised the perfume the intruder was wearing."

Pierre was silent for a moment.

"I think I do too," he said, thinking back to the interview room.

The officer showed them the hollowed out book and the empty safe in the office.

"No finger prints or other evidence?"

"We've found nothing so far. Whoever broke in knew what she was doing though. The front lock has been picked – not forced. It's old and not very effective. The intruder left via the door at the back which leads out into a courtyard and then into a side street."

"Has door to door yielded anything?" asked Patrick.

"One of the owners of the flats above did wake in the early morning – claimed he heard the sound like that of someone kicking a drinks can in the street. He looked out of his window, but there was only an early jogger heading down towards the river. He thought it was a woman. She was carrying a backpack. No chance of a facial description though – he only saw her from behind."

"OK," said Patrick. "Get as full a description as you can – height, weight, colour of track suit etc."

He turned to Pierre.

"Could be our girl – we know she's a jogger and she has the motive. It's somewhere to start. Shall I call her office?"

"No, let's go straight there," replied Pierre. "It'll save time and she won't have had time to fabricate a story. I'm sure she wasn't telling me everything at the interview. She was nervous and tried to hide it by getting angry and losing her temper at my questions."

They walked up the *cours de l'Intendance,* which was given up almost entirely to the new tram system, and entered the architects' offices which occupied a converted flat above a former bank branch. The receptionist showed them through to the senior partner, Marcel Bouvier.

"What can I do for you, Commissaire?"

Bouvier's office was light and airy. The large eighteenth century windows and high ceilings had received a modern touch, without destroying the mouldings and formalism of the past. Outside the street was quiet now that the tramway had been built and most other traffic diverted from what had been a busy thoroughfare.

Even with the windows open only a murmur of the activity in the street below reached those inside. In one corner near to the natural light of the window was an architect's drawing board. The other half of the room was furnished with comfortable, modern chairs, more suited to receiving visitors. Bouvier himself was informally dressed and took a seat after his guests had taken theirs. Pierre noted with approval that he didn't position himself behind his desk, but joined them in the armchairs.

"We would like to speak to you about Katja Kokoschka, Monsieur le Directeur."

'Now there's a talented young lady. I hope there is nothing the matter. She was due for some leave and has gone on holiday. She won't be back for ten days."

Pierre exchanged glances with Patrick.

"That was sudden, wasn't it? When did she leave?"

"Today. She only requested the leave yesterday, but we are not too busy at the moment, so I said yes. She's well up with her work and deserved a break."

"Did she say why she gave such short notice?"

"Just that she had spotted a cheap flight to Greece and wanted to book it straight away."

"How long has she been working for you, Monsieur Bouvier?"

"She applied about a year ago and, after an excellent interview, was offered a place in the practice. She had already organised a 'career break leave' as she described it, but we were so keen to take her on that we agreed to wait a few months before she joined us. In fact she started early this autumn."

"Do you know what she did during her career break?"

"She said she wanted to travel and to study styles and buildings in Greece. She's quite an expert on early Greek architecture. I felt it could only help in her work for us."

"And you are happy with her work here?"

"Indeed we are. It's early days yet, but in two or three years I can see us offering her a partnership in the practice. But what is this all about, Commissaire?"

"At the moment this is just background information. She was present by chance in a building where a man was found dead and we are doing routine checks on all the people who have associations with the dead man."

"May I ask who the man was?"

"He was a book dealer in the old quarter."

Bouvier laughed and relaxed back in his chair. He smiled as he said:

"Ah! That man Deveau! I saw it in the paper only this morning," he said glancing over to his desk where the morning's edition of Sud-Ouest lay open. "Katja was a great collector of early books on architecture and design and was always saying the man was a crook and charged her too much. I don't know why she kept going back to his shop really."

"Did she ever make threats against him?" asked Patrick.

"Oh! No, nothing like that. Just the usual sort of grousing about paying too much. She brought some of the books in here sometimes. They were fascinating and she was good at discovering real gems. She was quite an expert. But I'm sorry he's dead. Do you know how?"

Neither Pierre nor Patrick responded to the question and Bouvier continued having not really expected an answer.

"I met him once when I went with Katja to the shop – never thought he looked a fit type. Probably died of drink and lack of exercise."

Pierre got to his feet, followed by Patrick taking his cue. Putting out his hand, he said:

"*Je vous remercie, Monsieur le directeur*, you have been very helpful. We shall be in touch."

He and Patrick left the building and walked up towards the *place Gambetta*, where they went into a café.

The waiter approached as they pulled out chairs on the *terrasse* and Pierre ordered two coffees.

"Do you think Bouvier and Kokoschka are having an affair?" asked Patrick.

Before Pierre could answer, Patrick's phone went. He listened, closed it down and looked across at Pierre:

"We have a match on the computer. They are certain our old friend Isabella Marquessa has been in Deveau's flat. They found her finger prints."

Pierre stopped stirring his coffee and looked up.

"Isabella Marquessa, now there's a name to conjure with. What could she be doing here in Bordeaux? The last we heard of her she had disappeared from sight somewhere in Paris. Could she have something to do with Deveau's death?"

"I doubt it. The prints have been overlaid by others so hers are some days old. However it's an interesting link with someone we would very much like to interview after the events of last summer."

"Back to Kokoschka. I instructed her not to leave Bordeaux and now she's taken off without telling us. Get a search warrant and search her flat and the house at Saucats. See what perfume she uses. Try it out on the officer who recognised the perfume in the shop. See what belongings she has taken with her. And let me know if there is any more news over the identity of the jogger seen near Deveau's shop."

"Where are you going?" asked Patrick, seeing Pierre get up.

"To Deveau's place and back to the shop. There must be a clue somewhere as to what he was up to and I have a hunch that whatever it was, Kokoschka knows all about it now and is stepping in where he left off."

"So you do think she was the jogger and broke into the bookshop?"

"I'm almost certain it was," he said putting on his jacket. "And see if they can find a match for those other prints they found in Deveau's flat."

"Shall I put out an alert at the airports for when she returns from Greece – if that's really where she's gone …"

"Yes, do that."

Chapter 4

"*Che puttanaio!*"

Giovanni Lucca cursed loudly as he hauled himself out of bed. His leg was playing up and he had spent the night tossing and turning. He hobbled across the bedroom to the chair by the window and started the massage he was obliged to do each morning to get the circulation going.

As he rubbed his leg he looked through the window out over the sea far below the house and reflected on the events that had shaped his life over the past year. It had been a close call in Lyon. That *bastardo* Marc Lacroix had shot him deliberately in the leg while looking him full in the eye. The bullet had narrowly missed an artery and his leg had only been saved by the skill of the surgeon who had operated on him after he dragged himself into the hospital. He had only just made it inside with the help of the taxi driver.

Even now, months later, it would hardly support his weight. He hated being handicapped, but knew it could have been much worse. There was no way he could have put up with life in a wheel chair or even with an artificial leg. He was much too impatient for that and it would have put an end to his activities.

Lucca had always been a *tombarolo*. Even as a young boy he had roamed the hills bare-footed with a gang of friends and searched for anything the mythical Etruscans had left behind, well before he had any idea of who they were.

What he did know was that people would pay good money for the fragments of pots and figurines he brought back. One day when out with his best friend Vincenzo Samborini he spotted a hole in the ground where the earth had recently dropped away exposing an underground cave, as they had thought at first.

He remembered how they had wriggled in through the narrow gap and dropped down onto the floor of the cave. To their amazement Vincenzo's torch had revealed a treasure house of artefacts – vases, jars, small statues and paintings, even bows and spears. They never looked back from that moment and became the best and most respected band of *tombaroli* in all Italy.

Collectors and museum buyers trekked to their door, though not literally of course. All transactions were carried out with total discretion and the Italian police somehow, he chuckled to himself, never succeeded in proving anything against them. He and his band became expert at squeezing good money out of their willing buyers at meetings conducted well away from prying eyes. Lucca's house was still full of the spoils he had, literally, unearthed.

A year or so before, the gang had been tempted further afield by a commission they could not turn down – to find Achilles' battle helmet in the ruins of ancient Troy.

It had been their greatest coup and their worst nightmare. Lucca still could not quite believe that his oldest and closest friend could have betrayed them like that. Vincenzo sold out the whole gang to the Turkish authorities and made off with the helmet they had all spent so much time searching for. There was no way back. It had been the direst betrayal. One that could never be forgiven.

Lucca paused for a moment remembering with startling clarity the moment he had taken his revenge. He shivered as he recalled the blood spurting from Vincenzo's neck – after all, they had been best friends for as long as he could remember. But then he smiled to himself – it had all turned out well in the end.

In fact, after their arrest, the gang had become local heroes in Istanbul. When the Turkish authorities realised the value of all the other treasures they had unearthed, they made a deal. If Lucca showed them all the locations where the finds had been made, the gang would be paid for the objects they had found and released.

In this way a gang of Italian *tombaroli* became expert guides for the Turkish police and archaeologists from the national museum to the ancient sites they had discovered, including the main prize – Achilles' tomb. The archaeologists were delighted – the *tombaroli* were saving them years of work. He laughed at the irony of it all.

In the end they had made more money – legally, for the first time in their lives – than they would have made off-loading them to collectors and to those museums which were not too fussy about where the items they bought had come from.

Lucca got up from the chair and tested his leg gingerly walking slowly up and down the room. It felt better and he went back to the window to look out over the bay to the islands in the distance surrounded by the glittering blue sea.

But, he brooded, later that summer his business had not been so profitable. The deal over the icon in Greece had been a disaster. He'd been swindled out of half a million dollars by that *bastardo* Lacroix. He had finally caught up with him and his partner Isabella Marquessa in Lyon, but Lacroix had shot him in the leg and laughed in his face when he demanded his money back.

The fool let him go without taking his gun and later he read in the papers that when he fired into the room through the closed door from outside in the corridor, a lucky shot had killed Lacroix. But that bitch Isabella had escaped and the police were still looking for her. One day he would catch up with *la puttana* himself, he thought.

His only consolation was that the American collector who had paid him to steal the icon had been caught trying to smuggle it out of Greece. So perhaps there was a god after all.

He sat down and continued to massage his leg, more out of habit than necessity. He knew he could no longer work in the hills. He would have to change tactics and deal with collectors direct for the antiquities and works of art they craved. It wouldn't be hard to recruit others to do the spade work, no pun intended he smiled to himself.

In fact he hadn't had to lift a finger for this job. Deveau had come straight to him and asked him to find a manuscript that could still be lying somewhere in a remote monastery in Greece.

Deveau had droned on about the history of it. At first Lucca had only listened impatiently, but gradually he saw the point of the detail – it would make the job of finding it less difficult. According to Deveau local tradition had it that one of the knights making his way back to England through Greece after the Third Crusade, stopped with his retinue in a small village and announced to his followers he would go no further. He said he was too old and weary to continue the journey home and before he died he wished to record all he and they had witnessed during their battles to recapture Jerusalem from the Saracens. He had decided to retire to a monastery nearby to write his account.

The monastery he chose was hidden deep in the Lousiós Gorge. There, Deveau had told him, he is supposed to have dictated his story and there he died and was buried. Lucca could still recall Deveau's exact words – the ones that had made him finally sit up and take notice.

"No other eye-witness account of the Third Crusade is known to exist. The original manuscript may still be lying somewhere in the monastery which is now a ruin. Probably buried under the fallen roof of the monks' library. All you have to do is find it and smuggle it out of Greece. I've got a buyer ready and waiting."

The story held no romance for Lucca, but he saw good money in the deal and it was a challenge which pleased him.

Before his injury he would have gone to the site himself, but his damned leg made that impossible. For the moment however he was happy to gather as much information as he could from the girl who had accompanied Deveau.

In principle he hated working with women, but in this case Katja Kokoschka was turning out to be quite an asset. She spoke Greek and was an expert on the Crusades and old manuscripts. She had experience of this kind of operation and seemed hard nosed. Her cover was her profession as an architect – where better to go than Greece to see classical styles?

The stupid bitch had lost her temper when Deveau swindled her over the value of some trifling books and drawn attention to herself, but how was she to know the old fool was already dead when she went to his flat? In fact Lucca rather approved of her feisty character.

He got up and started to put some clothes on. Time to start the day. Pity about Deveau, but he had had to die. He was too greedy and knew too much.

"*Cinquanta percento – assurdo*! I no need some French fool to deal with the *Americanos*. I do it myself," he said aloud to the room. "*Bravo, Marco.* You did good work."

*

The coach full of tourists stopped outside a hotel in the small town of Dimitsána at the head of the Lousiós Gorge. The tour guide stood up at the front of the coach.

"Ladies and Gentlemen, I'm sure you're pleased to have arrived at our hotel where we will be staying for the next three nights. Please wait in the lobby while I hand over your passports and receive the room list and the keys.

"Enjoy your meal this evening, but make sure you have a good night's sleep as tomorrow will be a strenuous day. We will be walking down into the Lousiós Gorge, as you know, to visit the ancient monasteries."

As the travellers climbed down from the coach and walked across the road to the hotel, Katja studied the American couple again. They were a little older than the rest of the party and looked rather unfit for the type of walking which would be involved. But you never can quite tell, she said to herself. Some large people are surprisingly spry. Anyway the wife seemed to be enjoying herself and never stopped talking. Her husband was more taciturn.

The guide collected their passports and had gone ahead to pass them over to the receptionist in the little hotel. As Katja entered he was already reading out the names of the guests with their room numbers. Listening carefully, Katja was surprised to hear the Americans had a Greek surname. With a start she realised it was a name she knew from her time at the gallery in Paris.

The other travellers in the group were a mix of nationalities and there was much laughter as the guide did his best to pronounce their names. Everyone was in good humour, pleased to have arrived after the long coach journey from Athens and ready for the adventure into the Gorge. Katja liked most of them and the atmosphere in the coach had been good.

This was her first time on a package holiday and she did not really enjoy the herding around which went with it, but it did mean she could explore the Gorge without attracting attention. The guide, Nikko, was very knowledgeable about the area and had filled in a few details which she had not picked up from her reading. He was also young and quite handsome …

She realised with a start he was calling her name and coming towards her to hand her the key to her room. She picked up her backpack – just a small one with a minimum of clothes – and went into the lift. The American couple reached it just as the doors were about to close. She pressed the override.

"Oh! Gee thank you dear I'm just dying to go to my room and take a shower it's so hot here and I'm feeling real sticky do you think they do a massage in this little place? Perhaps not, it's so cute – we normally stay in the biggest hotel we can find don't we George but I guess this one is the biggest they have."

It had all came out in a rush – virtually one sentence Katja realised as she helped the woman push her huge suitcase into the tiny lift.

"That's kind, dear. George you'd better wait there and come in the next lift or we'll squash this young lady into a corner."

Her husband looked on in blank resignation as his wife sat on her case like a hen shuffling down onto her nest. The doors closed and Katja thought she glimpsed a look of relief on his face at the thought of a few minutes quiet.

"You must call me Mira, dear. My, is that all the baggage you have? How do you manage? I seem to need so much…"

"And I'm Katja," she replied as Mira appeared to be drawing breath. "I don't like having to carry lots with me on these trips."

The lift stopped on the second floor and Mira pushed out her suitcase, unfolded the handle and set off determinedly down the corridor tugging it behind her. Katja found her room and as she put the key in the lock, Mira reappeared, looking flushed, pulling her case and squinting at the door numbers.

"Ooh good!" she exclaimed. "We're just opposite you Kattie dear, that's real nice."

"See you downstairs in the bar later, Mira," said Katja quickly, as she went into her room and closed the door.

She slung her backpack onto the bed and took a look at the bathroom. The shower looked modern and she immediately stepped out of her clothes and ran the water. The coach was air-conditioned but still the journey from Athens had been long and hot. Every time they had stopped and left the cool of the coach, stepping out into the 38° C degree heat had been a shock to the system. Endless cans of cold sugary drinks and the subsequent 'comfort stops' required had done nothing to ease the fatigue of the travelling.

Under the shower the dust and heat of the journey were drained away and Katja stood letting the warm water run down her body easing the stiffness from sitting for so long. Feeling slightly guilty at using so much water in such a dry summer, her thoughts nonetheless turned to what she was doing there in this little town in Greece.

Though she had accepted the commission originally from Deveau, it was the slightly scary Italian, Giovanni Lucca, who had suggested, to her delight, that she should go to the Lousiós Gorge under cover of her research. Someone has to do it, she thought with a smile.

How odd that the opportunity had come about in a such a roundabout way via the gallery. What a strange coincidence that Deveau knew Isabella Marquessa and had contacted her when he needed an expert in old manuscripts. Knowing Katja had recently moved to Bordeaux after leaving the gallery and was on the spot, Isabella had recommended her.

Katja turned the warm to cold and stayed under the shower for as long as she could stand it before shutting the water off and stepping out to reach for the towel on the rack. She hadn't mentioned this other link to Deveau when Rousseau questioned her. It had nothing to do with his death after all, she justified it to herself. And she didn't want the police to look into her connection with the dubious side of the art world too closely.

When she had read through the file on the deal with Lucca, she had found nothing to suggest there was a rift between them, which is why she decided to contact Lucca herself. She had already met him once when she accompanied Deveau to the first meeting with Lucca out at his house on Sardinia. Everything had gone well until she mentioned her connection with the gallery in Paris and Isabella Marquessa. Lucca had flown into a rage and forbidden her to speak of *'la putana'* again. Both she and Deveau had sat there open-mouthed at the outburst, but Lucca recovered quickly and the incident was passed over. It was then that Katja had realised there was a darker side to the Italian than she had supposed. But it was none of her business and the possibility of finding an original manuscript account of the Third Crusade in the ruins of one of the monasteries in the Gorge was just too exciting to step away from.

Part of the process of checking the provenance of such items in Katja's view was to form an idea of where the item might have come from and under what conditions it had been kept. Though in the past she had kept well clear of items which had been so obviously spirited out of its country of origin, this time it was different.

It was the first time she had had the opportunity to locate an item herself and her first experience out in the field was giving her an adrenalin rush she had not experienced before. The tourist excursion to the very valley where tradition had it that the manuscript had been written was an extra bonus and provided excellent cover for her to look closely at the monasteries.

Wrapping the towel around her she went back into the bedroom and walked across to the window. Outside the dryness of the area was only too obvious. It had not rained for weeks and the ground was bare and rough. Below her a goat herder passed by marshalling his flock along the lane behind the hotel. In the distance in the valley she could see another herder sitting under an olive tree, his dog stretched out by his side. How do they manage to survive this heat, she asked herself.

Man and beast appeared to operate a system of minimum movement. The man stayed in the shade below the branches and the goats sought the shade by climbing the trees and perching there like woolly toys on a Christmas tree. How on earth they got up there on cloven hooves she had no idea. You never saw them do it. It was almost as if they did it secretly by levitation when no-one was watching.

Turning slightly she could see into the hotel garden. Some of the coach party were outside sitting on loungers under the split cane shades round the pool having yet another cold drink served by the hotel waiters. One of the party – a particularly amusing, but hyper-testosteroned Italian – looked up and mouthed *'bellisima'*, accompanied by a thrown kiss from his closed finger-tips. Katja laughed and retreated one step back into the room where she knew she was not quite out of sight.

I've got you now Marco Platini. The evening has potential yet, she thought with a smile.

A knock on the door made her instinctively draw the towel tighter round her as she called out:

"Who is it?"

"Just me dear," came the reply. "Shall we see you at the bar in a few minutes?"

"Let's meet at the pool. I'll be down soon. I'm dying for a swim."

"You are brave – maybe I'll join you in the water after a cocktail."

Katja wondered what cocktail Mira thought she might be able to order in this small hotel in the middle of nowhere, but then the staff were used to tourists and many coach parties stopped there on their way to visit the monasteries.

In fact she was in no hurry to join the others and stretched out on the bed to savour a few moments without the chatter she knew awaited her by the pool. Reaching over to the bedside table she picked up the guide book and began to reread the history of the Lousiós Gorge.

"Some of the monasteries are deserted and in ruins but others have begun to revive and to support small communities of monks. The monks originally chose this valley to build their monasteries centuries ago because of its remoteness. Many times in the long history of Greece this inaccessibility has favoured those who wished to hide from their enemies or to escape from marauding armies. In recent history it served as one of the bases for the Revolutionaries who in 1862 finally drove out King Otto, a Bavarian prince imposed by the Great Powers on Greece in 1832.

"Much earlier in the twelfth century the Lousiós Gorge served as a welcome refuge for knights returning to their homelands from the Crusades. For the monks this was a potential source of profit. They eagerly offered hospitality in the form of lodging and food to the knights as they passed by. Many found it so agreeable they elected to stay, being too exhausted or weakened by their injuries to wish to continue on the long and dangerous journey to their homelands.

"The monks knew well the knights were often in possession of the rich spoils they had captured or looted during the battles against Salah al-Din in the fight for the Holy Land. In return for an offer of permanent refuge and sanctuary in the monastery, the weary Crusaders were easily persuaded to hand their booty over to the safekeeping of the monks.

"The monasteries thus ironically became the repositories of many Islamic treasures which have for the most part remained hidden ever since ..."

The guide book fell from her hands with a thump and she woke up with a start.

"Enough history! Time for a swim."

Katja swung her legs over the side of the bed and dropped the towel to the floor. She quickly put on her bikini and, wrapping a *pareo* round her, left her room and went down to the pool and the outside bar.

Chapter 5

Sir Geoffroi de Vinsauf wiped his brow as he squinted forward into the sun. He and his retinue of companions and squires, shadowed by a gaggle of camp followers, had travelled far that day early in the summer of the year 1193. Many of their company had fallen by the wayside or been killed in the numerous skirmishes they had encountered as they fought their way out of Arab lands. Now, many months after leaving the Holy Land the previous year, the remaining Crusaders were reaching their, or rather his, destination in the Lousiós Gorge. The last stop before the Monastery of Filosófou was to be in the little village of Dimitsána where a modest taverna with rooms welcomed travellers, especially those returning from the Crusades.

Sir Geoffroi knew this was going to be a difficult evening. He intended to announce to his companions his decision to travel no further. They had been together for so many years and survived so many dangers that he feared their reaction. But they had witnessed great numbers of their fellow knights and squires cut down by the forces of the mighty Salah al-Din or die of grievous fever on the journey and he fervently hoped they would understand why he had chosen this path to seek some internal peace. Perhaps others would join him.

They all knew their so-called triumphal return to their homeland and their estates after five long years away would also be filled with sadness. They would be the bearers of the news of the deaths of those not returning. Tales of heroism would be scant consolation for grieving wives and mothers.

Sir Geoffroi pondered the fickleness of their allies in the Holy Land. The alliance had collapsed and Leopold of Austria and Philippe of France, had left the Holy Land to return to their native lands. King Philippe's treachery knew no bounds. The scoundrel had joined forces with Richard's own scurvy brother, John Lackland, to seize Richard's rightful possessions in Normandy and Poitou. So King Richard too was forced leave the Holy Crusade and to make peace with Salah al-Din.

Some of the Crusaders had left the Holy Land by boat with Richard in 1192, but there was not room for all and those who chose not to stay

in the Christian enclave had had to return to their homelands the way
they had come – on foot, under the guidance and leadership of Sir
Geoffroi.

He paused to mop his brow and his squire proffered him water from
his gourd. They rounded the last bend before the village of Dimitsána.
Ahead of him he saw the landlord of the taverna coming out to greet
the arriving company. Sir Geoffroi waited for him to approach. The
landlord bowed low to him and the other knights.

"Here's a truly slimy rogue," Sir Geoffroi muttered to his squire.
"Observe his every move with the eyes of a hawk, William."

The landlord studied the newcomers carefully. His was a dangerous
profession and many times he had been robbed or held prisoner in his
own inn. On the whole though he made a good, mostly honest, living
from the flotsam and jetsam of the Crusades and enjoyed listening to
the knights' tales. He knew this type of business would continue for a
few years yet and was keen to preserve his reputation so more parties
would follow enabling him to continue to make a healthy profit.

He always made sure the leader of the group had money or goods to
barter with before he risked providing food and drink.

"Welcome to our humble village, most noble knights. How can I be
of service to those who have fought so valiantly to recover our Holy
City for Christ?"

Wearily Sir Geoffroi handed over a bag of silver coins without a
word. The man felt the weight of the bag in his hand and smiled.

"Pray follow me, your Excellencies. You will not find our hospitality
wanting."

Accustomed as he was to receiving the tired and vulnerable stragglers
of the wars, the landlord directed the various ranks to their quarters
with practised authority.

The knights were given clean straw and places to sleep in the loft
over the taverna. The squires made do outside in the stables with the
horses and the followers set up their own camp nearby.

The knights and the squires threw off their tabards and flopped
down gratefully in whatever shade they could find under the olive trees.
They chased off the goats but the droppings on the ground still

attracted the flies which immediately turned their attention from the goats to the exhausted travellers.

The landlord dispatched his serving boys to ply the Crusaders with drink. The squires poured the wine into goblets and offered them to their knights, who gratefully took great gulps of the contents.

There was short moment of complete silence and followed by a roar as each one in unison spat out the sharp vinegary liquid.

"This evil piss is not fit even for the curs that follow us," exploded Sir Geoffroi. "Our silver has bought us the best wines and viandes, not this foul *vin aigre.*"

Turning to his companions he said: "Come with me my friends. We will soon find where the rogue keeps his best wines. But first he must drink the wine he dares to serve his guests."

They rose as one man and approached the taverna. The host was sitting outside on a bench and his face lost its tan as he saw them coming towards him, presaging nothing good. Before he could escape or protest, he found himself on his back, pinned down by four knights well used to administering this sort of punishment to landlords who dared to serve less than the best to returning knights who had fought the Turk in the Holy Land in the name of peasants like him who professed allegiance to the Holy Catholic Church of Rome.

Sir Geoffroi himself forced the man's mouth open and poured a generous dose of the evil vinegar down the equally evil looking throat of the victim. To avoid drowning the host was forced to swallow. Five minutes of this punishment sufficed for the man to reveal the whereabouts of the real fare his guests deserved.

Soon a long table had been erected outside the inn and the serving lads and wenches quickly laid out dishes of fruit and meat, fish and fowl fit for the noble knights and squires of their lord and master, Richard, King of England and Duke of Normandy.

The host was obliged to join them – squeezed between two burly Norman knights who made sure he was enjoying himself as much as the rest of the increasingly happy company. The lamb carcasses found hanging in the cellar were soon roasting on spits turned by the stable lads over open fire pits.

In a fit of generosity by the host, encouraged by a Norman sword at his throat, a whole roasted lamb was even sent over to the camp followers. The fine wine flowed generously and goblets were constantly refilled by serving girls who by now were becoming increasingly obliging as they drunk the wine freely offered by the revellers and helped themselves to the food off the plates of the noble company.

Darkness fell quickly and by the soft light of the fires the feast continued more quietly as weariness returned and the knights grew more melancholy. Realising the evening was drawing to a close. Sir Geoffroi braced himself to stand and address his companions.

He hauled himself slowly to his feet and struck the table with his fist to call his companions to order. In the sudden silence the knights and squires stopped their eating, set down their goblets and turned towards him. Seeing the expression on Sir Geoffroi's face, they impatiently pushed the frightened serving girls off their laps. The girls fell to the ground and scuttled away.

"My friends – we have come through many trials together and seen many things which civilised men should not see. We have marvelled at many brave acts committed in the name of our Saviour and in support of our noble King. But sadly too we have witnessed the slaying of many courageous companions in arms who fell at our sides. Let us remember them."

The knights rose as one and raised their goblets to their comrades slain on the field of battle. Hesitantly they sank back onto the benches and waited for the old knight to continue.

"We have seen the blessed towers and spires of Jerusalem itself. Our glorious King Richard, he of the Lion's Heart, defeated the mighty Salah al-Din in battle outside its very walls …"

The knights roared their approval.

"… but finally had to concede he could not enter the gates of the Holy City, without the assistance of our allies – Duke Leopold and King Philippe. But as you know all too well, those treacherous dogs deserted our holy mission."

The knights growled their disapproval at such cowardice.

"Philippe of France is even now attacking the lands of our sovereign King Richard in Normandy and Poitou. Our holy crusade is over and sadly despite our best endeavours the Holy City remains in the hands of the Turk. But you also know King Richard struck a treaty with the mighty Salah al-Din for Christendom to hold the coast for three years and to have the right to visit the Holy Shrines of Christ, as is their due."

The knights raised their goblets.

"But I am growing old, my friends, and have come to a decision. I will journey no further with you."

Every knight looked up at Sir Geoffroi and a stunned silence befell the whole company.

"I have made my decision to stay in this valley and to accept the hospitality of the monks of the monastery of Filosófou. I wish to write of all I have seen in order to preserve the memory for those who come after us to read and marvel at the valour we have shown and to know what Christian men will do in the service of the Holy Church of Rome."

There was a murmur around the table as the knights looked at one another and realised the import of what Sir Geoffroi was proposing.

"You, my brave companions, must all continue your journey homewards to your estates and families and carry the news of the Crusade to your loved ones. I have received news recently that my own dear Lady has succumbed to the terrible Black Plague which ravishes our homeland and has been laid to rest. Here, in this remote place, I hope to find peace and solace as I pray for her soul in heaven where she has surely gone."

At this his squire rose from the table and approached Sir Geoffroi, but before he could speak, the older man held up his hand and said:

"No, Squire William, you too must continue on your way. You are young and valiant and have all to live for. I grant you my horse and my sword and pray God that in your turn you may gain the noble status of knight and perhaps one day return to fight the Turk once more in the service of our king."

He turned back to the company.

"So, my valiant friends, let us celebrate our last evening in true Crusader fashion. Let us eat and drink and be merry for who knows what the morrow brings."

He clapped his hands.

"Landlord, bring back your prettiest serving girls and have them pour more wine – the best only mind, or we will slit your throat," gesturing with his fingers across his own throat and the knights roared their approval again.

The landlord looked pale and resigned as he rose to do as he was bidden, encouraged on his way by the knights on either side of him.

*

At the pool some of the coach party were relaxing stretched out on the loungers in the sun and accepting the cold drinks brought to them by the attentive hotel staff. Katja's appearance caused a few heads to turn – appreciative looks from the men and more critical ones from the women who were debating whether they could squeeze into a bikini that small and admiring the tightness of her behind compared with their own. The men looked away reluctantly, wary of being caught staring, and the women sighed as they came to their own conclusions, vowing to drop a dress size when they got home after the holiday.

Katja approached the bar and ordered a long lemon and tonic water. Mira Leontarakis was perched precariously on a stool at the other end of the bar and her husband was staring vacantly into space beside her, a beer on the counter in front of him. Katja went over to them.

"Sorry I wasn't able to talk much to you earlier, Mira. What brings you out to Greece and so far from home?"

"You're right, my dear. Boon, Ohio sure does seem a long way from here. Me and George" – she gave him a nudge in the ribs – "had heard so much about these old monasteries we just had to come and see them for ourselves," she replied gingerly taking a first sip from her glass.

"Me too. I really want to see the Filosófou monastery. It's supposed to have some wonderful frescoes."

Mira was making a face.

"George, don't just sit there. Ask them what's in this drink."

George blinked and sat up with a sigh.

"Yes," she went on. "We read that and there are lots of other monasteries in the valley too, of course," she added quickly catching her husband's eye.

"They say the welcome at Filosófou is simple but quite friendly," said Katja. "The monk who lives there is a bit stern looking, but likes the company of tourists and the site itself is beautiful. It's said there's also a library of old manuscripts which no-one except the monks are permitted to see."

"You don't say," said George, entering the conversation for the first time and turning towards her. "Are you interested in manuscripts?"

"Just in general. I find the historical details so fascinating, don't you?"

"Oh! I sure do, dear," Mira replied.

"We just like looking at the awesome scenery and the old monuments," George corrected her. "We don't know much about the early history around this place."

 "And you know how you love taking pictures of everything, George. He has so many wonderful pictures you know, and we invite all the folks back home round to see them. They just adore them, don't they, George?"

"Time we went to eat," interrupted George. "All I need right now is a good T-bone. And I sure don't mean goat either. Shift your butt, Mira."

He seized Mira firmly by the elbow and guided her away in the direction of the restaurant.

Thoughtfully, Katja watched them go. She had recognised their name and knew they were well-known as discriminating collectors of art. So why the act? George in particular seemed to want to hide behind the façade of being just a tourist.

She was finishing her drink when Marco Platini came towards her radiating teeth and smiles.

"*Buona sera, Signorina.* I see you are all alone. May I be with you this evening as I too am alone and I do not like to eat by myself. I am Marco."

"And I am Katja," she said, smiling at the chat-up line.

"Such a beautiful name, Signorina. How could such a beautiful woman be travelling alone for long?"

"Well, I am not alone now, am I Marco? *Grazie a Lei!*"

"So, you speak Italian too. *Magnifico*! We must eat together. I show you the best there is – the best there is in Greece, of course. Not like in Italia, but we will eat and drink quite well in spite of that."

They walked across to the restaurant. Entering, he clicked his fingers and the *maître d'* approached at once and showed them to the best table – as he had been generously tipped beforehand to do – with a spectacular view down the gorge. Flowers and candles were already arranged in the centre of the table. A bottle of champagne was cooling in the ice bucket by the side. Katja recognised with approval all the signs of imminent seduction and decided to enjoy the game.

"How lovely this table was free," she said. "But will you excuse me for a few moments, Marco?"

He stood as she got up and made her way quickly to her room to change. Ten minutes later she returned, dressed in a simple loose shirt and flowing skirt. Marco whistled softly and held her chair for her as she sat. He glanced across at the *maître d'*, who quickly came forward and poured the champagne. Marco raised his glass:

"To my beautiful guest."

The other members of the coach party were beginning to appear for the evening meal and soon there was a buzz which covered individual conversations. As they ate Katja was content to let Marco talk about himself and his family back in Italy.

He recounted how he had come to Greece on a pilgrimage to see where his dear grandfather had been during the Second World War when the Italians briefly occupied the country.

"After Italia joined the Allies, the Germans came in and occupied all Greece. They forced the great Italian army to surrender to them and made them all prisoners. My grandpapa was one of them."

He paused for effect.

"He was never seen again."

She placed her hand on his arm and leaned forward.

"I am so sorry, Marco."

"But enough of this sadness," he said putting his other hand over hers.

"Tell me about yourself and why you here."

"Oh! Nothing so sad. I'm just here for a holiday. I love old monasteries and walking, so this valley was the logical place to come," she replied retrieving her hand and picking up her glass.

"Then we shall walk with each other tomorrow, no? I too love the walking and it is so beautiful here. On feet is good."

"I would like that."

She got up from the table.

"We have an early start tomorrow and I am tired after the journey, so I thank you for your company and I will see you tomorrow at dawn," she said. "*Buonanotte.*"

"I like when you speak Italian! *Bravissimo!*"

Marco stood and bowed slightly.

"It is a perhaps a shame you go so quickly as the night is still young, but as you wish. *Buonanotte, Signorina. Dormi bene!*"

He watched as she left the dining room, and saw her turn at the last moment to look back.

*

Sir Geoffroi woke early in the small bare-walled cell he had been given by the monks. The monastery of Filosófou was already over two hundred years old when Sir Geoffroi had bidden farewell to his companions and climbed the narrow path up to the gates. He had stood for a moment looking back and watching the straggling procession snaking its way slowly up the valley, the banners with the red cross of St George fluttering in the light breeze seeming to bid him farewell. He saw his squire, William, turn for the last time and raise his sword in final sad salute to his master. Moist-eyed Sir Geoffroi rang the bell and the monk opened the gate to let him pass.

The monastery itself was almost invisible from a distance. The monks who had built it in those far off days knew well that the remoteness of the valley was not in itself sufficient protection from the lawless bands of brigands who roamed the area. They had chosen the site carefully for maximum camouflage and natural fortification.

The present monks welcomed him to their home and provided him with his own tiny cell. They were wise enough to leave him to his own thoughts for as long as he wished, allowing him to adapt to his new life in his own good time.

Sir Geoffroi was grateful for this period of calm to rest and reflect after the toils of the previous years fighting and several weary months travelling. So for some weeks he kept to himself and did not join in the routine of the life of the monastery. He would sit on the small terrace for hours catching the rays of the sun as it entered the valley and watch the changing colours of the scenery in the deep gorge below the rocky perch on which the monastery sat. Occasionally the silence was broken as the sound reached him of the bells of goats and the voices of peasants collecting the olives to make oil for their cooking.

Gradually he adopted the rhythms of the monks' regime and become accustomed to rising early. His strength returned with the peaceful passing of the days and his thoughts turned to the task he had set himself. He knew he must not delay the writing of his chronicle, but he still needed time to distance himself from the events and to form a plan in his mind as to how to organise the account.

Finally one fine autumn day in the October of 1193, he summoned the monk who had offered to be his scribe, went out onto the terrace to clear his head in the freshness of the morning air and began to tell his tale. By chance it was the very month that, unbeknown to the old knight, his foe the mighty Sultan Salah al-Din died, exhausted, in his capital Damascus.

The scribe settled himself at the table, placed the ink pot to hand and smoothed out the parchment. He waited expectantly. Sir Geoffroi began to speak:

Prologue

'It sometimes happens, that exploits, however well known and splendidly achieved, come, by length of time, to be less well known to fame, or even forgotten among posterity.'

He paused and watched the white mist hanging over the trees in the gorge below beginning to clear as the sun's warmth began the gentle process of evaporation. The scribe replenished his quill in the ink pot and waited patiently, pen poised.

'In this manner the renown of many kings has faded, and their deeds have sunk with them into the grave where their bodies lie buried — deeds which have been performed with great splendour, and were much celebrated in their own time, when their novelty brought them into favour, and unanimous applause set them up as models for the people.'

He paused to take a breath and looked up as a flight of birds flew overhead, black shapes against the pale blue of the sky.

'The ancient Greeks, aware of this, were wise enough to use the pen as a remedy against oblivion, and zealously stimulated their writers, whom they termed historiographers, to compile histories of noble deeds. Thus the silence of the living voice was supplied by the voice of writing, so that the virtues of men might not die with them.'

Sir Geoffroi hesitated once more as images of what he had seen on the fields of battle passed in rapid succession through his mind. How in the Lord's name was he going to convey to those who had not witnessed such scenes the true valour of the Christian knights of the Third Crusade? Knights who endured so much hardship to avenge the terrible slaughter of their brothers, so overwhelmed by the might of Salah al-Din and his army at the fateful battle of Hattin only a few years before. Knights who had striven and failed to retake Jerusalem.

He drank from the jug of cold clear water on the table beside him and took up the tale again. The scribe struggled to keep up as his words flowed faster and faster. Geoffroi continued working late into the evening, pausing only to take refreshment and finally retiring to his cell as the light faded.

Early next morning, the scribe read back to him the passages he had dictated. Pleased with the Prologue, his head cleared by the night's sleep, Sir Geoffroi began his true chronicle of the events leading to the Third Crusade:

'In the year of the Incarnate Word 1187, when Urban III held the government of the Apostolic See, and Frederick was Emperor of Germany; when Isaac was reigning at Constantinople, Philip in France, Henry in England and William in Sicily … the Lord seeing that the land of his birth and place of his passion had sunk into abyss of turpitude, treated with neglect his inheritance, and suffered Salah al-Din, the rod of his wrath, to put forth his fury to the destruction of that stiff-necked people; for he would rather that the Holy Land should, for short time, be subject to the profane rites of the heathen, than that it should any longer be possessed by those men, whom no regard for what is right could deter from things unlawful …

Even as he wrote news reached him of momentous events. His Lord and King, Richard, had been forced to continue his journey home overland after being driven ashore by a storm near Venice shortly after leaving the island of Corfu. The messenger recounted how despite travelling in disguise, Richard was recognised and had been taken prisoner on the orders of Leopold, Duke of Austria, his former companion of arms, shortly before Christmas the previous year. Worse was to follow for King Richard. Finding himself excommunicated for holding a Crusader against his will, Leopold handed Richard over to Henry, the Holy Roman Emperor. He too was excommunicated, but to no avail.

Despite his grief at the news, Sir Geoffroi pressed on day after day with his account. He spent his mornings dictating to the scribes and then retired to his cell to rest. The effort cost him dear, but such was his determination to record the events for those who would come after him that he drove himself on and would not rest until the task was done.

At night he prayed to God to give him the strength to continue and for the safe release of his king. His prayers were finally answered. News reached him in the following year that King Richard's mother, Queen Eleanor, she of Aquitaine, had raised the huge ransom demanded by the Emperor and that Richard had been restored to his rightful place as sovereign of England and of his lands in France.

Despite his failing strength, Sir Geoffroi was finally able to draw his account to a conclusion.

'… At last restored to his native soil and the kingdom of his ancestors, in a short time he restored all to tranquillity. He then crossed over into Normandy, to avenge himself on the wanton aggressions of the King of France, his rival; and when he had more than once defeated him, he powerfully recovered by sword and spear his alienated rights, even with augmentation.'

Sir Geoffroi struggled up from where he had been sitting and gazed out over the valley below. He heard a shrill cry far above him. An eagle was lazily circling on an updraft, its wingtips like outstretched fingers against the pale blue sky. Sir Geoffroi shivered as he felt the power of its piercing eyes searching for prey below. He turned to the scribe.

Here ends the book of King Richard's expedition to the Land of Jerusalem.

Now his work for those who would come after him was finished Sir Geoffroi was left bereft of all that was dear to him. His companions, his faithful squire William and his king were far away in distant lands. While he still had the strength he knew he must perform one last task. He bade the monks bring the best stone masons before him.

Following his instructions the masons set about making what was to be his final resting place in the little chapel.. They carved his likeness in stone – a crusader knight in full armour. The work was slow and meticulous. Sir Geoffroi was demanding in the detail he required of the panels decorating the sides of the sarcophagus and more than one attempt was abandoned. Finally he was satisfied and called the masons together.

"You have worked well and your skill has created a monument worthy of all those who gave their lives in the service of their God and their King in the Holy Land, of whom I am just one unworthy servant. Those to come will gaze at the tomb you have created and marvel at the story of the sacrifices made and so honour the memory of great men and their deeds."

It was late in 1199 when the news reached Sir Geoffroi that his king, Richard Cœur de Lion, was dead. During the siege of the castle of Châlus he was shot by chance through the neck by a bolt from an *arbalète*. His treacherous brother Jean sans Terre was now King of England, Duke of Normandy and Duke of Aquitaine.

This unwelcome twist of fate affected the knight sorely and soon after, the body of Sir Geoffroi de Vinsauf was conveyed to his tomb by the monks in the chapel of Moni Filosófou. They dressed him in his full armour, laid his accoutrements by his side and wrapped him in his banner as befitted a valiant crusader and defender of the true faith.

Chapter 6

The following morning the coach party assembled in the foyer of the hotel. Nikko checked no-one was missing and went round chatting to each of them to make sure they all were suitably dressed for the day's excursion into the valley.

"*Kaliméra*. Good morning everyone. I hope you all had a good evening and slept well. I think everyone is here. It will be hot today so I suggest you all have a hat and a bottle of water. I see most of you have already thought of that. We can buy refreshments at some of the monasteries, but I have also arranged for you to have a simple packed lunch."

He gestured to the table behind him.

"Please help yourselves. When you are ready we will make the short walk to where the path down into the valley begins. On the way I will tell about the history of the valley and about the monasteries we will visit."

Everyone clustered round the table and helped themselves to the lunch packs the hotel had prepared.

"Everyone got their pack?"

He looked round.

"Good, let's go. Follow me."

They followed him out of the hotel and along the road. After about ten minutes they reached the entrance to the path and started the steep walk down into the valley. The heat from the sun was already stronger and when they reached the small village of Palaiochóri Mira Leontarakis insisted on stopping.

"It sure is hot," she sighed. "Back home in Boon we don't walk too much, do we George? We have this lovely little car ..."

Since it was clear she was not alone in wanting to take a break, and, rather than see the whole party dip into their provisions so early in the day, Nikko gave in to the inevitable.

"There is a taverna further down the street where you can buy a drink and have rest," he said. "You do have another five or six kilometres to go before the next stop."

That decided it for most of the group who were already feeling the effects of the beating sun.

"Don't worry it will be cooler further down in the valley under the trees. I'll show you where the path continues down into the valley and anyone who wants to can go straight on. We'll catch you up at the first monastery, the Moni Filosófou."

George considered continuing on along the track to the monastery, but hesitated as he admitted to himself he would enjoy a break as much as anyone. When Mira grabbed him by the arm and dragged him towards the taverna the decision was made for him.

The others clearly felt the same way. Wiping the sweat from their foreheads, they followed Nikko towards the taverna hoping it would be air-conditioned and have ice for the drinks. Neither wish was fulfilled, but the shade of the terrace was a relief nonetheless.

Only Katja and Marco decided to carry straight on and they soon disappeared from view down the track.

"That is lucky, no? We are alone in this beautiful place, Signorina. We could not ask for more."

Katja laughed and strode ahead as they negotiated the steep rough path. The red cliff sides of the gorge towered a thousand feet above them, seemingly reaching as high as the morning clouds. Concentrating on keeping their footing, they said little as they descended into the valley.

After an hour's steady progress they stopped for a moment to look up at the monastery, just visible through the trees, perched high on the rocks and clinging dramatically to the cliff face like a swallow's nest to the eaves of a house. Ahead of them the view down the long valley was breath-taking.

"Let's stop for a moment," said Katja, shading her eyes to look at the view. "This is so much better than being in a taverna."

They sat down by the side of the track to drink from their water bottles and to savour the silence.

The noise of their boots on the rocky path as they walked had drowned out the quiet of the valley, but now there was not a sound. It was as if there was no other living soul on the earth. Katja had never experienced such complete soundlessness anywhere before. They sat side by side saying not a word: even Marco seemed awed into silence.

"If there was no-one there to hear them before man walked the earth, were earthquakes and erupting volcanoes silent?" she asked, remembering a sentence she had read somewhere.

Before Marco could reply, the familiar tinkling of goats' bells reached them from the valley and the silence dissolved with the question.

Marco stood up and put out his hand to help Katja to her feet. They shouldered their small backpacks and set off. A hundred metres along the track they turned off for the final climb up to the monastery. The path was steep and they were breathing hard when they arrived at the gates. Katja stopped for moment to look back down the track. The others were nowhere in sight. She turned and pulled on the bell rope.

There was no response and she was about to ring the bell again when a bearded face appeared behind the grill of the jalousie.

"May we enter, O Holy One? We have come to refresh ourselves spiritually. We wish to pray in the chapel and to give thanks for the holy frescoes."

Katja had asked Nikko beforehand what the accepted greeting was, but she nonetheless felt a tinge of conscience at the hypocritical overkill. Marco kept a straight face. The old monk was not fooled in the slightest, but nonetheless opened the gate enough to let them slide by.

Once inside the walls, they stood rooted to the spot. The little chapel was bathed in sunlight and the terraces round it were enlivened by bright red hibiscus and flowering trees. To say it was idyllic was to underestimate the impact on the eyes of the visitors. They slowly moved forward to one of the tables and sat on the bench. The monk shuffled away and when he returned he was carrying a jug of iced water and a plate of biscuits. He sat down at the table and began telling them about the monastery, but neither Katja nor Marco could understand his local dialect very well and soon he fell silent.

Katja indicated she wished to see the frescoes inside the chapel. That part of her speech at the gate at least had been true. The monk led them across the terrace and up some steps to the side door. The cool of the interior was a welcome relief after their climb and they stared in wonder at the biblical figures and scenes which covered the whole chapel from the cavernous ceiling of the nave to the floor.

The colours were as vibrant as the day they were painted more than three hundred years before. The silence of this colourful world acted like a spell and despite themselves they hardly dared to breathe or to move. Finally they backed slowly out of the holy place, feeling themselves in the overwhelming presence of a higher power.

The monk was waiting patiently for them outside, quite used to the effect the inside of the chapel had on even the most cynical of visitors. He led them back to the table on the terrace, where he left them, seeming to disappear without a sound.

The bell at the gate rang. The monk opened it wide and Nikko entered with the rest of the party. Their fellow coach travellers flooded in to the little courtyard chattering excitedly. The climb up had taken its toll and they headed gratefully for the tables and benches. Mira waved to Katja and Marco, but George steered her to another table as the last seats were taken up.

Everyone gratefully shouldered off their backpacks and the ground was soon littered with bags and bottles of water. For a moment Marco and Katja thought they were going to ask for the menu, but Nikko quickly took charge and begged the monk politely for a little refreshment.

He silenced the chatter by standing up and telling them about the history of the monastery and asking them to respect the holiness of the site. The group responded and the initial excitement calmed into quiet awe at their surroundings. The monk returned with water and biscuits and for a while the visitors remained at the tables looking around them, breathing in the heavy scent of the flowers and savouring the peacefulness disturbed only by the shrill calling of buzzards circling high above.

With the monk's permission Nikko took small groups of four at a time into the chapel. He asked them not to use their cameras, assuring them there were postcards for sale and the monk relied on these for the little income he had.

Marco and Katja watched the goings on for a while before requesting permission of the monk to visit the monastery library.

"*Ochi*, not possible," the monk replied immediately. "Books very old. Not strong."

"So we know there is one," Katja said to herself.

"How old are the books and manuscripts? How did they come to the library?" she said aloud.

The monk hesitated before answering. He seemed uncertain whether he should divulge the information. Finally he said:

"Many books from begin of new monastery here," he said finally, gesturing around him. "Some not good condition. Some from other monastery fallen down."

"So there are earlier manuscripts from before this monastery was built." said Katja. "Stories of the Crusades, for example?"

Marco stared at her in surprise at the question.

The monk shook his head.

"Maybe in old monastery."

He retreated into the local dialect again and they did not understand the rest of what he said.

"Of course!" exclaimed Marco. "This is the Néa Moni Filosófou, the new monastery. The original monastery is further on. We will pass it when we go to next one."

"That's the Agíou Ioánnou Prodrómou, isn't it?" Katja said stumbling over the name as she consulted her guide book. "I would like to see that one, but perhaps if we set off straight away we could see the old monastery too and still catch the others up," Katja said, trying to keep the excitement out of her voice.

"If you wish. But it's mostly a ruin, so there won't be much there."

"I know, but it so old and I'd love to see it, Marco, though it can't be as beautiful as this place. I can almost understand why the monk can stay here on his own in such isolation. Anyone would start to believe after spending time in that chapel."

"Time to go then," replied Marco with a twinkle in his eyes, "or I lose you here to the monk!"

Marco went across to Nikko to tell him what they planned. They offered the monk what supplies they had carried with them, purchased some cards and left the monastery to continue down the track south towards the old monastery, less than a kilometre further on.

The air was heavy with the scent of wild oregano and thyme and they heard the rustle in the grass by the track of tortoises foraging. The original monastery came into sight, clamped to the cliff-face, where it had clung since 960 – one of the oldest in the Peloponnese. The way up to it from the main path was overgrown and they almost missed it. They struggled their way up, having to help each other over the rocks blocking the way. Arriving slightly out of breath they entered through the remains of the gateway. Once again they were moved by the holiness and tranquillity of the site.

The chapel itself still stood, but much of the rest, had fallen into ruin. There was no way Katja could quickly identify where the library or the monks' cells might have been. With Marco there she did not want to give too much away and risk seeming too curious about their exact location.

Marco had wandered off and was clambering over the fallen stones looking intently around at the buildings. Suddenly he stopped and called to Katja. Over in one corner of the courtyard, lay a bunch of wild flowers.

"Who could have put them there?" exclaimed Katja. "Do you think someone in the valley still has some connection with this place and comes here to pray? How extraordinary."

"Why don't we just stay here for a while and let the others go ahead? We can catch them up at Gortys."

"But then we would have no time to see the next monastery. No, we should stick to what we told Nikko."

Marco reluctantly nodded his agreement, but moved closer to Katja as she stretched out on the warm stones.

"Not here in this holy place, Marco. Later," she said to head him off.

Pushing him away, she got up from where they were sitting and picked her way through the fallen stones across to the old chapel. Marco watched her carefully as she bent down to squeeze through the low doorway.

Inside the chapel it was dark but her eyes slowly adapted to the small amount of light streaming in through a window high up in the vault. She could make out the faded remains of frescoes with their images of the saints. The chapel was partly hewn out of the cliff face and at the far end beside the altar there was a tomb.

She called out to Marco to join her and went forward to look more closely. On the top of the tomb the effigy of a knight was beautifully carved. He was in full armour with his sword by his side. Marco arrived and held up his lighter. Katja knelt down and ran her fingers over the inscription on the frieze.

'*⬜i gît Le Sieur Geoffroi de Vinsauf, défendeur vaillant de la foi'*.

*

Back in the hotel in Dimitsána Katja took a shower, changed and went down to the bar by the pool. George and Mira and the rest of the party were back and most were relaxing in the pool or on the deck-chairs laid out round it. Katja went over to Mira.

"Hello, my dear. Wasn't that a wonderful day? Where did you go? We missed you for a while."

"Marco and I went to the old monastery of Filosófou before catching you up."

George raised his eyebrows and looked steadily at Katja, but before he could say anything Mira continued:

"My dear, that monk at the Filosofy monastery got quite cross with us after you left. I think he didn't like us using our cameras in the chapel. How were we to know he had postcards for sale?"

"Nikko did say …"

"All this funny Greek writing is very confusing. He looked so fierce in his beard – are you sure he isn't Ben Lardy?"

"bin Laden – the 'bin' means son of."

"Did you hear that, George? Kattie is so clever. You want to watch that Marco, my dear. He's only after one thing – he is Italian after all."

"Oh! I can handle Marco. Don't worry Mira. Let's forget the monk – he's definitely not bin Laden," she laughed, standing up.

"I'm going for a swim in the pool. Enjoy the rest of the evening."

George watched her thoughtfully as she left them.

Chapter 7

"So Marco, how is your plan to bring to me the manuscript?"

Giovanni Lucca was resting his leg on a chair. Marco sat opposite him in the main room of Lucca's house near the little town of Palau, on the island of Sardinia. The room was light and airy – unusual for an old house in an area where the houses had small windows and thick walls to keep them cool in summer and warm in winter. However with the money he had made over the years as a *tombarolo,* he had modernised the house. The windows offered breathtaking views over the Costa Smeralda and even, on a clear day, across to Bonifacio on Corsica.

The relative isolation of the house meant business could be discussed and deals struck without raising eyebrows. The terrace was the perfect place to receive and entertain his overseas guests without the danger of being overheard. He knew the Sardinian police were aware of his past activities and suspected some of his present ones, but they had failed to find any proof, or at least enough to take him to court. To protect himself Lucca had the house regularly swept for electronic bugs, although he was fairly sure that as long as he kept his head down and did nothing illegal on their patch the local police would not bother him.

Marco Platini stretched his legs and looked Lucca in the eye.

"There is no guarantee the manuscript is still there, Giovanni. It is possible the monks took it from the old monastery to the new one when they left it, but …"

He shifted uneasily as he felt Lucca's eyes on him. There was a smile playing round his lips which he did not understand.

"… but it could still be there under the ruins, perhaps even with more manuscripts."

Lucca still said nothing.

"But me, I think it also possible those monks make money from the gifts the knights give to them and sell them quickly after the knights die" – he crossed himself. "It is sad, but what can one expect from such people? There were many buyers for those treasures. Greedy vultures, I think."

There was a silence in the room as Marco's flow dried up and he was left perplexed at the lack of reaction from Lucca. The sound of the waves breaking on the shore below reached them through the open window.

"What does Signorina Kokoschka think?"

Lucca kept a straight face as he watched Marco's reaction. Marco froze completely for split second before recovering, but it was enough for Lucca.

"She did not tell you, no?" said Lucca, releasing a rare chuckle.

"Tell me what?"

"Tell you she work for me and watch you at same time?"

Lucca enjoyed the discomfort of the younger man.

"No, she didn't, *la putana.*"

Marco ran his mind back over the time they had been in the Lousiós Gorge.

"So the bitch knew who I was all that time and she never say anything!"

Lucca watched him with amusement. Marco's emotions passed across his face like a series of frames in a film. He saw the initial anger recede and change into a wry smile.

"*Allora, la bella donna* was not so innocent after all! She make a fool of me.*"

"You need not worry, Marco. She said to me you behaved like a perfect Italian man should do. She enjoyed how you tried to lure her into your bed. She knew how to keep you panting behind, like the little dog you are."

"*Bravo!* She did very well! But tell me, Giovanni, why you take on this pretty Signorina to help us. You do not usually trust the women, however beautiful."

"She knows more about Greek manuscripts than we do, Marco. She has told to me it is possible the manuscript is still there in one of the monasteries, I have to believe her. We make good money if we find it, Marco, especially since you kill that old fool Deveau. You did well."

Marco's face lit up as he accepted the rare praise and was about to say something when Lucca continued.

"It may be there. After all nobody thought Achilles' war helmet would be in his tomb, but …"

"… *si, si,* you have told me that story many times, Giovanni. Let us drink some wine and I tell you my opinion since you already have the woman's."

Lucca reached forward and poured the wine. He sat back to listen to what Marco had to say. Unusually he did not interrupt and Marco felt himself growing self-conscious again as he talked. Gradually he ran out of things to say in the face of Lucca's silence.

Lucca stood up painfully to stretch his leg and walked to the window. Looking out with his back to Marco, he said:

"So, Marco, I think from what you say to me you must go back to Greece on your own and see what you can find. But nobody must know you do this, not even the woman. *Capito?*"

"*Perfettamente!*"

*

Pierre stared at the reports in front of him, both elbows on the desk, hands under his chin. To his annoyance he had had to perch his newly acquired reading glasses on his nose, in order to be able to read the files. He still felt self-conscious wearing glasses and kept glancing at his unfamiliar reflection in the glass door to his office opposite his desk.

He needed to know exactly how Deveau died. Although it appeared at the moment as if it was a straightforward heart-attack, there were too many strange coincidences surrounding his death to accept that preliminary medical diagnosis. His instincts told him there was something strange about the whole business. He pressed the intercom.

"Ask Inspector Bruni to come in will you, please, Céline?"

There was a short tap on his door. Pierre quickly took off his glasses before saying:

"*Entrez!*"

Patrick Bruni came in, pretended not to notice the spectacles half-hidden behind one of the files, and settled in the chair in front of Pierre's desk. Pierre reached into the cabinet behind him, took out two glasses and a bottle of *pineau*.

"From my cousin in the Deux-Sèvres," he said by way of explanation. Removing the cork, he paused, the neck of the bottle above Patrick's glass. Patrick nodded. They raised their glasses briefly, sampled the bouquet and took a first sip. Both raised their eyebrows appreciatively and settled back in their chairs.

"So, what do you think?"

"Excellent!" replied Patrick, deliberately misunderstanding, and then continued: "We didn't find much when we searched Deveau's shop, but enough to show he had a separate doubtful line of business with outside clients. No identifiable names yet, but we found files with what seem to be codes for the different names. He clearly bought and sold valuable illuminated books and manuscripts at auctions and to private buyers. Nothing illegal in that on the surface, but why would he want to conceal the clients' names?"

"And the jogger?"

"Nothing to connect her with Kokoschka, but it still remains a possibility. We have no forensics yet to show whether or not she was in the shop."

Pierre consulted the reports on his desk.

"The travel company has confirmed Kokoschka joined an organised tour to Greece."

He paused and took another sip.

"And?" said Patrick, recognising a prompt when he heard one. "Bouvier told us she was away in Greece."

"The group she was with toured monasteries and other sites in the Peloponnese, especially in the Lousiós Gorge."

"And?" he repeated.

Patrick recognised the usual signs that his boss was playing with him.

"Well, by coincidence, Antonia has just called through from Athens to say there have been strange goings on in one of the long abandoned monasteries in that very valley. A former colleague of Eleni's uncle Kóstas reported that someone had disturbed the ruins and overturned stones inside the old buildings. He regularly visits the site to lay flowers in memory of a friend who died there."

"But how does that affect us? Is there something significant about that monastery?"

"It was already old by the time of the Crusades. The gorge became a stopping off place for some of the knights returning home from the wars."

Patrick was growing more and more puzzled as to where all this was leading. Thank goodness the *pineau* is good, he thought impatiently, taking another sip. Pierre was continuing and he tuned in again.

"The monks offered hospitality to knights who decided not to continue the journey home. Some of them wrote about what they had seen and done in the Holy Land. The scribes made copies and sold these accounts on in the nearby towns such as Dimitsána and Stemnítsa. They made a nice income from these manuscripts."

"And Kokoschka is interested in old books and manuscripts," said Patrick making the connection.

"Antonia has put a watch on the old monastery and will let us know if anything else happens."

"Lousiós Gorge. Wasn't that also a base for the partisans in the War of Independence against the Turks?"

"You have been brushing up on your history! Eleni is educating you! Yes, it did. Dimitsána was the headquarters and where the campaign started."

Patrick looked pleased with himself until Pierre continued:

"But much more recently it also served as a hideout for the resistance against the Colonels."

"Hence Kóstas' friend spotting the disturbance."

"Exactly."

"So, you think the disturbance might have been caused by Kokoschka looking for something there? An old document perhaps? "

"It's possible. But don't forget Isabella Marquessa may be behind this too. Her fingerprints were also in the flat. She could have been the jogger."

"I contacted Paris and they say they are aware Marquessa is running a gallery there under a different business name."

"Have them check whether Kokoschka ever worked there."

Pierre finished his glass and looked at Patrick, who shook his head.

"So, I suggest we ask the O.C.B.C. to give us a list of the sort of manuscripts that have been reaching the markets recently. See if they can make a link with any of the files you found at Deveau's. Meanwhile I'll give Chief Superintendant Lýtras a call in Athens."

Pierre's phone rang and he reached out to pick it up.

"*Rousseau à l'appareil.*"

He listened for a moment and put the receiver down.

"Kokoschka's been spotted in Italy. She flew in to Rome airport from Athens yesterday."

"Do they know where she is now?"

"No. They lost her."

*

It was not until several months later that the Abbot felt able to reveal his feelings and to speak his mind to the monks on a subject weighing heavily on his heart. He brought the early morning mass to an end and moved down to the centre of the aisle. The monks raised their heads and waited in silence for him to address them conscious of the break in the normal order of events.

"Brothers in Christ, the earthly remains of our great benefactor now repose in a tomb befitting his status. His earthly remains will be venerated by generations to come. His spirit is with God.

"Sir Geoffroi gave us of his generosity many treasures for the benefit of our communion. These are in safe keeping and we will cherish them as they deserve. Although many of these objects are not of our faith, they deserve our respect."

The Abbot bade the monks sit.

"As you are aware Sir Geoffroi spent many months recounting the events he witnessed in the Holy Land. Our scribes laboured long and hard to record faithfully his every word for it was his will that in generations to come men should marvel at what sacrifices were made for our faith.

"Our energies will henceforth be devoted to producing copies of Sir Geoffroi's words in a fashion worthy of those great events. I charge you to use your best skills to adorn his words and to furnish the account with illustrations of the great scenes he witnessed taking your inspiration from the descriptions he bequeathed to us. In this way many more of our faith all over Christendom will be able to read of the Holy Crusade to rescue our Holy City, in accordance with Sir Geoffroi's wish.

"The value of these works, wrought by your hands, will bring welcome income to our monastery and will spread word of our art and skills to those who follow."

The monks bowed their heads as the Abbot moved down the aisle and left the chapel. He paused half way along and spoke quietly to one of their number who left his place and followed the Abbot to his cell.

*

Katja arrived in Civitavecchia, just outside Rome, having managed to shake off Marco in Athens at the end of their tour of the Lousiós Gorge. It had been fun stringing Marco along, but enough was enough. He had become an irritant. Still, it had injected some extra amusement into what was already an exciting assignment.

The real question in her mind, which she could not quite resolve, was whether Lucca had sent Marco there to check on her, or whether she was there to check on Marco. She had reported what they had found out to Lucca over the phone, he had seemed satisfied and invited her to go out to Sardinia again to discuss in more detail how they were going to proceed.

As she boarded the ferry for the crossing to the island, she reflected she was being paid to do exactly what she loved doing. How good was that? Back in Bordeaux Marcel Bouvier would be shocked to know what she was up to on the side, but then life had to have its exciting moments, otherwise what was the point?

The crossing was uneventful and she passed the hours lazing on the deck soaking in the sun and the warm breeze raised by the speed of the boat. The ferry docked in the little port of Olbia, which has not got a lot going for it, she reflected, as she waited for a bus to take her on to Palau on the northern tip of the island. She was very tempted to take a taxi when she saw the state of the bus and the number of passengers, but knew that would draw attention to herself and Lucca had warned her to be as discreet as possible.

She climbed on board the ancient vehicle and made her way down the bus squeezing past the locals who were laden with goods bought at the market and finally found a seat near the back. The bus pulled away and soon they were outside the town, giving her glimpses of the rocky countryside as they climbed and descended the narrow road leading north.

Palau was not far, but it took a good hour by the time the bus had meandered through little villages and stopped at the entrance to tracks which apparently led to some isolated habitation. The driver seemed to know most of the passengers and lengthy conversations took place at the door of the bus at every stop before the travellers alighted.

In Palau, Katja struggled her way to the front of the bus and climbed down. She stood for a moment looking round the little square. On the far side there was a car waiting, the driver leaning against the door, smoking. He looked up as she got off the bus, threw down his cigarette, and started to walk towards her.

"You are the Signorina who visit Signor Lucca, I think?"

"Yes," she replied removing her sun-glasses.

"You get in car and I take you to 'is 'ouse."

"*Grazie.*"

"*Prego,*" he said opening the door for her.

The journey was a short one and driven at speed by a driver who had done the journey many times before and knew every twist, turn and bump in the road. Lucca's house was high up on the cliffs and as the car swung into the drive Katja was again awestruck by the sight of the wide bay and the grandly named *Archipelago della Maddalena* spread out below. Lucca himself was waiting for her on the steps. She got out of the car and paused to admire the view stretching across to the *Isola Caprera*, where she knew Garibaldi had finally made his home and was buried in the garden beside his wife and sons.

Lucca watched her reaction to the view as she got out of the car and gestured her to follow him in. She noticed he walked leaning heavily on his stick and remembered he had injured his leg badly. He went ahead leading her into the main room where the view was maintained through the French windows.

Outside on the terrace a table was set up ready with water and glasses. A bottle of white wine stood in an ice bucket by the side. Rather out of character, Lucca waited till Katja had sat down before he took his seat. He poured her a glass of water and then wine for them both. Katja kept her surprise at this gentlemanly behaviour out of her expression as she raised her glass in response to his.

"Well, how was it, Signorina? You did well with Marco. *É molto frustrate*! He was very cross when I tell him you knew who he was all the time."

He leaned forward towards her.

"But to serious matters, Signorina. I want to know what you find out. Do you know where the manuscript will be?"

"What we do know, Signore, is that the original was written in the original Filosófou monastery and copies were made and sold to passing travellers and visitors.

"The story goes that the effort of recounting the details of the crusade took its toll on Geoffroi de Vinsauf's health and soon after he finished dictating he passed away and was buried in the chapel. That much is definitely true. His tomb is still there. We found it in the chapel."

"The manuscript, did they bury it with the body?"

"I doubt that. The monks had excellent business sense and would have kept the original in order to make further copies. The manuscript was too valuable to them to give it up like that. They would have kept it in their library."

"So, it is still there?"

"The library's in ruins so everything depends on what happened when the old monastery was abandoned centuries later."

Lucca looked thoughtful and picked up the bottle to replenish their glasses. Katja waited as he looked out to sea and analysed what she had said.

"So what do you think?"

"It is possible it is still there, but it is more likely they took all the manuscripts with them when they moved to the new monastery, but we can't know whether any were lost or destroyed."

"So we search for this manuscript in the new monastery?"

"That would be difficult without attracting attention. The monastery is like a fortress. All the monasteries were built like that, but at the same time they are very exposed. Any strange goings on would be immediately spotted. Anything short of murdering the caretaker monk would not work."

Lucca fractionally raised an eyebrow at this remark, but quickly continued, covering his reaction by raising his glass to his lips.

"So, we start first with the old site?"

"That would be best, Signor Lucca, but it would not be easy without attracting attention. Any disturbance would be noticed. We found fresh flowers there, so the place is still visited by the locals."

Katja had noticed Lucca's reaction to her passing remark about the monk and felt her unease growing. Once more she had the feeling this man before her was more dangerous than he appeared. Surely he had not taken her seriously? She wondered again how Lucca had damaged his leg.

"Tell to me about the copies, Signorina? How can you tell them apart from the original?"

"The original would be much simpler in presentation than the copies. The scribes would have spent some time making the copies more marketable by illuminating them and writing in a fancy script. They would possibly have included pictures, drawing on Sir Geoffroi's memory to help them draw some battle scenes."

Lucca fell silent. Her mind racing, Katja grew more nervous as she sat by this strange Italian, who could behave like a gentleman, but who had depths of steel which she preferred not to think too hard about.

Lucca was weighing up the options and considering how far he might have to go. Marco was a good man, but could he do what he had in mind? More to give himself time to think than because he was really interested, he asked:

"How is everybody so sure this manuscript ever existed?"

Katja relaxed a little. She was on safer ground now. She had done her research well and kept her nervousness under control by recounting what she knew.

"The first complete printed version was made in 1687 in Oxford. The printer based his text on a copy of the original, but that copy has been lost."

"Are you sure this was not, how do you say, a trick, *un falso?*"

"As sure as I can be. John Fell, the printer, was a great scholar who set up the first university press. He even designed his own type faces. He was also Vice Chancellor of Oxford University and Bishop of Oxford."

"So, *un Grande!*"

"Indeed. Fell wouldn't have risked his reputation by printing a fake. He must have come across a copy and decided to print it. There had also been fragments of Geoffroi's account around before that. Most notably," she continued, slipping automatically into the precise jargon of her trade, "in a work by Jacques Bongars, a French diplomat and scholar. These fragments have been used to verify parts of Fell's text. As we would say, the provenance is good."

"*Bravo*, you have done well, Signorina, I am very impressed. You make your money. I contact you when we have the manuscript."

The meeting was over.

At that Lucca got up, bowed slightly to Katja and walked off the terrace without no further word. Katja stood for a moment slightly bewildered and made her way to the front of the house. To her surprise the car was waiting for her and the driver was holding the door open. She got in and was driven back to Palau.

Rather than go on to Olbia and take the ferry back to the mainland that evening she decided she deserved some relaxation after the strain of the meeting with Lucca. The nearby upmarket resort of Porto Cervo beckoned. She found a local taxi in the village square and settled back to enjoy the short drive into another world.

*

The Abbot entered his cell and sat at the simple table at the far end. He poured himself a glass of water from the jug and motioned to the monk who had followed him in to sit. As there were no other chairs in the cell the monk settled himself cross-legged on the stone floor and pulled his robe around himself.

"Brother Simeon," the Abbot began slowly, choosing his words carefully, "I need not remind you the Lord in his wisdom has granted us a bounty which is not given to all the holy communities in this valley. The words Sir Geoffroi has left us are of great value to all those who believe in the Our Lord's Holy Mission to bring all people into his embrace. It falls to us to spread abroad the tales of valour and sacrifice which Sir Geoffroi describes for the edification and instruction of those who will follow and who will also take up the sword to rid our Holy Places of the Infidel."

Brother Simeon shifted slightly on his haunches as he listened silently to what the Abbot was saying.

"Our brothers must strive to work diligently and with all speed to produce worthy copies of Sir Geoffroi's words. I place the burden of seeing this is done on your shoulders. I also charge you with ensuring that these manuscripts reach all those of the faithful who desire to read of these events. The donations you will seek in return will be used to the benefit of this place and to the glory of God."

The Abbot took another sip of water and nodded his dismissal of Brother Simeon.

Chapter 8

On the same day Katja flew back to Bordeaux from Rome, Pierre and Patrick flew to Athens to join Chief Inspector Antonia Antoniarchis and her deputy, Inspector Eleni Tsikas. Both men were looking forward to working with their opposite numbers in Greece again. They settled back in their seats, neither saying much, preoccupied as they were with thinking about the Deveau case and possible further developments in Greece.

Patrick soon dozed off, but Pierre could not prevent his mind whirring. Switching on the in-flight film had no calming effect, so he gave in to the speculating and tried again to make sense of the pieces of the jigsaw.

Was Kokoschka just who she said she was? What was she really doing in Greece and Italy? Did she have anything to do with Deveau's death or was that just a coincidence after all? Had she broken into Deveau's shop? What was she looking for? Or was it Isabella Marquessa? Is there a link between the two of them? What deal was Deveau involved in?

Pierre finally dozed off just as the cabin crew announced their imminent arrival in Athens.

Patrick felt refreshed as he walked down the steps onto the tarmac. Pierre much less so. They waited at the carousel to collect their luggage and were ushered quickly through the formalities. Antonia and Eleni were waiting for them with the official car and they were escorted through the Athens traffic by outriders to the Hôtel de Police for a briefing with Chief Superintendent Lýtras.

"Welcome Commissaire, Inspector. I am pleased to be working with you both again. After what you told me on the phone Commissaire about your Deveau case – have I got the name right? – we think there may be links with a new case we have here in Greece. That is why Chief Inspector Antoniarchis and I thought of reconstructing such a successful team and inviting you back."

He paused for a moment and looked at each of them in turn as they sat in the chairs arranged in front of his desk. Pierre gave him a moment to continue, but when Lýtras remained silent, he asked:

"We are delighted to be here and will help in any way we can, Chief Superintendant. Can you explain in what way there may be a link between the two cases?"

"Chief Inspector Antoniarchis will brief you in detail, but I can tell you it involves the monasteries which your Mademoiselle Kokoschka recently visited. And there is also a complication which involves the sensitivities of the Orthodox Church here in Greece."

"Concerning the monasteries in the Lousiós Gorge?"

"Indeed, Commissaire."

Lýtras fell silent for a moment and looked at each of them in turn.

"The gorge is not just famous for its monasteries, it is also well known as the place where the Revolutionaries hid out during the rebellion against the Turkish occupation …"

Pierre glanced at Patrick by his side.

"…and later it was a haven for those involved in the resistance against the Colonels."

Lýtras' gaze hovered over Antonia for a second. Then he rose from his chair, looked at his watch and said:

"I am sorry to be a little mysterious, but I have another meeting and must leave you. Welcome again, Commissaire Rousseau, Inspector Bruni. I will leave you in the capable hands of my colleagues who will brief you more fully on the details so far."

They all stood and shook hands before leaving the office. Outside, Pierre looked at Antonia and Eleni and said:

"What on earth was all that about? Why did he look at you like that at the end?"

Ignoring the question, Antonia smiled.

"Right, now the formalities are over, time for you to sign in at your hotel."

Both men could not prevent a brief flash of disappointment showing on their faces, at which Antonia's tinkling laugh echoed in the corridor.

"Don't worry – it's just for the sake of form. We're all dining at Kóstas' tonight. There we'll tell you what all the mystery is about. Afterwards, we shall see what we shall see."

A car was waiting for them outside the building and Pierre and Patrick were driven away to their official hotel. The car drew up at the door of the hotel and the driver helped them with their cases. The two men approached the reception desk to complete the formalities of booking in. Professional instincts and training cause them both instinctively to scrutinise the people waiting in the foyer. Pierre thought there was at least one watcher. How could that be? he thought. No-one is supposed to know we are here and yet we are being followed already.

They took the lift up to their rooms on the fourth floor and arranged to meet in the bar an hour later. Pierre knew the watcher would be observing the numbers flashing up over the lift doors in the foyer and pressed the number 6 on the operating keypad. Patrick nodded his understanding. At the sixth floor they pressed the number 2 on the keypad and the lift headed downwards. On the second floor they left the lift and walked back up to their own floor.

"It won't work," said Pierre, "but we mustn't make it too easy for him."

"How many do you think?" asked Patrick.

"One definite, possibly a couple, I'm not sure" Pierre replied.

"You mean the one on the first floor landing looking down over the banisters. He never took his eyes off us. So, someone is interested in our presence here. Who do you think they are?"

"I have no idea, but I'll let Antonia know."

They reached their floor where they had adjacent rooms and automatically checked the corridor before letting themselves in. Nothing.

An hour later both men were perched on bar stools, sipping an early aperitif and discussing what had happened since their arrival – which wasn't a great deal.

"So what was Lýtras hinting at? It's unlike him to be so mysterious, his word," asked Patrick.

"We'll have to wait until this evening to find out. Antonia also likes to tease by not revealing what she knows. She holds it all back until the right dramatic moment."

Just like someone else I know, thought Patrick, unable to prevent the grin showing on his face. Pierre read his reaction and responded with a chuckle.

'OK! I know what you're thinking, Patrick."

*

A car arrived for them at eight and they were whisked off to the restaurant run by Eleni's uncle, Kóstas Chatzidákis. He welcomed them warmly and led them to their table towards the back of the restaurant, where Eleni and Antonia were waiting. The table was already covered with a selection of *mezés* and an open, half-empty bottle of wine was a clue for the two French detectives to gage how long their Greek colleagues had been waiting at the table.

"Our apologies," said Eleni getting up to welcome them. "But we could not wait with so many good things to eat in front of us. It's my uncle's fault. Kóstas is really pleased you have both returned. So we drank a toast to the villains without whom you would not need to be here!"

Pierre and Patrick took their seats and raised their glasses in mock salute to the villains.

At this Kóstas returned with further supplies and pulled up a chair to sit with them. Several more toasts were drunk. Some even to the gods of Ancient Greece, who, according to Kóstas, needed a boost to their morale as he felt they had been neglected by mere mortals for too long.

The serious business of choosing from the menu resulted in Pierre and Antonia staying with fish, knowing the *psária plaki* would be superb. Patrick went for *mousakás* and Eleni for the *kléftiko*, goat being her favourite meat when done well as she knew it would be.

"So, come on," said Patrick aiming his fork at a dish by his side. "You can't keep us waiting any longer. What's been going on and why are we here – not that I am complaining ..." *Loin de là*! he thought to himself.

He took a bite of the *mezés* he had chosen, nodded his appreciation and added:

" .. except that you should know we were tailed to our hotel. There was at least one, possibly more watchers."

Antonia didn't seem surprised at the news and picked up her phone. She spoke rapidly to the person on the other end, snapped her phone shut and nodded to Pierre. Eleni had helped herself to more *mezés* and looked at Antonia as she put the phone down. Receiving her assent, she began:

"Well," she said, addressing Pierre and Patrick, "it seems we may be about to experience another attempt to steal part of our country's heritage, which as you know we are passionate about preventing. We believe some of the main players may be the same as those whom we foiled last summer. Those who survived of course."

Pierre reached across for more olives.

"You mean Giovanni Lucca?"

"We haven't seen him yet, but the Leontarakis are back and were seen spending time with someone you will recognise."

Eleni drew out a photograph from the folder on the table and laid it before the two men.

"Well, what a surprise!*"* said Pierre, not looking at all surprised, as the smiling face of Katja Kokoschka looked back at him sitting beside the two Americans at a hotel bar.

"Yes, that's Kokoschka …"

"And there are our old friends George and Mira Leontarakis with her," said Patrick. "All we need is Isabella Marquessa to complete the picture."

"Has she resurfaced too? And what more do you know about this Kokoschka woman?" asked Antonia.

"Yes, she has. I'll tell you more about Kokoschka in a moment. Where was this photo taken, Eleni?"

"In a hotel in Dimitsána. We followed the Americans there after they re-entered the country. They took the same trip to the Lousiós Gorge as your Kokoschka woman. Is that a coincidence?"

"In theory it could be. We have nothing definite yet on Kokoschka. But it's possible they knew each other before the trip. The Americans are collectors and Kokoschka once worked in a gallery in Paris. But it's not a crime to meet someone on holiday and chat to them. What makes you suspect them of evil again?"

"More her than them for the moment. She made an unusual detour to visit the the Palía Moni Filosófou, an old monastery which is now in ruins."

"So? Why unusual?"

"It's not on the usual sight-seeing trail and she was accompanied by an Italian who was also on the trip by the name of Marco Platini. We don't know much about him yet ..."

"... but possibly an associate of Lucca?"

"Exactly."

Eleni looked across at Kóstas to fill in more of the story. For a moment Kóstas looked grim, but soon recovered and began:

"Well, my friends," he said, looking at the two Frenchmen, "the Lousiós Gorge, as you know, means more to someone of my generation than just monasteries. It was very inaccessible until relatively recently and was a useful hiding place when we were opposing the regime of the Colonels in the seventies."

Pierre had had reason to be grateful the previous summer to Kóstas and his fellow patriots for the skills they had learned during that dark period of Greece's history.

"We established several hiding places, one of which was in the old Filosófou monastery which was abandoned in the seventeenth century, when the monks moved to the new site."

He paused for more wine and to let everyone serve themselves from the dishes which had just arrived at the table.

"We lost a great friend there during those troubled times and my cousin Dmitri regularly goes to lay flowers at the spot where he died. A couple of days ago he realised others had been there too and been disturbing the ruins."

"Disturbing?" asked Pierre.

"Someone had been moving stones, as if they wanted to make a tunnel into where the old library was."

"Has Dmitri any idea of who has done this?"

"Not yet ..." said Kóstas.

"Is there anything valuable left in the monastery?" asked Patrick.

"The only objects of value would have been in the chapel, but those were removed long ago," replied Eleni.

"So why would anyone be trying to tunnel into the library … ?" asked Patrick through a mouth full of *mousakás.*"

"…wouldn't the monks have taken all the treasures and books to the new monastery when they left?" Pierre continued for him, noticing Kóstas was listening closely.

"Nobody really knows, but that's a fair assumption," said Antonia. "This is why we have called you both in. It looks like a similar attempt to last time is being made to find an artefact and to smuggle it out of Greece. Some of those involved, as you have seen, are familiar faces."

"I would have thought the Americans got their fingers burnt enough last time," said Patrick, busy using the bread to soak up the last of the sauce on his plate.

Kóstas slapped him on the back.

"I see you have not lost your appetite since your last visit, Patrick. Maybe it is time for you to dance it off?"

As if on cue the balalaika players picked up their instruments and began to play. Some of the regulars were already leaving their tables and heading for the floor. Eleni took Patrick's hand and dragged him off to the join the growing circle of dancers.

At the table Kóstas looked serious.

"There is more I'm afraid, Pétros, my friend."

Antonia nodded, as if to give him permission to continue.

"Yesterday Dmitri followed the track up to the new monastery – the one the monks moved to. It is almost abandoned too, but normally there is one monk there to look after it. He acts as caretaker and says mass regularly in the chapel. He also receives the many tourists who come to see the site and the frescoes which are quite famous. This brings in a little money for him to live on."

"When Dmitri got there," Antonia took up the story, "he found the gates wide open and the chapel unguarded. He searched around and found the monk's body half-way down the cliff where he had clearly been thrown."

"Thrown?" asked Pierre. "Couldn't he have slipped gathering herbs or something?"

"Indeed, but he was badly beaten before he fell."

"And you suspect the same person or persons who disturbed the ruins in the old monastery had gone to the new one to find what they were looking for?"

"Yes, and the poor old monk was probably beaten before he was pushed off the cliff by his attacker who tried to make him reveal where what they were looking for was hidden in the monastery."

"So, what do you think they are after?" asked Pierre.

"Possibly part of the treasure given to the monastery by the Crusaders. But it could be a manuscript or a book hidden in the old libraries."

Pierre was about to say something when Patrick and Eleni returned to the table in a flurry of laughter. Patrick flopped down into his seat looking hot and out of breath. Eleni remained standing with her hands on her hips looking down at him.

"He has quite a talent, your inspector, Commissaire. He just needs to get fit and we shall turn him into a real Greek yet."

Patrick downed a glass of water in one gulp and took his seat. Ignoring the interruption, Pierre refilled his glass and went on in a serious tone.

"What you have told me," he said looking at Antonia and Kóstas, "fits in with what we know."

He picked up his glass and continued to voice his thoughts.

"Despite what I said earlier it's too much of a coincidence that Kokoschka and the Americans should turn up in the valley at the same time, at the same time as a possible henchman of Lucca's, especially when soon afterwards the places they visited are disturbed and a monk is murdered."

He nodded to Patrick who had quickly recovered and regained his concentration on hearing Pierre's last remark. He took up the story.

"Kokoschka works as an architect in Bordeaux. But she also had dealings with a book dealer who we have been keeping an eye on for some time. We suspected him of dealing on the side in stolen rare books and manuscripts"

"Suspected …?" said Antonia.

"He was found dead last week in his flat. We don't know how he died yet. Later his bookshop was broken into. We think it might have been Kokoschka who broke in. She left for Greece at short notice immediately afterwards despite being told to not to leave Bordeaux. So it's possible after what you have told us, that she found something in Deveau's files indicating some sort of deal concerning an early book or manuscript. Her present employer says she is an expert in the field."

Pierre continued:

"The murder of the monk has Lucca written all over it, especially since this Platini was there too and Kokoschka went straight on to Italy after leaving here …"

"… to Italy?" interrupted Antonia.

"Yes, so we need to establish whether she went there to meet someone – Lucca, most likely if our theory is correct. That would be the link we're looking for."

"So where do we go from here?" asked Eleni, glancing at Antonia.

"I suggest, if Pierre agrees, that you two," said Antonia looking at Patrick and Eleni, "dress up as tourists and take a trip to the Lousiós Gorge."

"Good idea. You can check the monasteries and find out if anything is missing. I'll follow up on Platini – there will no doubt be a picture on file if he is known to the Italian police. And I'll ask the Italians to trace exactly where Kokoschka went after she left Rome," said Pierre.

"And we will find out where the Leontarakis are now," said Antonia.

Kóstas clapped his hands and announced:

"That's settled then. Enough work for tonight, my friends. Now you must pay more attention to the food I have prepared for you and to the dancing."

Looking at Antonia, he added softly: "We will talk more later about how I and my friends can help."

*

Much later that evening the four of them left the restaurant. Patrick and Eleni took a taxi back to her flat via the hotel. Pierre and Antonia decided to walk.

"I don't have anything with me," said Pierre as he took her arm.

"That sounds promising! I've bought you some shirts for tomorrow. We'll collect your stuff from the hotel later."

"Whatever you say, madame."

"That'll be a first!"

They entered her flat and Pierre looked around to see if much had changed since he was last there in the late summer. Antonia had moved a few pictures about and there were one or two he didn't recognise. Seeing the direction of his gaze, Antonia said:

"One of the perks of being welcome at the museum is that they let me have the odd picture on loan as they would if I had my own office there."

"*Magnifique*," Pierre said, pursing his mouth in appreciation. "Not something we are entitled to in Bordeaux."

"The wine is in the fridge. Help yourself while I take a shower," she said retreating into the bedroom.

Pierre took two glasses and the bottle out onto the balcony. The air was still warm despite the lateness of the season and he was content to look out over the cityscape and the lights spread out below him. He must have dozed off for a minute, as when Antonia returned he opened his eyes with a start.

"I thought you would like to see one of the shirts I bought you," she said standing there in the doorway to the balcony striking a modelling pose.

"I'd love to see the rest," he replied.

"I assume you are referring to the shirts, monsieur."

"Unless there's something else you're wearing I can't see, madame."

"Follow me to make sure."

He picked up the glasses and was making his way to the bedroom when his phone rang.

"*Merde!* Why didn't I switch off?" he groaned, as he pressed it to his ear.

"What is it, Patrick?" the irritation showing in his voice.

"Sorry, *chef*, but you'd better come over here. Both our rooms at the hotel have been given a thorough going over. Someone is keeping a close eye on us."

"So we were right. This definitely has Lucca written all over it. O.K. *J'arrive.*"

*

It was the year 1601 when the Abbot gathered the monks together on the very terrace where four centuries earlier a lonely knight had gazed his last out over the valley and where the Abbot's predecessor had called his flock together in the same way. The sun was beginning to show itself but the morning chill was such that the monks' breath showed like puffs of smoke on the still air.

"Look around you, my brothers. Our home is in sad need of repair. It is no longer worthy of our mission to preserve and spread the words of our Lord."

The wide sweep of his gesture took in the extent of the desolation.

"The Lord in his bounty has come to our aid. Brother Benedict has discovered treasures the like of which we could not dream of. The spirit of the great Crusader we honour in this place has come to our aid. The gifts he gave to our predecessors have been rediscovered hidden away for safe keeping. Amongst the many gold and silver objects both of our own faith and of that of the Turk we have discovered an ancient manuscript, perhaps the very first copy, of the knight's witness of the Crusade.

"These riches will enable us to begin our long desired endeavour – the building of a new monastery to the glory of God."

The assembled monks turned towards each other and a low excited murmur spread through the brothers as they shared the import of the Abbot's announcement. He quickly called them to order.

"My brothers, first there is much work to do. You will devote your time to making copies of the manuscript we have found just as I believe your brothers did long ago. These we will take to our brothers in Stemnítsa for printing. Brother Benedict has already made contact with a French man - Monsieur Jacques Bongars — who will take our books and sell them in all Europe."

One of the monks listening dared to interrupt the Abbot and raise a hand.

"Yes, Brother Ignatius. What is it?"

The Abbot did not appreciate the increasing tendency of the younger monks to ask questions.

"My Lord Abbot, you said there were also treasures not of our faith. What will happen to these?"

"That need not concern you Brother Ignatius. They will be disposed of and the proceeds will enable us to purchase the materials we need to build our new home.

"The Lord has provided for us and we will work in his great name."

Chapter 9

Marco got into the front seat of the car waiting for him at the ferry port of Olbia and sat back as he was driven up to Lucca's house. He had plenty to report. He knew he had done a good job of tracking the arrival of the two French detectives in Athens and of searching their hotel rooms, but he was less certain of Lucca's reaction to what had occurred when he returned to the Lousiós Gorge.

He was always nervous coming out to Sardinia. He sensed he didn't know enough about what had happened the previous summer and why Lucca was so obsessed with the two Frenchmen.

The higher the car climbed into the mountains and the closer they came to Lucca's, the lower he sank into his seat. Perhaps I went too far with the monk, he thought, but how did I know the fool was going to be so stubborn? All he had to do was to tell me where the door to the library was. *Cretino!*

Lucca was nowhere to be seen when he stepped out of the car. He stood for a moment looking about him. One of Lucca's dogs stood outside the front door glaring at him and daring him to climb the steps to enter the building.

He shouted at the dog, which immediately meekly lay down. As he started up the steps, Lucca appeared in the doorway.

"Well done, *molto impressionante*, Marco! Few people would have dared do that, let alone succeeded."

He dismissed the dog, which slunk away head down, his tail between his legs, but wagging slightly.

"Come in – I've something to show you."

He led Marco in to the dining area. On the table several Greek newspapers were spread out. All showed the same photograph and had similar headlines deploring the death of the monk who was the sole guardian of one of the best preserved monasteries in Greece.

The next thing Marco knew, his head was against the wall and Lucca's hands were around his throat, his face centimetres from Marco's as he spat out:

"That is what you call *'discreto'* is it, *imbecille*? You go to the monasteries, leave a trail of destruction and a monk who is dead. Everyone know what you have done and will guess why you do it. Maybe I kill you right now."

Marco slid down the wall as Lucca released his grip. He rubbed his throat gasping for air.

"The stupid monk did not say to me what I wanted to know," he managed to rasp out.

"So you kill him, *pezzo di cretino*! Now he can not tell us anything, can he? Did you think of asking him nicely, you fool?"

Lucca viciously kicked the cringing form on the floor and leaned over him.

"I give you one more chance to look for the manuscript. If you fail this time, for your good health it is better we never met again. No mistakes this time, *capito?*"

"*Si. Giovanni.*"

Lucca turned sharply on his heel and left the room. Marco remained slumped where he was for a while longer. He could not stop shaking and his throat still ached from where Lucca's fingers had tightened round it.

He slowly pulled himself to his feet and shuffled towards the door and out onto the drive. No car was waiting for him this time, so he had no alternative but to set out on the long walk back to Olbia. Behind him he heard the dog growling.

*

The previous night had been a long one after the discovery of the break-ins at the hotel. Pierre and Antonia had arrived to find the forensic team already at work in the rooms. When the team had finally finished up and they were able to return to the flat and fall into bed exhausted, it was five in the morning.

Later that day Patrick and Eleni packed their bags for the tourist trip to the Lousiós Gorge. They had taken advantage of a late cancellation on the next trip out leaving the following day.

"Thank goodness we have the rest of the day to recover from last night before going," complained Patrick. "Why do we have to go undercover anyway? We might just as well make it an official visit and then we can avoid having to be with a tourist group. You know I hate that."

"You didn't complain about being undercover last night I seem to remember. I can arrange it for not being undercover tonight if you prefer!"

Patrick gave her a shove and she fell laughing over the suitcase onto the floor.

"You know what I mean…"

"Yes, you're saying you don't want to come with me on a free holiday to a beautiful Greek valley … But seriously, despite your horror of tourists we may learn something from the tour guide about which monasteries the Americans visited and of course whether Kokoschka and Platini went to any others. I checked to make sure it's the same guide. Later Pierre and Antonia will interview him formally if we find out anything."

"Since we are being watched so closely, do you think we will be followed?"

"That's for us to find out, but I think whoever it is will be reluctant to show their hand again so soon."

"Who do you think is behind this?"

"Well, after last time when Pierre and Antonia were both kidnapped, I'm sure it's Lucca again. He has the motive."

She looked at her watch and phoned for a car to take them to the police headquarters.

"Time for the briefing already," she said. "Perhaps we will also find out more from forensics about who searched your rooms in the hotel."

Chief Superintendent Lýtras was waiting for them with Antonia and Pierre. They had already been discussing the case for a while before the others arrived.

"Sorry we are late, Chief Superintendent," said Eleni. "My colleague is a slow packer it seems."

"Not at all, Inspector Tsikas. We were just reviewing the case so far, before your arrival. It seems you must be getting close and that someone wants to know how close. However now we have a murder to investigate too."

"Have forensics come up with anything in the hotel rooms?" asked Eleni.

"We have evidence which will yield DNA, but have no match as yet. The DNA has been passed to Europol and Interpol," Lýtras replied.

"We want you and Inspector Bruni to look carefully round both Filosófou sites. They have been reopened to the public so your visit will not attract attention. We also want you of course to keep your ears open for the local talk and anything the guide may remember about those on the last trip before the attack on the monk," said Antonia.

"Meanwhile we will have the archives searched for any material indicating where the library was in the older monastery and whether there are any records of what was taken over to the new site," said Lýtras, looking down at a folder as he spoke.

"Do we have any further proof whether it is a book or manuscript or some other artefact the thieves are looking for?" asked Eleni.

"An astute question, Inspector. No we don't, but our French colleagues have strong suspicions this case is linked with events in Bordeaux of which you are aware and therefore it is likely that it is a manuscript which is at stake."

He looked across at Antonia to continue. She shifted in her seat and addressed Eleni and Patrick directly.

"In view of the history of the Gorge at the time when the monasteries were more of a going concern, if I may put in that way, the chances are there were several original manuscripts written by Crusaders who took refuge in the monasteries. We can rule out paintings and icons as the target of the collectors, since these were not common in the early monasteries. They were mostly confined to the richer village churches and were very vulnerable to looting."

Patrick, who had remained quiet up to this point, asked:

"What about the murder of the monk? Has a weapon been found? Do we know exactly how he was killed and when?"

"A good point, Detective Inspector," answered Lýtras. "A slow packer perhaps, but not a slow detective."

He paused and smiled at his own joke.

"No, we found no weapon, for the simple reason that he was badly beaten, probably with fists and boots, before being thrown over the cliff. He was still alive – it was the fall which killed him."

He looked round at each of them.

"Well, if that is all, the meeting is at end. Thank you all for coming. You will keep me up to date, Chief Inspector."

"Of course, Chief Superintendent."

Once outside, they went down to the canteen in a sombre mood thinking of the fate of the monk. Patrick and Pierre reached for the *baklavá* to have with their coffee.

"Not too many, you two," remarked Eleni. "We are due at Uncle Kóstas' this evening."

Looking round, she added softly:

"He has offered to help – unofficially of course."

*

Katja arrived back at Olbia airport in the afternoon to find Lucca's chauffeur standing at the exit holding out a placard with her name on it. He raised his hand when he saw her and led her to the car. Katja tried to start a conversation but the driver did not respond so she fell silent and was left with her thoughts.

She had received a second summons from Lucca to go to his house in Sardinia and this time had managed to book a flight over a long weekend. That way she did not have to ask Marcel Bouvier for leave so soon after her last absence. She had been able to report back for work looking refreshed and rested after that trip and he had said he had never seen her looking better.

His compliments had come close to flirting. That had caused her to wonder what his home life was like. She had not been long enough in the firm yet to have found out much about her colleagues. Bouvier was a good looker and Katja had always assumed he was spoken for. She had never seen him go for a run or noticed any other signs of his taking part in sport, but it was obvious he kept in good physical shape.

Not for the first time since her appointment she couldn't stop herself musing on what he might be like as a lover. Perhaps she would get the chance to find out one day.

Her reverie was abruptly broken into by Lucca's driver announcing their imminent arrival at the house. As they approached the iron gates, the dogs began to bark. The chauffeur operated the gates from inside the car and indicated to Katja with a jerk of the head that she should not step out of the car. Followed by the still barking dogs they drove up to the foot of the steps leading up to the main door. Lucca appeared and silenced the dogs with a snap of his fingers. They stopped barking immediately and raced up the steps to sit by him.

"*Buongiorno,* Signorina Kokoschka. *Ben arrivata.* Good of you to come over again so soon."

"*Buongiorno*, Signor Lucca. Thank you for sending the car to meet me."

Lucca led her into the main room and she stood at the window marvelling at the view across the bay. Lucca watched her for a few minutes without saying anything and then motioned to her to take a seat. He took his seat opposite her in the other armchair and flicked his fingers in what was evidently a pre-arranged signal, as a servant appeared immediately with a tray of *baci*, slices of *zuccotto*, and a bottle of Orvieto Abboccatto. He looked pleased at her surprise.

"I hope you enjoy sharing this little vice of mine, Signorina. I have a weakness for what we Italians call *baci* – kisses – and, what to true Tuscans like myself tastes like home, a slice of *zuccotto*. They are *fantastico* with a small glass of sweet, but not too sweet, white wine."

Katja viewed with some misgiving the enticing slices of sponge cake with its filling of nuts and chocolate and cream.

"That will cost me a long run tomorrow, but I accept your kind hospitality," she said with a smile, wondering all the time what was behind all this politeness.

Marco had told her about the *tombarolo* tradition of breaking into tombs and selling the artefacts found inside to collectors all over the world. Judging by some of the objects she could see displayed around the room, Lucca had been or was still successful in that side of his affairs.

"Now, down to business, Signorina."

Lucca settled back in his chair and looked across at Katja.

"As you know I want to find an old manuscript written by this Crusader. When I have it, you will say to me if it is genuine. However since you last went to Lousiós Gorge many things have changed. I must ask more money than before from the buyer."

"I don't understand. I thought the manuscript was for you. That is what I was told."

"No, I find it for another person. I want you to talk to the *Americanos* you met on your trip and to explain them the price is half a million of their dollars, not a quarter of a million."

Seeing the look of surprise in her eyes and mistaking its origin, he added with a smile:

"Your fee of course remains the same percentage."

"You mean the Leontarakis are the ones who want the manuscript? They are involved in this?"

"*Certo.* Yes, they are not so innocent as they seem. They are the buyers. Their act is very convincing, no?"

"Yes. I did recognise their name as collectors, Signore, but I thought this time they were there just as tourists. Perhaps I should have read the signs better."

"Don't worry, Signorina, why should you suspect them? They are professionals – that is what they do."

"But why me? Where do you want me to meet them? How will they react when I tell them I know the real reason why they were there?" asked Katja warily, taking another piece of the *zuccotto*.

"That's easy. We are fortunate they are in your Bordeaux town visiting an old friend of mine, and of yours of course – Jean-Louis Deveau. He help me from time to time and he recommend you, Signorina, as you know. The *Americanos* will be surprised, but not angry, I think."

"But Deveau has had an accident."

"Jean-Louis? How strange," Lucca said sitting up in his chair and picking up his glass. "What sort of accident?"

"I don't really know, but he was found dead in his flat only a few days ago. You didn't know?"

"No, I had no idea. That's very sad."

"Does that change things?"

"It is sad, but I think not. You will still see the *Americanos*. I tell you where they stay and you arrange meeting for next week in the evening."

He handed her a slip of paper and got to his feet. The interview was at an end. His usual style, thought Katja. A long way to come for such a short meeting.

The car was waiting for her outside and the drive back to the airport gave her time to reflect on what she had been told. Was Lucca lying about Deveau? He hardly reacted to the news he was dead, she said to herself. Why did he ask me to deal with George and Mira and not ask Deveau? He must have known Deveau was already dead, otherwise why involve me?

The driver looked round at her and she realised she must have spoken aloud.

But how had Lucca known? She thought, being more careful not to voice her thoughts aloud. And why didn't he admit it? What am I getting myself into? Smuggling is one thing, but am I being sucked into something more sinister?

*

Dawn that day started grey and cold, unusual for the time of year. It was over eighty years since the monks had embarked on their enormous task to build a new monastery on the other side of the valley. Three generations of monks had been and gone during the construction and none of those who had taken the decision to start the building were still alive to see the result of their decision. Those who were preparing to leave the old monastery had only a hazy idea of how it was the community had found enough money to fund the project.

They knew from the older brothers that previous generations had laboured long and hard to produce wondrous manuscripts and these had caused their monastery to be become famous throughout Europe for the quality of the illuminations. The story the manuscripts told was the marvel of the age. Kings and Emperors had sent emissaries to the gates of the monastery to be sure of having copies specially bound for their libraries, complete with their personal coats of arms and dedications. As the new techniques of print-making had spread across the lands the monks had learned the skills needed for preparing the texts and illuminations for the print-makers.

But this industry on the part of their brothers had not been enough on its own to raise sufficient funds to make the building of the new monastery possible. They heard that many treasures brought from the Holy Land by the knights of old and presented to the monastery were sold to the great families of Europe. Some were even purchased by the descendants of those in the Saracen lands who had fought the Christian knights and were returned to their rightful places in the mosques and holy places of Palestine.

But on this fateful day in the year 1685 their Abbot declared the new monastery ready. Many of the stones from the old monastery had been used in the building of the new one and it was time to leave what remained. After the early mass, the monks assembled on the terrace in front of the chapel and waited patiently for the Abbot to appear before them. They were dressed in their best robes and stood shivering until the sun broke through the morning mist and shone brightly down upon them. Bundles of belongings were heaped all around.

When the Abbot appeared he too was wearing his best robes and carrying his staff. The senior brothers stood by his side. He stood for a moment his eyes blinking in the sunlight.

"Brothers in Christ, today is a momentous day for today we leave this ancient place and move to our new home. You and your predecessors have devoted your energies to creating a chapel worthy of Our Lord and even as I speak the walls and ceiling of God's House are being decorated with scenes of the life of Our Lord Jesus and His disciples.

"We will not neglect the chapel in this place however. The tomb of our great benefactor Sir Geoffroi de Vinsauf lies therein and we will continue to honour his last resting place. Every Sabbath we will return and give thanks.

"Our new library contains the works and manuscripts which have made this wondrous enterprise possible and we will devote our time to preserving these treasures without which we would not have had the means to embark on this holy work.

"I bid you gather your belongings and we will progress to our new home."

The route they took was lined with local villagers, many of whom had helped in the building of the monastery, hauling the stones and other materials up the steep slopes. The construction had provided much work for the families in the valley and they were fearful this source of much needed wages would no longer be available to them. They watched the procession approach as it left the old monastery and wound its way up the steep path to the new site. They lowered their heads in respect as it passed, but there was both fear and sadness in their eyes.

Chapter 10

That evening in the Yiántes restaurant, Pierre couldn't help thinking how good for the spirit it was to have the chance to leave the job behind and to have relaxing company and music. Ever since his separation and divorce he had found the evenings the most difficult time to fill. He had fallen into the habit of working late and shutting out the rest. His new relationship with Antonia had brought him back out of himself and reminded him there was a world outside work.

However he knew that Kóstas had become an unofficial undercover agent for Antonia and Eleni and so discussion of the present case would still form part of the evening's proceedings.

"So, you two are going on holiday I hear," Kóstas was saying, looking at Patrick and Eleni. "It's a beautiful place, especially at this time of the year. But take care, my young friends. Remember the valley hides many ghosts and holds many secrets."

"I think most of the ghosts will have been frightened off by all the visitors, Uncle," said Eleni laughing. "Anyway we're going with a tourist group. We want to hear the local gossip and to find out more about the people who were on the last tour. There must be some talk amongst the locals about the attack on the monk and the digging around at the old monastery."

"Ah, yes. That poor monk. I knew him from the old days. He was a young man then and he hid us when the Colonels sent in soldiers to flush us out."

"Really? You've never mentioned that before," said Antonia. "I thought the bishops blessed Papadopoulos and his dreadful regime."

"They did, but it did not go down well with all the priests and monks, especially the younger ones. And that made it even more dangerous for them to help us."

Pierre stopped dipping into the *mezés* and looked up.

"You said the monk hid you from the soldiers?"

"Yes, quite a few times. Even the officers did not dare to order their men to search too hard in the monasteries, so it wasn't too difficult to hide away even in such a small monastery."

"Where did you hide exactly?"

"Well, at the back of the altar in the main chapel there's a small door behind the arras. This opens onto a room where the treasures of the monastery are kept."

At this all four of them suddenly stared at Kóstas who was looking thoughtful.

"What sort of treasures?" prompted Pierre.

Kóstas remained silent for a moment before he answered.

"Well," he said carefully, "remember all this is nearly forty years ago. When you talked about manuscripts last time, it made me think back. The room was quite big and dug out of the rock behind the chapel. It was ventilated by ducts to the outside, but the temperature remained cool. On the one side there were piles of old books with leather bindings and some scrolls. These we were not allowed to touch. On the other side the books were less old and we were allowed to read these to pass the time."

"How could you see to read?" asked Antonia.

"That was a problem as the monks were afraid of fire if we lit candles and there was also the smell which might give us away, but there was some light at times when the sun shone down the vents."

He paused to take a sip of wine.

"Sometimes they let us bring out the later books and read them in the chapel itself. Whenever soldiers were spotted we went back into the hidden room and the monks lit candles in the chapel to cover any possible smell from our presence. Normally we stayed there in the dark until the soldiers had gone."

"Did the soldiers never suspect there was a hidden room?"

"Oh! I think they always knew there must be a hiding place somewhere, but they were in awe of the monks and usually left as quickly as they could. Mostly they were just young recruits."

"Did you ever have a look at the books on the forbidden wall, Uncle? Or remove any of them?"

"Of course, we looked at some. Curiosity, and boredom, got the better of us at times as we waited there sometimes for hours. We never tried to take them out to the chapel though and to my knowledge none were ever damaged though they were very fragile. The monks were risking their lives for us after all and to have broken their rules would have been the ultimate ingratitude."

"Can you describe any of them?"

Antonia tried in vain to keep the excitement out of her voice.

"There were scrolls, others just sheaves of pages tied together. Some were histories, probably accounts of battles, and of course there were a lot of religious writings. Most were quite plain – just writing – but a few were superbly coloured and decorated with all sorts of pictures and fancy scripts. We didn't unroll the parchments as they were very dry and brittle and we didn't want to damage them."

"How easy would it be for a thief to find them?" asked Eleni.

"Frankly, very easy. All they have to do is to know where the hidden door is – and it's not that difficult to find."

Eleni turned to Antonia.

"Would it be possible for the Museum to obtain permission to look at them and to catalogue them officially?"

"I'm really not sure. They are the property of the Orthodox Church and it might be difficult, but I'll look into it."

"Is the monastery guarded now the monk is dead?" asked Patrick.

"No, just locked. I have one of my men keeping watch on it though."

Eleni looked at Patrick thoughtfully as she picked at the *mezés*. She knew they were both thinking along the same lines.

"OK. We'll go under cover of darkness. Can you keep your man there, Uncle, until we arrive?"

"Of course, we want to catch whoever is doing this. We owe the monks that at least after what they did for us all those years ago."

"I didn't hear that, Kóstas. And I don't want to know more, but be careful," said Antonia. "Don't do anything you may regret, my old friend."

*

Later when they walking back to Antonia's, Pierre remarked:

"Were you a bit brutal to Kóstas with your warning?"

"*Ochi*. No, he is used to me and I have to remind him he can go too far sometimes and that it might be dangerous for him. He knows I would never – how do they say in English – grass him up, but he also knows it would be difficult for me, and of course Eleni, if he revealed too much of how he achieves his results when he does help us. I just hope Lýtras never finds out."

They were nearing her flat and despite the warm evening were pleased to be going inside. Antonia brought out a bottle of white wine and they sat and talked over the case again for a while.

"There's not much to go on at the moment, except the coincidence of some of the main players from the last case gathering," said Antonia, curling her legs under her as she sat by him on the sofa.

"True, but we do have a dead book dealer who was only discovered so quickly because of a woman with an apparently small grievance banging on his door late at night. We also have Marquessa's fingerprints in his flat and others which we have not yet identified ..."

"… then your woman with a small grievance, as you put it, turns up on a visit to a monastery, the ruins of which are later disturbed. The Leontarakis are on the same tour and an Italian gigolo, who may lead us back to Lucca…"

"…who Marquessa hates with a passion. So the circle is complete. That gives us enough pieces of a jigsaw to keep us busy for a while."

Pierre took another sip of his wine and looked at Antonia.

"Do you think we're putting Eleni and Patrick in danger by sending them on the tour with no back up? Remember we were followed here and our rooms were searched at the hotel."

"No. Don't worry. Kóstas' men will look after them better than any protection we could provide. We still don't know who broke into your rooms. There's no match on the data base for the DNA we got from the hairs forensics found."

Later as they lay side by side with just a sheet over them, Pierre's mind was still racing. Outside through the open balcony window he could hear the owls calling to one another. It was an eerie sound and their message seemed to confirm his feeling that, despite Antonia's reassurance, something bad was going to occur in the Lousiós Gorge and they were exposing Patrick and Eleni to danger.

Chapter 11

"You look as if you had a good long weekend in the sun somewhere, Katja."

Marcel was standing beside her in the main drawing office studying the designs on her drawing board. Katja had done most of her preliminary work on computer, but like many of her colleagues, liked to see an enlarged hard copy on the drawing board in the traditional way.

"Yes, thanks. I went out to Sardinia and spent most of the time walking on the cliffs or running along the beaches. It's warmer there than here on the Atlantic coast, though I do love the dunes here, at Pyla in particular."

"I can see it hasn't taken you long to find your way around the area here – you don't miss Paris too much then?"

"No," she replied, swivelling round on her chair to face him. "Perhaps a bit – the theatres and cinemas and of course the restaurants."

Marcel was tall and, despite Katja being perched on a drawing board chair, was still a head higher than her. He laughed and hesitated before visibly plucking up courage and responding:

"We have restaurants second to none in Bordeaux. If you have nothing on for lunch, may I take you to one?"

"I'd love to," she replied more quickly than she had intended. "But I can't today as I have so much to catch up on."

"Tomorrow?"

"That would be great. Thank you, Marcel."

"Excellent! I'll leave you to your work so you will have no reason to change your mind tomorrow."

He walked over to one of the other architects and was soon engrossed with him on the computer.

Katja had wanted to play for time before accepting the lunch invitation, so she could ask around the other women in the office whether he asked all the new females out to lunch. Her previous boss in Paris had defined lunch as an hour at the table followed by a couple of hours in a pre-booked nearby hotel room. Marcel Bouvier didn't seem the type to try that on. But would I mind if he did? she mused.

Anyway she was too distracted by thoughts of the meeting she was going to have with George and Mira Leontarakis that evening to pursue that line of thought very far. They were staying in a small hotel half hidden in a side street between the *cours de l'Intendance* and the *Porte Dijeaux*. The choice of this discreet, small but comfortable hotel, when they could certainly afford the biggest and the best, was in itself curious, but it suited Katja not to meet them in a more public place.

She turned back to the drawing board, but could not really focus on her work. She was still worried about quite what she was getting into with Lucca. The assignment to meet the Americans was not the problem. She did feel anxious about what their reaction would be when she revealed that she was working for Lucca. But then again they had played the same game on the trip, not letting on why they were so interested in the monasteries. Perhaps they had been more astute than her and seen through the role she was playing herself. She would soon find out.

*

Early that evening she left her studio in the *rue du Palais Gallien* and walked the short distance across the *place Gambetta* to the hotel. The receptionist called up to their room and the two Americans came down to meet her.

"Gee, how nice to see you again Kattie. How did you know where we were staying? I'm so glad you contacted us," she went on without waiting for an answer. "What a cute little town Bordeaux is – all these quaint streets and such great buildings. It's not like this at home."

Mira gave her a huge hug and Katja was enveloped in the heavy scent it seemed Mira had bathed in before coming down to greet her. George shook her hand more formally, but seemed in a good mood and watched his wife's effusive welcome without comment.

"Now dear, where can we take you for supper as our guest? I'm sure you know of quaint little places to eat and we're feeling quite faint. Back home we eat much earlier than this," Mira said, glancing at her wrist watch.

"It is still a little early for France but I know where we can go. It's not far. Just round the corner, off the *place Gambetta*."

"Oh! I do love that accent, don't you George?" gushed Mira taking Katja's arm.

Katja led them across the road to the restaurant and upstairs, where they settled down at a table near the window. She persuaded them to have an aperitif first while they decided what to order. The waitress returned with the drinks and the *kir* went straight to Mira's head as Katja knew it would.

"We don't drink much back home in Boon," she said, mopping her forehead with the napkin. "I feel quite giddy already. You are a naughty girl."

"So, what have you been doing since we met in Greece?" enquired Katja.

"Just looking in museums and galleries. You know, we like to collect nice things and there's just so much art over here."

It was George who replied as Mira was recovering from a coughing fit brought on by the remains of the *kir* going down the wrong way.

"And here in Bordeaux itself, where have you been?"

"You have that cute gallery in the old winery warehouse," said Mira, between gulps for air. "I simply loved that old building. All those arches. How clever of you people to use it as a gallery. We would have surely knocked it all down and built a new one."

The waitress had come across to their table and they fell silent as they looked at the menu, while she waited impatiently. The restaurant was quickly filling up around them and the buzz of conversation would neatly cover their own, thought Katja.

"Oh dear," sighed Mira. "I don't know what to choose. You order for me, dear. Nothing too fattening now."

George just muttered something to himself about it being too late and then, aloud, that he would have the steak and he wanted it cooked this time.

"That last place we went to, they hadn't cooked the meat and I had to keep sending it back," he complained, looking at Katja.

"I'll make certain it is cooked this time, George. Don't worry."

She looked at the waitress to see if she had understood, mouthing '*très bien cuit*'.

Katja ordered a *bouillabaisse* for herself and Mira and a bottle of Entre-deux-mers. She chatted with Mira about what they had seen in the gallery, before asking:

"And I think you told me on the trip to Lousiós Gorge you were interested in old manuscripts. Anything in particular? There are several old bookshops in Bordeaux I could take you to."

"Well, we just love the illuminated ones, but they don't come on the market very often," said George leaning back and the waitress started to put their meals on the table.

"Bring me a glass of milk and a cold Budweiser."

Katja glanced up at the girl who a had fixed smile on her face and asked George if Heineken would do. George's sigh said it all, but he looked pleased with the steak as he cut into it.

Mira took one look at the bowl of steaming *bouillabaisse* and exclaimed:

"Kattie, you wicked girl – I can't eat all of that!"

"Don't worry – it's for the two of us."

"Oh! I'm sure glad you said that," she said immediately helping herself from the bowl.

"But whatever you do don't put too much of that sauce on yours – it's very spicy."

For a while they busied themselves eating. Mira needed some persuading that all of the pieces of fish were edible, and that the mussels and pieces of crab could be picked clean using the tools provided. With much laughter she eventually got the hang of it, helped along by the wine, but drew the line at pulling the large crayfish bits apart. George meanwhile plodded steadily and silently through his steak.

Katja and Mira finally gave up on the *bouillabaisse*. They dipped their fingers in the finger bowls and used the wipes to clean their hands. Katja prepared herself to take the plunge and to tell the Americans of her link to Giovanni Lucca.

"I have a bit of a surprise for you," she said. "I am working for Signor Lucca. He wants me to authenticate the manuscript he is trying to find for you."

George looked up from his steak with a start and stared at her, his eyes narrowing.

"You mean you knew all along why we were in the Lousiós Gorge and you said nothing?"

"No, not at all, I promise you," said Katja quickly. "I've only just found out and had no idea you were anything more than interested tourists. It was a huge surprise to me!"

George seemed to relax slightly on hearing her reply and Mira cooed:

"Well, that's just what we are, my dear. Obviously we would like Mr Lucca to find us a manuscript about the Crusades, but we went to the valley just to see the wonderful country ..."

"...and the monasteries where the manuscripts were written – that is if they exist," interjected George, adding quietly. "Lucca's a slimy devil."

"How is it you are involved in this, dear?"

"Well, I trained in authenticating manuscripts during the time when I worked in a gallery in Paris. I loved doing the research, but it didn't pay well enough, so I returned to my real profession as an architect."

"So how do you know Lucca?" asked George, eyes narrowing.

"Lucca knew a book dealer here in Bordeaux called Jean-Louis Deveau. I often asked Jean-Louis to look out for any books to do with Greece and so we got to know each other quite well. He found out about my background in manuscripts and it was he who mentioned me to Lucca."

"So, it's you who will – what was that word you used – authenticate – the sort of manuscript we want," asked Mira, who despite looking as if she was asleep, had been following the conversation closely. "So now we will be know for certain whether it's genuine. That's wonderful, dear. Isn't it, George? I never trusted that man in the bookshop."

It was Katja's turn to look surprised as she realised they knew Deveau.

"So you know Deveau? You asked him to find you a manuscript?"

"We'd dealt with him before and he said he could find an old manuscript for us. He must have contacted that devil Lucca to do the job. If we had known that before we wouldn't have started all this," said George, barely containing his anger. "When Deveau told us Lucca was involved I was real angry, but it was too late. We've had trouble with that bastard before."

"George, mind your language in front of Kattie."

She turned to Katja. "Didn't I see something about Deveau in the paper recently?"

"Yes. He was found dead in his flat. I think that is why Lucca wants to deal directly with you and why he asked me to pass on a message. Otherwise of course it would have been Deveau – I'm not used to doing this sort of thing."

"Did you hear that, George? The poor man – he's dead."

"I bet it was that bastard Lucca," he muttered to himself. "Do the police know how he died?"

"Not yet," said Katja, who had heard the aside. "At one point they thought I had something to do with it. It was quite scary because I happened to go to his flat and knock on his door when he was lying dead inside."

"You poor girl," said Mira reaching out and patting her hand, "that must have been a terrible shock."

George suddenly sat up and looked intently at Katja.

"You just said something about passing on a message – what message?"

Katja looked anxious for an instant under George's intense stare, but faced him squarely as she replied.

"Don't shoot the messenger, George, but he told me to tell the manuscript is going to cost you more – half a million dollars …"

"What …!"

The whole table shook as his fist crashed down on the table. The other guests in the restaurant turned round in shock. Katja breathed a sigh of relief as at that moment the waitress returned and started collecting the dishes. The buzz of conversation from the other tables resumed and George angrily pushed his chair back and fell silent.

Mira picked up the menu the waitress had handed her and exclaimed:

"Ooh! They do cream broolie here, George."

George sighed angrily and looked at his wife in the way husbands do as they contemplate the contrast between their wives and the slim figure of the waitress.

He ordered a coffee for himself and took no more part in the conversation between the two women who had both opted for dessert.

Chapter 12

Eleni and Patrick joined the other tourists leaving from Athens and boarded the tour bus bound for Lousiós Gorge. For both of them it was a strange experience, half holiday, half undercover and going away on an organised trip with other people for the first time. They were treated as a couple by the guide and by the other travellers and could not help laughing, partly in embarrassment and partly in amusement, so much so the other members of the group assumed they were on their honeymoon.

The journey out to the head of the gorge at Dimitsána took most of the day. First there was a stop in Kórinthos where more travellers joined the coach, so they were able to leave the coach for an hour or two and wander around the ancient ruins.

"You know I've never seen the Corinth Canal," Patrick said as they wandered arm in arm through the old city.

"Neither have I," Eleni said.

"What! It always takes a visitor to show the natives their own area," he grinned, looking at his watch. "We've just got time to go there if we take a taxi."

Grabbing her hand he ran towards the exit of the site and hailed one of the taxis waiting in the street.

"We'll have to be quick. Antonia will never forgive us if we miss the coach to the Gorge," said Eleni breathlessly as she climbed into the back.

"And Pierre will put me back on traffic duty!" said Patrick leaning forward to speak to the driver.

They made it back to the coach with minutes to spare and had to face the amused smiles of the other passengers who clearly thought they had been involved in a different sort of sight-seeing. They found their seats and slid down to avoid the glances and hide the embarrassed smiles on their faces.

"This is the best cover we could have asked for," said Eleni. "No-one will bother us or wonder why we are wandering off away from the others."

The guide was speaking to everyone and they both sat up and looked over the top of their seats to hear what he was saying. The coach started up and headed south towards Argos and on along the coast. The views from the windows on either side were spectacular and every now and then the guide pointed out ancient sites as they drove by, including Mycenae.

"That's where Agamemnon was murdered by Clytemnestra when he returned from Troy," said Eleni, nudging Patrick who by now was dozing off.

The roads soon became narrower and more twisty as they turned inland and after they left Tripolis they were only just wide enough for the coach. There were frequent stops to let cars and farm carts by. The hills were dry and the gnarled olive trees clung onto the stony ground digging deep to find enough water. When they finally drove into Dimitsána everyone on the coach was tired and thirsty and badly needed to stand up to stretch their legs after sitting for so long.

Their suite in the hotel was large with armchairs in a sitting area and a separate bedroom. They went out onto the small balcony and stood side by side looking out over the deep and heavily wooded valley below. The heady mix of scent from the cypress trees, the wild thyme and the fruit orchards reached them on the warm evening breeze and the early dusk lent a mystical air to the view. They knew they were looking into an ancient valley full of mystery and ghosts from long ago. Full of danger too.

Eleni turned, leaning back against the balcony rail.

"I wonder what it was like for Uncle Kóstas and the others on the run from the Colonels' soldiers all those years ago. It must have been terrifying as they hid for their lives."

"No wonder Kóstas was so upset about the death of the monk," said Patrick. "His men are out there somewhere guarding the site."

He looked out past her over the valley as if he was hoping to spot one of them.

"And they will be protecting us too, don't forget," said Eleni. "This is not the first time he's helped us, as you know."

"Probably best if I don't know the details," Patrick replied with a smile. "Last time was a close enough call for me."

Downstairs the diners were gathering for the welcome drink and the briefing from Nikko, the tour guide. As Eleni and Patrick mixed with the other travellers, they weighed each one up looking for signs of anyone not conforming to the typical tourist profile. They came from all over the world as tourist parties often do. Australians and Canadians, Americans and Japanese, British and French, Italians and Germans. Most spoke passable English and the babble of conversation became more and more lively as people introduced themselves, helped by the *ouzo*, which to many was a new experience.

Nikko called them to order for moment to say they would be on an early start the next morning. This brought forth the predictable ironic groans and smiles. Everyone was keen to see the old monasteries and no one really objected to being up early.

The party went through to the dining room and gathered round the table containing the buffet style *mezés*, helping themselves before crossing to the tables and taking their seats. Eleni and Patrick headed for the same table as the guide where a group of Italians were sitting. The evening passed quickly with much laughter at everyone's attempts to fathom the menu with its mix of Greek and sub-titles in English.

The Italians all knew each other and often broke off into their own language as the wine took hold, giving Eleni and Patrick the chance to talk to Nikko. They stuck to standard tourist talk and found him to be knowledgeable about the early history of the area. He was particularly fascinating about the early Crusaders who had sought sanctuary in the valley.

"On my last tour there was another couple who were keen to know more about the Crusaders. A French girl with foreign sounding name – Katja, I think. And there was an Italian who spent most of his time trying to get her into bed. But she was good at both leading him on and fending him off."

He laughed at the memory.

"There's a lot of that on these sorts of tours."

"Were they interested in any monastery in particular?" asked Patrick.

"Yes, I think they were. They left the party behind at the Néa Moni Filosófou and climbed up to the older site further down the river. They caught up with us and came back to the hotel on the coach with everyone else."

There was a pause as Nikko turned to the Italians who were asking him about the itinerary for the next day and what they should take with them.

The waiter took their orders for the next course. Patrick could not resist the yoghurt with honey, though it was a hard choice between that and the *baklava*. Eleni ordered a *výssino,* as she loved the delicate mix of Morello cherries, syrup and *kaséri* cheese.

"Did we hear there had been an incident at one of those sites?" asked Eleni, when Nikko turned his attention once more to them and nodded his approval of their choice of deserts.

"Yes. It was very strange. Firstly, a local shepherd reported someone had disturbed the old monastery site. Only the chapel is still standing, the rest is in ruins, so it's a mystery why anyone should think there is anything there worth taking after all these centuries of neglect."

He broke off his account and seemed to concentrate on his desert. As he appeared to be engrossed in thought Eleni and Patrick waited for him to continue. Making a decision he looked up and said:

"After that it became much more serious. At the newer monastery – that means the seventeenth century – the old monk in charge apparently slipped and fell down the cliff. But now they are saying he was beaten before he fell."

"That's terrible. The poor man. Do you mean he was murdered?" asked Eleni.

"I don't know."

"So, is the monastery is closed?" asked Patrick.

"No, it's open again, though there's a soldier on guard. Tourism is too important it appears to be interrupted even by a death. "

He looked round anxiously for a minute as if to see if anyone had over heard and then added:

"Please don't mention this to the others. I don't want to spoil their trip."

Later, they went up to their room and looked out onto the valley dotted with the occasional light twinkling in the distance. The sound of goats' bells carried up to them on the light breeze, banishing the suspicion the ghosts of the past were roaming abroad in the darkness below.

"So, now we have confirmation of the presence of the main players on the trip, though that doesn't mean they were the murderers."

"I really can't see Kokoschka carrying out a brutal murder like that," replied Patrick. "The local papers have been discreet it seems. And anyway we know she was back in Bordeaux when the monk was killed. It fits more with Italian style killings."

"I agree – that means we need to know where Marco was at the time. And we must ask Nikko about the Leontarakis too, but I thought we had asked enough questions for one evening."

She took his arm and turned him towards her, relaxing her whole body against him and putting her mouth to his ear.

"Time to go undercover. We have a long day tomorrow."

Patrick ran his hands slowly up from her waist, along her spine and up to the back of her neck and felt her quiver slightly, before pulling away suddenly with a laugh.

"You're not to tickle," she said taking his hand and moving towards the bedroom. Patrick went in to the bathroom to shower. When he came out wrapped in a bathrobe, Eleni dodged under his arm and darted into the bathroom herself.

When she returned Patrick had turned on his side and was asleep. No stamina, these Frenchmen, she thought as she slid in beside him and gently matched his body position, feeling his warmth from head to toe. The next moment she found herself facing him in his arms. His hands moved down her spine again.

This time he heard no complaints.

*

The morning following her meeting with the Americans, Katja reached her office at the usual time and sat at her desk to continue the design task she was working on. For a while she concentrated on the work in hand, feeling more relaxed about the business with Lucca. Apart from George's initial anger, he and Mira had said no more about the rise in the cost of obtaining the manuscript – if indeed it existed – and she had emailed Lucca to say she had passed on the message. He had sounded pleased.

Was she simply being played along and enticed into his web like a fly to a spider, or was she letting her imagination get the better of her? Either way there was nothing more required of her before the manuscript was found and needed authenticating. The fate of the monk still bothered her, but she put it out of her mind and returned to her work.

By eleven o'clock she had nearly completed her project and was about to embark on the routine responses to emails and phone calls when Marcel came across to her area.

"Are we still on for lunch?" he asked.

"Thank you, yes. I'm looking forward to it. While you're here could you just look at something on this plan which I am having trouble with?"

"Of course. What's the problem?"

They spent the next half hour discussing and trying out solutions, before Marcel returned to his office. Katja went across the open floor area past a colleague's desk towards the washroom. She caught Katja's signal and a few moments late got up and followed her in.

"So, what's the gossip on you and Marcel? Has he asked you out?"

"Well, yes he has – to lunch," she added quickly. « That's all, Marie-Anne. Stop grinning like that ! »

« Who's the lucky one then? He doesn't usually do that. In fact I don't think he's asked anyone else – you're the first."

"That's what I wanted to know. I wondered whether he tried it on with every woman here."

"Not at all. The old goat here before him used to, but not Marcel. More's the pity."

"Not enough harassment going on, you mean?"

"Definitely not!"

"But is he married? I don't want to be involved in anything like that."

"He was, but they split up years ago. I met her once – she had an affair and they broke up."

"Thanks, Marie-Anne, at least I won't put my foot in it now."

They turned to leave the washroom and at the door Marie-Anne put her hand on Katja's arm.

"He's a genuinely nice man, Katja, not a '*chaud lapin*'."

She opened the door and started back to her desk, whispering as she passed Katja:

"But be sure to tell me all about it when you get back!"

*

Later, Katja found herself in a little place off the *cours de Verdun* with Marcel. She did not often treat herself to such an upmarket restaurant and was enjoying the atmosphere.

"Do you come here often?" she asked him. "Or is that your line?"

He laughed in return.

"Only on special occasions. The food is always good and the menu changes regularly. But I'm afraid I always choose the hot oyster profiteroles with chive butter when it is available. It's the chef's speciality."

"I'll go for the same since you rate it so highly," she said, fingering the menu. "But you do realise I'm not going to do much work this afternoon, especially if I choose the *Choc'orange* with the ginger sauce afterwards?"

"No problem," he replied with a wave of his hand. "You have done a great job on the Mérignac airport project and we are well on schedule."

The waiter approached their table and greeted them.

« *Bonjour, Monsieur Bouvier. Bonjour, madame. Vous avez choisi?* »

He took their order. Katja drew the line at wine and settled for sparkling water.

"The chef here used to work at the *Palais de L'Elysée* for Mitterrand when he was president."

"Really? I'm impressed."

"But tell me about these visits to Sardinia, Katja. Do you know someone there?"

"No, not really. When I worked in the gallery in Paris I had to check the provenances of paintings and so on before they could be entered in our catalogues."

"It sounds exciting."

"Well, yes and no. Mostly it was simply a matter of following a paper trail. Occasionally though the trail petered out, or was obviously false."

"So, where does Sardinia come in?"

"There's a dealer on the island who has asked me to authenticate an old manuscript."

"Have you seen it yet? Is it very old?"

"Yes, it is. But no I haven't. He wants me to look at a manuscript from the time of the Crusades."

"Is that your field – can you do that? It sounds very specialised, I'm impressed."

"Don't be. I've looked into the background history and I'm sure it won't be difficult to see if it is genuine ..."

She hesitated and picked up her glass to give herself time to think. How much should she tell him?

"... only, he won't tell me exactly how he expects to get hold of it. To be honest with you, Marcel, I am beginning to wonder what I have got myself into. Whether the whole thing is entirely legal."

"Can't you just walk away from it?"

"Not really. I accepted an advance payment and that has locked me into the deal. The dealer involved is rather intimidating and I'm frankly a little afraid of him."

"That seems unlike you!"

Marcel immediately saw his mistake.

"Sorry! I can see you're genuinely worried."

"I'm probably just being silly, but there is so much illegal exporting going on and the fact it will be coming from Greece makes me think it can't be above board."

"Won't they have to obtain some sort of export licence? You could ask to see it first."

"Somehow I don't think Signor Lucca is the sort of man to bother with little details like that."

Marcel looked at her with concern as she fell silent and avoided looking him in the eye. He put his hand over hers on the table and said gently:

"If you really think you're involved in something illegal, the best thing to do is to go to the police and tell them what you have told me. They can run checks on this Lucca fellow and see if any export licences have been issued."

Katja thought for a moment staring into the distance. She shook herself, sat up and gave him a grateful smile.

"You're right, Marcel. I should do that. Thank you."

She saw their waiter approaching, withdrew her hand and was relieved to be able to change the subject.

"Here comes the food. Let's talk about something else and enjoy the meal. Tell me about yourself, Marcel."

Chapter 13

Early the following morning the coach party gathered in the dining room and settled down to breakfast. Late-comers rushed in looking flustered and grabbed a coffee to wake themselves up since those who had left their rooms on time were already getting up from the tables and heading for the coach waiting outside.

Inside the coach Nikko walked up the centre aisle counting heads and then there was a delay as the whole party waited for a couple who were missing.

After a short bumpy ride the coach stopped opposite the steep path above the village of Palaiochóri which led to the Néa Moni Filosófou. Patrick and Eleni got off with the others and Nikko led the way up the track towards the monastery. The final part was a steep climb and they stopped a couple of times to rest and let the stragglers catch up. When they arrived, they gathered in front of the ancient wooden gate. Nikko rang the bell and passed his identity card through the small window to the army guard on duty. The guard pushed it back through and opened the gate.

Some of the group were surprised to see soldiers there and without mentioning the death of the monk Nikko explained there had been attempts at stealing items from monasteries in the area and the army were there to strengthen the security.

Everyone gratefully put down their back packs and found a seat at the tables. Nikko gave them his usual short talk about the history of the monastery and the move from the old site. He then took them in small groups into the chapel to see the frescoes.

The heat of the day was beginning to build and Nikko suggested that before it became too hot he would take anyone who wished to go to see the remains of the old monastery. He added that it was not far along the valley, but the climb would be steep.

At that most of the party elected to stay put and sit in the sun on the terrace savouring the peacefulness of the place. The rest followed Nikko on to the older site. Patrick and Eleni watched them go. They joined the others at the tables for a few minutes and then quietly got up and re-entered the chapel on their own.

They both stood silently in the middle of the nave glancing up at the frescoes, but their minds were focussed on the structure of the building rather than on the decoration.

"So, according to what Kóstas told us we know there should be a door through to the library behind the tapestry at the back of the altar," said Patrick, walking towards it. He slid behind the tapestry and edged his way along the back wall, carefully running his hands along the stones searching for the break.

Eleni did the same from the other side. She had almost reached the middle with no success, when she heard Patrick call softly to her.

"Viens! C'est ici."

He ran his fingers round the contour of a low door-frame let into the wall and found an iron ring set into a wooden door. He turned the handle slowly and pushed against the door which opened grudgingly, the bottom edge snagging on the rough floor. He had to bend low to squeeze through into the room beyond, closely followed by Eleni.

They found themselves in a large chamber hollowed out of the rock and with none of the decoration seen in the chapel. The room was dimly lit by daylight filtering in from a small window high up in the roof and it took a few moments for their eyes to grow accustomed to the low level light. Then they could make out the rows of rough wooden shelves piled high with books and manuscripts which lined the rough walls.

They could see clear signs the monks had spent time in the room. The books and manuscripts on some of the shelves were neatly arranged and were free of dust. But the majority of the shelves were piled high in dusty confusion.

"So what exactly are we looking for?" asked Patrick looking round helplessly at the chaos.

"The first signs of disturbance were made at the old site, so we can assume Lucca thinks the manuscript he wants was written there – so it must be an early one. If it has anything to do with the Crusades, say twelfth or thirteenth century."

"Over here, on this side," said Patrick brushing away the cobwebs clinging to his hair.

Eleni gently removed some of the manuscripts from the shelf and started turning them over. The velum was delicate and dried out. She dared not unroll them for fear of them breaking apart in her hands. She looked at Patrick and started putting the manuscripts back on the shelf.

"Time to leave before the others return. We've found what we're looking for and without more information, we can't do any more. It could be any one of these."

"We must arrange for a stronger guard to protect the site though. Whoever killed the monk will be back and it won't take them long to figure out where this room is," said Patrick. "The only sure way is to put these manuscripts in a safer place."

"We'll need permission from the Greek Orthodox Church, if we want to remove any items."

"At the moment we don't know what to remove, but the security here is not good enough. Either we suggest they remove everything to another location or they let us increase the guard in the hope of catching the villains," said Patrick.

"I know you're right, but you don't appreciate the politics of the relationship between the State here and the Orthodox Church."

"Of course. I'm sorry. I'm out of my depth here."

"Not at all Patrick, I didn't mean that," she said putting her hand on his arm. "But it's not easy all the same. I would rather try to catch the thief than take on the Orthodox Church!"

"O.K., I understand, but it's time we went back outside and rejoined the others before Nikko arrives and starts counting heads. It must be a nightmare trying to keep track of everyone. It would drive me mad!"

They opened the low door slowly and listened to make sure the chapel beyond was empty. They slipped through and pulled the door to, edged their way along the back of the tapestry and emerged into the chapel proper. For a moment they were dazzled by the relative brightness, but quickly made their way outside where those who had remained were still sitting on the terraces watching Nikko's group walking slowly back along the narrow path below them.

The returning group were clearly hot and bothered after their half-walk, half-climb up to the old monastery. They all flopped down in whatever shade they could find and took out their bottles of water. As they recovered they chatted with those who had stayed behind, determined to convince them they had missed a great sight. Although there was not much left of the old monastery, they had experienced an unexpected surge of emotion as they stood on the spot where, centuries ago, returning crusading knights had trodden the same stones and gazed out over the same valley. There was even a Crusader tomb in the old chapel.

Eleni and Patrick listened carefully to their tales and noted the presence of the tomb, which confirmed everything Kóstas had told them. After a short rest Nikko rounded them all up and they set off for the next site. The rest of the day was spent being ushered in and out of other sites until they felt unable to take in any more. The way back along the trail was long, hot and dusty. A brief stop at the village of Palaiochóri was a welcome break and it was a tired but happy group which finally rejoined the coach for the short trip back to the hotel.

"Now I understand why we had that short coach trip on the way out," said Patrick, wiping his forehead. "This ride back is very welcome."

Once back in their room, Eleni spoke on her mobile to Antonia and described what they had discovered in the chapel.

"Well done. At least we know where the manuscript might be, even if we don't know which one is targeted. I'll try and persuade the Church authorities to allow a stronger guard on the monastery twenty four hours a day. Have a good evening; we'll speak again later."

Eleni put down the phone and went into the bathroom where Patrick had just stepped out of the shower.

"Let's go down to eat soon – I'm starving," she said, her voice half-drowned out as she turned the shower back on and gasped as the cold water fizzed on her hot skin.

In the dining room they sat with Nikko and chatted about the Gorge and its treasures.

"How do foreign tourists react to the sites?" Eleni asked, helping herself to the last of the *mezés* with a glance at the others.

Nikko laughed.

"Oh! Just as you would expect, depending on their nationality. On the whole they are appreciative, but the old hands who have seen other sites all over the world tend to glance at the real thing, take a picture of themselves in front of it like a trophy, check the guide book and move on. Another one ticked off the list as it were."

"I can sympathise with that to a certain extent," said Patrick. "We all receive an overload of information even when we're on holiday and supposed to be relaxing."

"True. But perhaps it would be better to do fewer trips and to stay longer. I blame the coach culture really."

He laughed.

"Which of course is how I earn my living. I too am part of the culture I'm critizing. It makes everywhere visitable too rapidly. But at least when I see people writing everything I say down in a note book – it's mostly American visitors who do that – I know they'll probably look at it again when they get home. Let's just hope they don't check it all on the internet and find I've got it all wrong!"

"Were there many Americans on your last trip?"

"No. Just one couple. They spent a lot of time with the French girl I described last night – and the Italian who followed her about."

He paused and picked up another olive.

"They looked like normal American tourists, but I got the impression they were sharper than they appeared at first."

"What made you think that?"

"Oh! Their questions were more searching than most. They were interested in old manuscripts and asked about the knights returning from the Crusades."

"They had done some preparation before the trip then?"

"Definitely. At least that was certainly my impression."

Eleni saw they were in danger of giving themselves away to this perceptive guide and changed the direction of the conversation to discuss the arrangements for the coming three days till the end of the visit.

The meal arrived and they realised how much of an appetite the day's exertions and the fresh air had given them. Nikko went round the tables several times to check all his charges understood what they were eating and, when necessary, amidst some hilarity, how to eat it. Returning to his seat he said:

"It's a good group this time. They're all enjoying themselves I think."

"Everyone is happy thanks to all the attention you pay them," said Patrick.

"That's kind of you to say so. I enjoy talking to people and I like to see them laughing. If I didn't, I guess I shouldn't be doing this job."

Towards the end of the main course the traditional floor show began and people left their tables to join over-enthusiastically in the dancing. Patrick and Eleni decided to help themselves to the dessert and to take it to their room.

Later as they slid between the sheets and zipped up the mosquito net, they could still hear the rhythm of the balalaikas through the open window from the floor below.

"It doesn't come much more romantic than this," said Eleni, as she turned towards him.

"Ouch!" Patrick exclaimed as he felt her light slap on his behind.

"Sorry, just thought I saw a mosquito."

"Liar!"

Much later in the early hours of the morning feeling the chill of the night air on his back, Patrick stirred and was instantly wide awake. He could hear a sound coming from the next room. He slipped noiselessly from the bed, pulled on some shorts and went over to the door to listen. Eleni had also woken, disturbed by the movement, and was watching him. He signalled to her to get up and put some clothes on. When she was ready he jerked the door wide and flung himself low into the room. He just had time to glimpse the silhouette of the intruder against the moonlight coming through the window, before he felt something buzz past his head, heard the pop of a silencer and the sound of a bullet crashing into the door panel above him.

Without taking a second shot the intruder rushed straight out onto the balcony and vaulted over. Patrick made it to the balcony in time to see him land as lightly as a cat on the lawn not far below and disappear into the darkness. Cursing, Patrick turned and went back into the room only to see Eleni sitting on the floor and holding her shoulder. Blood was seeping through her fingers and running down her arm. He rushed towards her, but she looked up at him and groaned through gritted teeth:

"It's alright, Patrick. Just a splinter from the woodwork."

*

For the rest of the night their room had been full of officials. The Greek police had searched the grounds of the hotel with dogs, but found nothing. The trail had dried up near the road and they assumed the intruder had left a car there for his getaway.

Inside the room the forensic team had retrieved the bullet and dusted everywhere for finger-prints. It was six in the morning before they finished their work and reported to Eleni before leaving. An inspector took statements from both of them. But Patrick had only had a glimpse of the intruder's back and apart from confirming the person was male and being able to guess his height could supply nothing more in the way of a description. They would have to rely on whatever forensics could come up with. Maybe a fingerprint or ballistics match.

By the morning the story of the break-in had spread fast throughout the hotel and people crowded round them at breakfast wanting to know more. The wound in Eleni's shoulder was not serious and the local doctor had cleaned and dressed the cut. Nothing showed on the outside of her T-shirt, so no-one was aware that she had been hurt.

Once some of the excitement had died down and the other guests had left them alone to continue their breakfast, Eleni asked Nikko to join them.

"Nikko, we didn't want to deceive you, but we have to tell you we are from the police."

"No problem, I knew it already," he said with a smile.

"Was it that obvious?" asked Patrick rubbing his chin.

"No, but I am a guide. I learn to sum people up very quickly."

"Well, the reason we are here as you will have guessed is to look into the death of the monk, who was killed last week."

"I don't know any more than what I have read in the newspapers."

"OK, but could you describe in more detail the Italian who was on your last trip? The one who was so friendly with the French girl?" asked Patrick.

When he had finished, Patrick nodded when Eleni looked across at him. Picking up on their glance, Nikko asked:

"Do you think he was the one who broke into your room and shot at you? What was he looking for?"

"I think it would be a good idea if you said something to the group about taking care of their belongings and locking their rooms," said Eleni, ignoring the question. "Nobody knows about the gunshot except you, so don't mention it please."

"OK. Then we go out into the valley and have another nice day. Agreed?"

"Of course, Nikko."

He got up to go round the tables.

Chapter 14

Marcel and Katja avoided the subject for the rest of the meal. The food was delicious as Marcel had said it would be. Katja kept a clear head and stuck to water, whereas Marcel relaxed a little with a glass of wine. He asked her about herself and she was happy to reveal more about her past.

He returned the compliment but seemed wary of saying too much and only mentioned his ex-wife in passing. Katja pressed him a little, but he evaded her questions and she didn't insist.

Katja ordered the *Choc'orange* as promised and finally put down her spoon with a satisfied look on her face. Marcel ordered coffee and suggested a walk along the embankment to help them digest.

"You're the boss," Katja replied. "How could I refuse!"

Later they returned to the office and Katja went over to her desk. She could feel the eyes of all the others in the room on her back. Marie-Anne would want to know all about it later and then of course the whole office would know too.

She stared at the design on the board but her mind was far away going over her conversation with Marcel at the restaurant. The others would be surprised if they could have read her thoughts. She was not thinking what they guessed when they noticed how preoccupied she was. She was debating with herself whether to follow Marcel's advice and go to the police.

By the end of the afternoon she was still undecided and, just saying a quick good night to her expectant colleagues, she returned to her flat to look again at the file she had taken from Deveau's bookshop.

Later that evening she made up her mind.

*

"Pronto?"
"Giovanni, sono io. Marco."

Marco was feeling nervous. Although he had gone over again and again what he was going to say, he knew the tremor in his voice would give him away to Lucca's ever perceptive antennae.

"I search their room in the hotel, but there was nothing. They found nothing in the monastery."

"*Non è vero*, Marco. You fucked up, no?" barked Lucca. "Tell to me what happened really."

"I swear to you, Giovanni, on the life of my mother …"

"Do not lie to me, Marco, or it will be the last you tell."

"The stupid Frenchman, he wake up and he come into the room when I am searching. But no problem, I jump off the balcony and he not see me properly. He will not identify me, Giovanni."

"*Cretino*! How can you be sure? And I think you use your gun, you idiot. Tell to me it is not true."

"No, I … But how … ?"

"So I am right …"

Marco held his breath in horror, his hand over his mouth. He knew he had fallen for the oldest trick in the world.

There was silence on the line and Marco waited in dread for his sentence to be pronounced.

"Marco, listen to me carefully. If the police really have found nothing, they will go back to the monastery. So, you follow. You watch to see where exactly they go inside. If they come out with nothing, you go there yourself and you keep looking. If they come out carrying something you know what you must do."

There was a click on the line. Nothing more to be said. Lucca sighed and aimed a kick at the chair in front of him.

"I am surrounded by imbeciles. But I cannot go there myself, so … what can I do?"

*

"Commissaire Rousseau?"

"*À l'appareil.*"

"It's Katja Kokoschka."

"*Bonsoir, mademoiselle.*"

There was silence on the line for a moment as Katja hesitated before continuing.

"May I come and see you?"

Pierre could hear the nervousness in her voice and sat up, his attention sharpened.

"Of course, mademoiselle. May I ask what about?" he replied gently.

"I'd rather not explain on the phone, Commissaire."

"I understand. When would you like to come? I'm free this evening."

"Thank you, Commissaire. That's perfect."

Again there was some hesitation.

"I would prefer not to come to the *Hôtel de Police* if you don't mind."

Pierre considered for a second before replying.

"How would the *Café de Paris* in the *place Gambetta* suit you? Say around seven?"

"Perfect, thank you, Commissaire."

Katja put the phone down and breathed a long sigh of relief. She hoped she had made the right decision.

Pierre's fingers drummed on the desk as he tried to second guess what Kokoschka wanted to talk to him about. He reached for the phone and asked his secretary to put him through to Chief Inspector Antoniarchis in Athens. Antonia was in her office and sounded rushed.

"Can I you ring you back later," she replied on hearing his voice. "I'm tied up at the moment."

"Of course. It's just to say Kokoschka is coming to see me of her own accord this evening, so perhaps we will find out more about what's going on."

"Let me know what she says. When are you coming out?"

"I don't think I will make it tonight. Perhaps tomorrow morning. I'll let you know."

"*Antio, Pierre.*"

"*À bientôt, Antonia.*"

*

Pierre sat back in his chair and gazed out through his office window, from where he could see across to the *Cathédrale St. André* where Aliénor, duchesse d'Aquitaine married Philippe of France in 1137. What a magnificent sight that must have been, he thought. The lords, ladies and knights of France and Aquitaine assembled with all banners flying. Years later she brought her new husband, Henri, comte d'Anjou, to Bordeaux. Barely two years later she became Queen for the second time, this time of England.

As if to give further colour to his imagination the newly cleaned statue atop the separate bell tower gleamed down at him, a brilliant gold in the sunlight. Why, he wondered, did he have to wrestle with such intractable problems when everything outside was so perfect?

There were many unanswered questions and they had not progressed very far in the investigation. They had not even established a solid link between the death of Deveau and what was happening in Greece. He hoped he would have some answers when he met with Kokoschka. He still might be able to fly out to Athens that night despite what he had said to Antonia.

He pushed back his chair and stood up. He found increasingly that he stiffened up if he sat too long. Time I spent more time in the gym, he thought. Or any time at all, he corrected himself. He paced the room for a moment and went over to the small fridge where he kept a bottle of water. The freshness revived him and he stood at the window to continue his mental review of the case.

What Bouvier had told him about Kokoschka had certainly given them a new perspective on her. According to him, Kokoschka was a talented and knowledgeable architect, so there was nothing suspicious on the professional level. Or was Bouvier covering up for her? After all he had let her go on holiday at very short notice. Perhaps he was involved in this too. Were they having an affair? Why should she need to visit Sardinia twice in such a short time? Who was she seeing out there?

Lost in his thoughts and going round in circles, he was hardly aware his phone was ringing. He reached over to his desk and picked up the receiver.

"Rousseau."

"Patrick here, Commissaire. I have some news. Last night our room here in Dimitsána was broken into. The intruder was looking for something when I disturbed him early in the morning. He took a shot at me, but missed. I only saw his back, but what I did see fitted with the description of the Italian who was on the trip with Kokoschka."

"You mean Platini?"

"Yes. The Italian police have confirmed he is one of Lucca's men and are sending a photo."

"*Enfin!* That's the link we need. What do we know about him?"

"*Attendez!* There's more. Forensics here found finger prints in our room and they match the ones found in Deveau's flat. That puts Platini in the frame for murdering Deveau."

"Well done, Patrick. I'll start things rolling right away this end."

A police car, siren going, screeched round the corner in the street below and he looked out through the window to follow its progress.

"Are you still there, Commissaire?"

"Yes."

"When are you coming back out here?"

"Probably tomorrow. I may have other news for you though later tonight."

"What …?" started Patrick, but realised Pierre had already put the phone down.

"Why does he always do that to me?" he said to himself with a sigh.

Pierre felt like punching the air on hearing Patrick's news. At last a firm link between the two cases. He picked up his hat as he prepared to go out to the café in the *place Gambetta*. He would be far too early, but decided to treat himself to a celebratory drink. At the door of his office, he hesitated and went back to his desk, where he picked up a large brown envelope.

As he strolled along the *rue des Remparts*, he paused and looked up at Deveau's flat. On a sudden impulse he turned in and went up to the landing. The door was sealed with police tape, but he ripped it off, let himself in and stood in the middle of the living room looking round. He had no idea what he expected to see, but wanted to try to get into Deveau's mind. He was certain that whatever deal he was involved in, it also included Lucca. Did Kokoschka know what it was? Was it Lucca she was seeing in Sardinia? He would soon have an answer to that one at least, he hoped.

Although he knew the flat had been searched thoroughly already he roamed about turning pictures round, opening drawers and looking under furniture. He left the living room and went into the bedroom. He stood for a moment, his eyes searching round. One of the drawers of the bedside cabinet was not flush with the front. Idly he pushed it to square it up with the others, but it wouldn't move.

He opened the drawer to see what was catching, but it was half empty – just some keys, an old watch and a bottle of aspirin. He pulled the drawer out and placed it on the bed. Taped to the back was an envelope. Putting on the gloves he always carried, he opened it carefully, his heart beating faster. Inside was a wad of $100 dollar bills – around a hundred he judged. There was nothing else in the envelope – no clue as to what the money was for.

Pierre put the whole envelope carefully into an evidence bag and sealed it up. Taking out his phone he gave instructions for the envelope to be picked up from the flat and for a detailed new search of every room to be undertaken. He refrained from demanding to know why the hell they hadn't done their job properly the first time. He could hear their red faces anyway.

He looked at his watch. There wasn't time for him to wait for the team to arrive. He couldn't risk not being there for Kokoschka. He let himself out and slowly went down the stairs. Pierre knew it wouldn't be unusual for someone in Deveau's line of work to have a quantity of cash around, but nonetheless ten thousand dollars was a considerable sum.

Out in the street he took a deep breath in the warm evening air and set off up the street to the *Porte Dijeaux*. He was still deep in thought as he turned mechanically to go through the arch into the *place Gambetta*. Maybe Deveau was simply murdered for money. Was his death the result of a simple burglary gone wrong? That was too easy – there was no sign of the flat having been searched. Burglars are just not that tidy. There must be more to it. He was brought back to the present as he walked into a woman standing gazing into a shop window. He apologised profusely.

He waited at the pedestrian crossing and crossed to the café opposite on the other side. The awning over the *terrasse* shaded the seats at the back from the glare of the sun, but he chose a seat at the side just catching the warmth of the sun's rays. He waved the waiter away indicating he was waiting for someone and sat watching the people and the traffic, still lost in thought. The sun was in his eyes so he did not see Kokoschka at first as she approached his table with the light behind her.

He stood up and pulled out a chair for her.

The waiter hurried across from another table and took their order. Coffee for him and a sparkling water for her. Katja took off her jacket and hung it over the back of the chair. She busied herself finding a tissue in her bag. Her confidence had deserted her now that she was face to face with him and she needed to make space for a moment.

Pierre watched her and waited for her to steady her nerves and speak to him. He could see her confusion, but experience had taught him the best tactic was to let the other person speak and not to ask questions, at first at least.

Katja closed her bag and looked at him.

"I'm not sure where to start, Commissaire. I'm beginning to be worried I may have got myself into something I can't handle."

She paused and twisted her bracelet nervously round her wrist.

"What I told you about Deveau was true – I really didn't know he was dead when I went to his flat. I was simply furious about how much he had given me for a book I sold him. I had been on my computer that evening and I looked on the Internet to see how much he was advertising it for. It was ten times what he'd given me for it! I'd been drinking and when I saw your officers arrive I just acted on a stupid impulse and jumped into my car."

Pierre knew all this already since it was in her previous statement, so he waited patiently for her to reveal why she had suddenly decided to arrange to see him.

"So that's the reason you left the scene?"

"Yes. It was nothing to do with Deveau, I swear," she said looking him. "I didn't want to lose my licence and thought that if I could shake them off, I wouldn't be breathalysed. It was just stupid. I wasn't thinking straight."

"In fact, you weren't over the limit, just over the speed limit!" said Pierre with a smile. "But you are right – you weren't thinking straight, mademoiselle."

Pierre put a packet of cigarettes and his lighter on the table and nodded towards them. Katja did not react.

"But we are not here to discuss your traffic violations, are we?"

Although she didn't smoke any more, Katja picked up the cigarette packet and took one out. Pierre leaned forward to light it for her, resisting the temptation to take one himself.

"What I didn't tell you, Commissaire, was that Deveau knew what I had been doing in Paris before I came here. I worked in a gallery for a while after I graduated and he knew I was experienced at researching provenances of items we were selling. We did sometimes use auction houses and had to show proof of the origin of the items before they would accept them."

"Not all auction houses are quite so scrupulous unfortunately," remarked Pierre, as he watched her stub out the cigarette she had not put to her lips after the first draw.

Katja turned to face him for a moment to see if he was implying anything before continuing.

"We mostly used them when old books or manuscripts came into our hands. In the gallery we just sold paintings and other art work."

"But would I be right in assuming that occasionally you did some dealing of your own?"

She looked at him in surprise. Did he really know about her under the table deals or was he just guessing?

"You're right – I did do some dealing on the side after hours."

She looked at him again realising he was not trying to trap her, but was waiting patiently for her to tell him of her real connection to Deveau.

"Sometimes, I admit I suspected that some of the items we bought and sold had been stolen or smuggled out of somewhere illegally, but I couldn't prove it. In a way that was what made it exciting, but I have never knowingly given a false authentication."

Pierre did not react and remained silent, just watching her.

"I guessed Deveau too was involved in deals which were not always legal, but when he said he was going to recommend me to an Italian called Giovanni Lucca, who he said was a collector of illustrated manuscripts, there was no reason for me to think there was anything dodgy about it. Very few genuine manuscripts reach the open market and so any collector would want to be sure he was not buying a fake. I accepted the commission to authenticate it, especially since the fee was good."

She ran her fingers back through her hair to sweep it off her face. It promptly fell forward, but she didn't seem to notice as she continued:

"Now of course I realise Lucca is not the buyer, but a middleman being paid to steal a manuscript to order."

"So, what exactly happened," he prompted gently when she fell silent.

"When Deveau died I had no way of contacting Lucca as Deveau had always acted as the go-between."

"So you went to Deveau's shop hoping to find out more about the deal?"

"I found the file with all the details of exactly what the collector is after. I didn't want the job to fall through, so I rang Lucca myself. He immediately invited me out again to his house in Sardinia. He didn't even ask me why I was contacting him directly. I wasn't suspicious at the time. I just thought he didn't know Deveau was dead and saw a way of cutting him out.

"When I got there he was charming in an Italian sort of way and said I should go on a visit to the Lousiós Gorge as part of my research into the circumstances surrounding the particular manuscript he was looking for as he couldn't go himself. I noticed he had a limp, so perhaps that was the reason."

He saw her hesitation and raised his eyebrows to encourage her to continue.

"You said 'again'. It was not your first visit then?"

"No, the first time I went with Deveau. It was a bit like going for an interview for a job, which I suppose it was really. I told him about my past experience in Paris in authenticating manuscripts and mentioned the name of the owner of the gallery I had worked for. He flew into a violent rage and told me never to mention her name in his presence again. Both Deveau and I were completely taken aback. I thought that was the end of the commission, but he recovered his good humour immediately, apologised and the whole thing was forgotten."

"What was her name?" asked Pierre, eyes widening in anticipation.

"Well, it was called the Sophie Cavalier Gallery, but that was the name of the previous owner. The present owner is Isabella Marquessa. She was the one who recommended me to Deveau."

"And that was the name Lucca flared up at?"

"Yes. It was quite frightening."

Pierre could almost hear the pieces of the jigsaw falling into place.

"Go on. What happened on the second visit?"

"Well, Lucca gave me more details and said the manuscript was an account written by a Crusader knight – Geoffroi de Vinsauf – who went on the Third Crusade. It was thought the original manuscript had been written right there in one of the monasteries in the gorge. That confirmed what I had read in Deveau's file."

Pierre asked her to repeat the name. She leaned forward as he wrote it down and helped herself to another cigarette. Pierre picked up the lighter and held it for her. He took a deep breath and reached for some chewing gum in his pocket.

"Oh! I'm so sorry. Are you giving up? I'll put it out. I thought …"

"*Non, non, ça va,*" - he held his hands up. "At least I can enjoy the smoke if not the real thing," Pierre replied. "Please go on with your story."

"Well, Lucca told me there would be one of his accomplices on the trip to the gorge too, but if he, Marco, made contact with me as he surely would, being a bit of a gigolo, I was not to let on I knew who he was."

"Didn't that strike you as odd?" asked Pierre.

"Yes, but I was so excited to be going on the trip to the gorge and about the research I didn't really take much notice."

"There were some Americans on the trip too I think."

"Yes, George and Mira. I didn't know at the time they were involved too in the deal, but later Lucca asked me to contact them here in

Bordeaux and to tell them the price had gone up. That was when I began to be worried."

"Why? Because you were being asked to do a lot more than just validate the manuscript?" asked Pierre.

"Yes. Obviously it should have been Deveau who did the negotiating. Lucca said he didn't know Deveau was dead, but I'm sure he did. So he needed me to negotiate with the Americans."

Katja stubbed out her cigarette and Pierre signalled to the waiter to bring another coffee and a sparkling water. He began to speculate on whether the dollars he had found were instead some sort of down payment from the Americans to Deveau. The waiter returned with their order and the silence between them continued for a moment.

When Katja raised her head, there was fear in her eyes. She began hesitantly.

"I am worried Lucca may have something to do with Deveau's death. I'm scared I might be becoming involved in murder."

"That's why you have done the right thing coming to see me. You have not broken the law apart from entering the bookshop and Deveau is not around to press charges."

He smiled, but got no response.

"Go on telling me what you know. For example, tell me more about this manuscript. What exactly are they hoping to find?"

Katja calmed her nerves, helped herself to another cigarette and took a deep breath.

"I expect you know that some of the returning Crusaders decided not to go all the way home and settled in the countries they travelled through?"

"And this Geoffroi de Vinsauf was one of those?" he asked looking down at the note he had made.

"We know he stopped at the old Filosófou monastery and wrote an account of his experiences on the Third Crusade. His tomb is still there in the chapel."

She poured herself some water from the bottle and took a sip as she warmed to her story.

"Knights like him also gave the monks some of the treasures they had looted in the Holy Land and it's possible these treasures, assembled over the years, enabled the monks to build a newer monastery across the gorge and to abandon the old one. But I am speculating. There's no way of knowing."

Pierre gave in and picked up a cigarette. Katja held out the lighter to him.

"Once the original manuscript was complete, the scribes would set about copying it. Some were real works of art with complex illuminated pages and even whole tableau pictures."

"Like the Books of Hours?"

"Exactly. But very few of the simpler originals survived. In Geoffroi's case we are lucky to have a complete text intact and printed, in Oxford as it happens. But the original source has long since disappeared."

"So, the original manuscript would be worth a fortune?"

"It would be impossible really to put a monetary value on it. That is, if it still exists."

Pierre sat back, relaxing from the forward position he had gradually acquired as he had become engrossed in her story. An idea was shaping in his mind, but he would need to discuss it with Antonia first. And as soon as possible.

He stood up.

"I won't detain you any longer, mademoiselle. You have been extremely helpful. Thank you for telling me all this. I shall be contacting you again in the near future. I take it you will be in your office during the daytime?"

"Of course," she said slightly surprised at the abrupt end to the meeting.

"In the meantime please phone me immediately if Lucca contacts you again. Don't worry, we will make sure you are in no danger."

As he turned to go, he looked back and asked:

"One last question, mademoiselle. Does Monsieur Bouvier know about this?"

"Yes, Commissaire. It was he who suggested I should come to see you."

"Thank you, mademoiselle. Could you come in to the *Hôtel de Police*, perhaps during lunchtime tomorrow, to look at some photographs."

"I'll be there. And thank you, Commissaire."

"Oh! I almost forgot ... Do you know where Mademoiselle Marquessa is now?"

"No. In Paris, I suppose."

He left the café and started to cross the road. Looking back he could see her still sitting there ringing someone on her mobile. He pulled out his own phone and made a quick call to the office to set up the efits for the next day and to tell them to expect Kokoschka's visit.

Chapter 15

As Pierre left the restaurant and started to walk back to back to his flat, his phone went.

"Commissaire Rousseau?"

"*À l'appareil.*"

"Inspector Bureau here. I thought you would like to know one of our uniforms identified Isabella Marquessa in the *rue Sainte Cathérine*. She has changed her appearance, but he is sure it was her. He followed her into the old quarter around the *place du Parlement*. She walked down towards Deveau's bookshop and stood outside for a few seconds before continuing on her way to the embankment."

"Congratulate him and circulate all officers with the details. She is not to be approached and must not realise she has been spotted. Just keep a log of her movements and try to trace where she is staying, Inspector."

"*Entendu, Commissaire.*"

Pierre was just about to close his phone as he weighed up the new information, but just in time he realised the inspector had not finished.

"I have heard from Paris, Commissaire. They confirm the Sophie Cavalier gallery is owned by Isabella Marquessa."

"Thank you, Inspector. That ties in with what I have heard from another source."

More food for thought. What is Marquessa doing here in Bordeaux? The usual suspects are gathering. But why? Does Kokoschka really not know she is here? He looked at his watch. He would just have time to grab his bag and make it to the airport to catch the last flight to Athens that evening after all if he moved fast. He looked down the road as he strode on determinedly. Why is there never a taxi when you need one?

*

Antonia picked him up at the airport just before midnight local time. She seemed preoccupied and said very little during the journey to her flat as Pierre updated her on what Kokoschka had told him. She hardly even commented when he told her Platini's finger prints matched some found in Deveau's flat as well as in Patrick and Eleni's hotel room.

Discouraged by her lack of reaction to what he had told her, he did not mention that Isabella Marquessa had been sighted in Bordeaux. The rest of the journey passed in silence and left Pierre feeling uneasy

They dismissed the driver outside her block and went up to her flat. Antonia had made a salad, which they ate, talking about nothing in particular. Pierre was puzzled about her almost listless behaviour, but sensed that whatever it was, had to be worked out in her own mind before she would share it with him.

They went into the bedroom and she smiled gently and said:

"Pierrot, do you mind if we …"

"No problem. I'll sleep in the living room if you want."

"Don't be silly, it's nothing like that, I'm just very tired tonight, that's all."

"Me too frankly. It's been a long day."

She kissed him on the cheek and was soon in bed and apparently asleep. Pierre followed her, turned on his side and mulled over the events of the day. They seemed to know so much more than before. But in fact, apart from the details of the manuscript everyone was so keen to find, had they really advanced in the murder of Deveau? Platini may have nothing at all to do with it after all.

Antonia lay awake too, unable to sleep. What Pierre had told her added a few details, but she was worried Eleni and Patrick were still in danger and would be attacked again.

Chapter 16

Any predatory watcher would have recognised the signs: tourists visiting a town for the first time look around them, raise their eyes to gaze at the buildings above shop front height, occasionally stopping to admire an exceptionally elegant piece of architecture. They glance down side streets, look both ways, twice, before crossing roads and wait at the pedestrian crossings for the lights to change.

Locals do none of these things. They walk determinedly from one place to another hardly aware of their surroundings and often cross streets relying on their hearing alone, rather than bothering to look for traffic. In many towns, including Bordeaux, there were accidents when the near-silent trams were first introduced. The authorities had to fit the trams with bells to warn pedestrians of their approach.

Isabella was well aware of all this, but it suited her to act like a tourist. She had changed her appearance as an extra precaution against recognition by the police. She was confident they would not recognise her from the pictures they had of her from the previous summer.

Her hair was darker, frizzy and with blond highlights; she wore jeans and a T-shirt like many other young women of her age, and a fashionable beret. Her fake Chanel shoulder bag completed the look. No-one would suspect her of carrying a small hand gun in the false compartment at the bottom of the bag.

It was some weeks since her first visit to Bordeaux. It had not been a great success. That fool Deveau simply would not tell her where Lucca was hiding out and she had had no luck afterwards trying to locate him. He had covered his tracks well and kept a low profile ever since their clash in Lyon the previous summer. Both she and Lucca had bullet wounds to recover from after the shoot-out. Her shoulder still gave her some trouble, but she had pulled through thanks to the efforts of a doctor friend who patched her up without asking questions.

A long period of rest and recuperation had allowed it to heal. She had used the time well and with the money they had tricked Lucca out of, she had bought a gallery in Paris and traded under the professional name of Sophie Cavalier. As far as she knew the police had not connected Sophie Cavalier with her real name. In fact the O.C.B.C. fraud squad had once inspected her gallery. She smiled at the memory, although she had been on tenterhooks at the time.

Her second visit to Deveau much more recently had been no more successful than the first. He had just laughed in her face when she demanded to know where Lucca was. She had not meant to hit him so hard, but he fell against the chair in the corner and was knocked unconscious. Fearing the worst, she had gone round the flat wiping her finger prints off everything she had touched, phoned an ambulance and quickly left the flat.

It was only a week after she had returned to Paris that she learned from the papers that Deveau had been found dead. For a moment she thought she must have killed him, but then worked out the dates more carefully. Nor did the report indicate suspicious circumstances. She breathed a sigh of relief when she realised his death had nothing to do with her, but it had given her a jolt all the same.

Later that day as she packed up a picture for a client it suddenly occurred to her that Deveau's death was also an opportunity. So she had returned a third time to Bordeaux knowing her best chance of finding out where Lucca was might be in Deveau's bookshop. What shady deals the murderous bastard was involved in were only of interest if they enabled her to catch up with Lucca. Then she would know what to do.

As luck would have it there was an empty flat in the same block in the *rue du Palais Gallien* where Katja lived. She had persuaded the owner to let her have a short let and taken it over. She planned to use Katja's link to Deveau to her advantage. On her way up the stairs to her floor, a young woman in a track suit rushed past looking very fit and obviously going out for a run. Isabella realised it was Katja and felt a tinge of jealousy – running still hurt her arm and shoulder too much to do much exercise. It made her hatred for Lucca burn even deeper.

She entered the little studio, pleased Katja hadn't immediately seen through her change of appearance, and flopped into the only comfortable chair. As she sat her mood changed. Her energy and will to fight deserted her and she felt lonely and vulnerable.

Before buying the gallery, she had been part of a gang of jewel thieves. There had been four of them – Sergio, Lucca's cousin, and two brothers – the Lacroix twins, Paul and Marc. In the good times, Lucca had been their fence.

"What fools we were – one job too far and it was all over," she said aloud in exasperation.

The fall out had been violent. Sergio gave evidence against Paul at the trial. Paul escaped from jail and she had gone away with him. Later Sergio caught up with them, there was an argument and Paul killed him. From then on they had always had to watch their backs, since Lucca was bound by the code of the vendetta to avenge his cousin and to hunt them down.

Tired of thinking about the past, Isabella got up, stretched and walked across to the window to look out over the roof tops of Bordeaux. The past would not go away though and she knew it was then she had begun to dislike herself for what she had become.

The fear of becoming a victim of Lucca's revenge had proved too much and she had known the only way to placate Lucca was to murder Paul herself. So she had done the unthinkable and calmly cut Paul's throat as he slept. But she knew in her heart it wouldn't be enough for Lucca and that the only way to be free was to kill him too.

She must have fallen asleep, for the next thing she knew was that someone was knocking on her studio door. Only half awake, and not on her guard, she went across the room and opened the door to see Katja standing there.

"Hello, I'm your neighbour from the floor below," sad Katja. "We passed each earlier on the stairs?"

Katja stared for a moment not being able to believe her eyes.

"Oh! my god! It's you! Isabella! What on earth are you doing here? You've changed your hair and everything!"

She moved forward to give her a hug.

"I wanted to give you a surprise," said Isabella. "I've business to do here in Bordeaux and thought I would spend a week or so catching up. By chance this studio was free in your block."

"That's wonderful! It's so good to see you!"

"You're looking good yourself, Katja. Tell me there's a new man in your life!"

"Look, we have so much to catch up on why don't you come down to my flat in about half an hour and we can have lunch, or if you prefer we can eat out."

"That would be great – eating in, I mean. Are you sure it's not too much trouble? You must tell me all about your new job – and your new man!"

"That's settled then. My place – flat 4 – in about half an hour to give me time to shower and change."

Isabella closed the door and returned to her chair to think. Now she was face to face with Katja, getting information out of her didn't seem so easy without giving away her real motives. How much was she going to tell her? She needed to find out everything she knew about Deveau, but mentioning Lucca to her was quite another matter.

It would be good cover to have a friend to go about with though. It would look much less suspicious and attract less attention if the police were looking for her as they surely were. They wouldn't be expecting her to be in the company of anyone else, so two young women out together would not stand out so much as a single female.

Later over lunch, Isabella relaxed and asked Katja lots of questions about her new life in Bordeaux. Gradually she turned the conversation round to Deveau.

"I came down partly here because I read in the papers that Jean-Louis had been found dead…"

"Yes, and I was almost there when he died," interrupted Katja.

"What do you mean, you were almost there?"

"Well, I had gone to see about some books he bought off me and knocked on his door. There was no answer, but I later found out he had had a heart attack or something and was lying dead inside."

"How awful. I never liked him that much, but we did business together as you know."

"I never thanked you properly for recommending me to him, by the way."

"No problem. What was all that about anyway? Why did he need you? Was he involved in something big? He never told me exactly what it was."

Katja felt the hairs on the back of her neck rise. There was something about the urgency in Isabella's voice that unsettled her. She remembered Lucca's reaction when she had mentioned Isabella's name. She hesitated a fraction before replying.

"No, nothing serious. Just an old manuscript he wanted me to check. Why don't you let me show you around Bordeaux," she said changing the subject. "It would be fun."

"OK, that sounds good."

"I can show you where the best bookshops are in the old quarter," Katja volunteered. "I promised Marcel…"

"…so that's his name."

"… I would go in to work this afternoon as we have a lot on, but he won't mind if I am a little late. We could stroll down there now if you like – it's not out of my way. In fact we will pass my office."

"In that case why don't I come with you as far as your office and you give me directions from there?" suggested Isabella. "I don't want to make you late unnecessarily."

"Alright, that would be better."

"You must let me take you out for something to eat this evening. Then you can tell me more about this boss of yours! You haven't told me anything like enough yet."

*

Early next morning Pierre's phone vibrated and he went into Antonia's living room so as not to disturb her. He listened to what he was being told by Inspector Bureau at the Hôtel de Police in Bordeaux. There was confirmation the cigarette end Kokoschka had stubbed out during their meeting at the café and the glass she had used had been successfully retrieved after they separated, but her DNA did not match the DNA on the cigarette found in Deveau's flat.

But Pierre's attention was really awakened when Bureau reported Katja Kokoschka had been seen in the street with Isabella Marquessa and that Marquessa had taken a flat in the same block as her in the *rue du Palais Gallien.*

"*Merci, Inspecteur.* You were right to contact me straight away. Your men have done well. Keep the watch on the two women. I shall return to Bordeaux this morning."

With a sigh he turned his phone off, as Antonia emerged from the bedroom. One look at his face and she burst into laughter.

"You look as if someone has just taken your favourite toy away ! What's the matter?"

"I have to return to Bordeaux this morning," he said ruefully, putting his arms around her. "But the news is good. I didn't tell you last night that Isabella Marquessa has been seen in Bordeaux. And now she has been spotted in the company of Kokoschka."

"Do you think they are working together?"

"No, I don't think so. I suspect Marquessa is in Bordeaux trying to locate Lucca, but now that Deveau is dead she's at a loss as to how to find him."

"So will Kokoschka help her?"

"Perhaps, but … I'm not sure," he said, thinking aloud. "She knows there's bad blood between Lucca and Marquessa, so she may be cautious."

"Could we use her?"

"I think we could. Despite breaking in to Deveau's shop, she's not really a villain, more an amateur experiencing a thrill from sailing close to the wind. She's genuinely afraid of what she has got herself into. She confided in her boss and it was he who suggested she come to see me."

"So what will you ask her to do?"

"If I could persuade her to drop Lucca's name into the conversation, Marquessa is sure to take the bait."

"Then you must go, Pierre – I'll phone for a car to take you to the airport."

She gave him a quick kiss, freed herself from his arms and picked up the phone.

＊

Pierre had chosen a different café to meet with her the second time, feeling the previous venue was too close to the *place Gambetta* where Marquessa might see them together and recognise him.

"Thank you for meeting me again so soon, mademoiselle. And for looking at the efits. You have been a great help. I have to ask you some more questions however."

Katja shuffled uneasily in her seat and looked at him, trying to keep the nervousness she felt from showing on her face.

"You were recently seen in the company of Isabella Marquessa."

Seeing the shock which registered on Katja's face, he corrected himself.

"Or, rather, she was seen in your company, since it is Marquessa who is under surveillance, not you I can reassure you."

"But why, Commissaire? She's just a friend. I didn't even know she was coming to Bordeaux. Has she done something wrong?"

"What do you really know about your former employer, mademoiselle?"

"What do you mean? She runs a gallery. I worked there. I told you all about it before."

Katja was beginning to feel frightened.

"Can I order a coffee?" she asked to steady her nerves.

"Bien sûr, excusez-moi!"

Pierre hailed the waiter and ordered two coffees. There was a pause as they waited for the drinks to arrive. Pierre fiddled with the cigarette packet in his pocket.

"Why has she come to Bordeaux?"

"She told me she felt like a break and is just travelling round France visiting auction rooms looking for pictures to buy. She also is interested in old books and jewellery."

"She recommended you to Deveau, if I remember correctly. Did she ask about what it was Deveau wanted you to do?"

"Well, yes of course."

"And what did you tell her?"

"Could I have a cigarette, Commissaire?" she replied.

Pierre pulled out the crumpled packet and offered her one.

"I'm getting you into bad habits, mademoiselle!"

He leaned back and waited while she lit it.

"So, what did you tell her exactly?"

There was no response.

"Let me help you, Mademoiselle Kokoschka. She asked what it was Deveau wanted you to authenticate and what the deal was. You remembered Lucca's reaction when you mentioned her name to him and so you said you didn't know. Am I right?"

"Pretty well, Commissaire. The way she asked me about the deal scared me for a moment and I suddenly realised, as you said, that I didn't really know much about her before she owned the gallery. Her arrival here so soon after Deveau's death suddenly seemed odd. So I said nothing about Lucca."

"So what do you know about her?"

"That she trained as a jeweller, but found it boring working in shops. She decided to simply buy and sell for herself. She inherited some money when her mother died and bought the gallery. Now she is going round auction houses to increase her stock."

"But she's also interested in old books and manuscripts, you said."

"Yes. So I showed her the way to the old quarter where most of the old bookshops are."

Pierre raised his eyebrows and leaned forward. He automatically looked around him and lowered his voice.

"Listen carefully, mademoiselle. We would like you to do something for us. You will be in no danger. But it would be of great assistance to us."

Looking distinctly worried, Katja nodded and said:

"If I can help I will, Commissaire."

Pierre explained quietly to her what he wanted her to do.

Chapter 17

"There's a new development, Eleni – Marquessa is in Bordeaux. As you know fingerprints were found in Deveau's flat. Not recent, but it does show there's a link."

Eleni had been woken by the sound of her mobile on the bedside table in their hotel room and by now was wide awake listening to what Antonia was telling her. She signalled to Patrick by her side that she needed a coffee.

"Marquessa has rented a studio in the same block as Kokoschka and they have been seen together. Pierre is convinced Kokoschka is an innocent in a dangerous position. He has persuaded her to report to us on Marquessa's movements. She hasn't mentioned her link with Lucca to Marquessa yet, but is going to reveal she has to go to Sardinia to see an Italian buyer."

"Isn't that dangerous?"

"We're banking on the fact Marquessa wants to take her revenge on Lucca and has no quarrel with Kokoschka."

There was a crackle on the line and Antonia was cut off.

"Damn these mobiles," said Eleni out loud.

"Talking to yourself," said Patrick poking his head round the door and receiving a rude gesture in response.

Her phone went again.

"Damn these mobiles. Can you hear me, Eleni?"

"No problem, go on."

"Kokoschka has given Pierre a description of the manuscript she has been asked to authenticate – if and when it's found."

"That's great. Give me the details."

"It's an eye witness account of the Third Crusade by a knight called Sir Geoffroi de Vinsauf."

"That's the Richard Coeur de Lion Crusade isn't it?"

"Now you are showing off, Inspector!"

Eleni laughed. "Can you spell the name?" she said reaching for the pad by the bedside. OK, so now we know exactly what to look for in the monastery library."

"Yes. I want you and Patrick to go back and see if you can find it. But be careful, Platini will tail you again. After the break-in to your room he must be fairly sure you haven't found the manuscript yet and will want to follow you to see if you go back."

"What do we do when or if we do find it?"

"Even if it is not there pretend to be bringing it out and make it clear you are carrying it in your backpack. If Platini is watching he'll wait till you're back at the hotel and search your room again."

"I don't understand. Do we just let him take the real manuscript – just like that! Assuming of course we have found it. What if we haven't?"

"No, we've got a facsimile for you to leave in your room, so the plan will work whether or not you find the original."

"Not the first time we've used that trick. Won't it take a while to make?"

Patrick came into the room with the coffee and sat beside Eleni on the bed. He handed her a cup and tried to hear what Antonia was saying.

"Don't worry. It's already being done ..."

"...sorry, Antonia, can you repeat that, Patrick is making too much noise and I missed it."

Patrick made a face and moved even closer.

"... it's done already, using text from an old copy they have in Oxford. Platini won't know enough to be able to tell it's not the real thing. He'll only see what he wants to see. Pierre will bring it to your hotel later this evening."

"Do we take it with us to the monastery?"

"No. Mr Constantine will take care of that."

"Who ...? Never mind! How do we enter the monastery, now there are guards there? Will they let us in late at night?"

"They have been warned to expect you. Kóstas' men will be there too for your protection, but I doubt you will see them."

"That sounds rather dramatic!"

"After the break-in to your room, we need to give you maximum protection especially on your way back from the monastery in case Platini tries anything."

"Do we try to lose Platini if he does follow us or do we lead him there?"

"Let him follow you to the monastery. He won't try to attack you on the way there. But he must be convinced you have the real manuscript when you come out."

"What if he does try to take it from us on the way back?"

"He won't. Kóstas' men will see to that. But take care, Eleni. I don't want anything to happen to you and Patrick."

*

After Antonia had finished giving instructions to Eleni, she called for a car and went straight to Kóstas' restaurant and chose a discreet table in a corner at the back. As soon as he could Kóstas joined her and a waiter brought the *mezés* and a bottle of wine. Antonia put her hand on the older man's arm and her eyes told him this conversation was completely off the record. He nodded and poured the wine.

"Don't worry any more, Antonia. They will be completely safe. My men will take care of everything. Eleni and Patrick are very dear to me. But where is that nice boyfriend of yours? How can he leave you on your own like this? If I was twenty years younger ..."

"... I would be 15 and you would be a child molester!"

"At last a smile! I would have only a year or so to wait and then ..."

"You are completely incorrigible, Kóstas my friend," she said, taking his hand in hers. "... but I feel a lot better now!"

They both touched glasses and Kóstas left the table.

A few minutes later Pierre arrived looking travel weary after his flight from Bordeaux. He greeted Antonia and sat down, ready to enjoy an evening of relaxation. He started to tell her more about the meeting with Kokoschka and was helping himself to the wine and the *mezés* when he realised Antonia was not listening to him.

She was signalling to a courier who had arrived from the Athens Museum and was standing hesitantly just inside the doorway. Antonia waved him over and he placed a package on the table.

"As you requested, Chief Inspector," he said, "there's a car waiting outside."

"Sorry to rush you, Pierre, but you must go soon. Patrick and Eleni are going back to the monastery tonight and will need this. When you arrive at the hotel one of Kóstas' men will be there waiting for you. Just put the package in your briefcase and leave it at the reception to be collected by a Mr. Constantine."

Kóstas returned as she was finishing and seeing the expression on Pierre's face, slapped him cheerfully on the back.

"It is good you are here, Commissaire."

"My feet have hardly touched the ground since I left here last time," Pierre responded, shaking Kóstas hand. "And now she's sending me away again."

"You drive him too hard, Antonia," said Kóstas with a grin. "Never fear, Pétros, you can have a nice rest in Dimitsána hotel tonight and we will all meet back here tomorrow evening to celebrate the success of our little game."

Regaining his seriousness, he added, looking at Antonia:

"My men will not let you down. This is a great adventure for them and make them feel young again – like back in the days of the Colonels."

"Lýtras will have my head on a plate if he ever gets to hear of this," admitted Antonia, with an anxious glance over her shoulder.

"Don't worry my dear Antonia, my men, they are invisible. They have not forgotten their skills and know Lousiós Gorge like the backs of their hands, as the English say."

*

In the early evening as the light started to fade Marco watched Patrick and Eleni leave the hotel and walk down the road leading to the Gorge. He was about to follow when he heard the sound of a car approaching the hotel. Curious someone should arrive at that hour. Marco went back into the hotel. He took a seat in the hall to observe the new arrival.

Pierre entered the hotel and immediately caught sight of Platini sitting in the foyer. Careful to show no recognition, and keeping his head turned away, he went straight to the reception desk and began to check in.

Marco watched as he signed the form and took his key from the receptionist. Still with his back to the foyer, Pierre picked up his briefcase and a porter took his heavier suitcase. They stood side by side waiting for the lift. The lift doors opened, slid shut behind them and the lift started to rise. Marco saw the numbers glow one after the other above the lift entrance and rise to five. There was a pause, before the lift began its descent for the next guest already waiting on the ground floor.

Seeing nothing unusual in these comings and goings, Marco cursed himself for being so on edge and quickly left the hall to head out in the direction Eleni and Patrick had taken.

Pierre waited in his room for an hour before descending the stairs to the reception desk and leaving his briefcase there as arranged.

After about twenty minutes Marco caught them up and slowed to get his breath back. He could hear them talking a short way further along the road. Keeping well back out of sight, he heard them turn off the paved road onto the track leading to the monastery. He followed at a safe distance knowing he would not lose them as the path led directly to the monastery. After an hour's steady climb, he watched the two detectives arrive at the gates of the monastery and go in.

Marco had prepared well, as he knew Lucca would not tolerate failure this time. He had concealed a trail bike the previous day by the side of the track, well hidden in the undergrowth. About ten metres further on there was a spot where, by withdrawing into the trees at the side, he could see anyone approaching the sharp bend he had picked as the best spot for an ambush on their return. He made the bike ready for a quick escape and settled down to wait for Tsikas and Bruni to reappear. If all went according to plan they would be carrying the manuscript, he was sure. Why else would return to the monastery unless they were sure the manuscript was there? Knowing he would hear them approaching down the rocky path, he allowed himself a few moments of relaxation and sat savouring the success he anticipated and the subsequent praise from Lucca.

*

Eleni and Patrick approached the Nea Moni Filosófou in the fading light. The ghosts of the past weighed in on their imaginations and each rustle in the trees and the undergrowth made them aware Platini might be behind them somewhere observing their every move. The old buildings were in total darkness and only the torches they were carrying allowed them to pick their way up the final stony path to the gates. Through the bars of the *jalousie* they could make out the faint glimmer of a light coming from a lantern near the chapel.

Patrick pulled on the chain hanging down by the side of the door and the sound of a bell in the distance broke the silence of the night.

"That'll tell Platini we've arrived, if he's out there!" said Eleni quietly.

The light came closer and a young soldier appeared, seemingly unsurprised by the presence of visitors at that late hour. Eleni showed him her ID and the small door cut into the old gate swung open. They both stepped in and the guard quickly secured the door.

He saluted and said:

"Welcome to the monastery, Inspector. I'm not sorry to have some company – it's spooky here at night and the owls terrify me."

"I know what you mean, Corporal – it was very scary too climbing up here in the dark," said Patrick.

"I can offer you coffee," said the soldier, reluctant to be left on his own and wanting to delay the new arrivals.

"Perhaps when we have found what we are looking for, Corporal," said Eleni quickly before Patrick could accept as she knew he would if given the chance. We would like to go to the chapel straight away as it is late."

They left the soldier and entered the chapel. Eleni went round lighting the candles and the little nave of the chapel was lit up to advantage. The flickering yellow light made the frescoes come alive and the ancient figures appeared to move and to converse with another. The colours stood out as they must have done to countless generations of monks and pilgrims.

Patrick stood for moment taking in the spectacular sight before Eleni urged him back into action. The arras behind the altar swayed slightly in the draft from the open door. At that moment they heard a stifled cry from beyond the monastery walls. The soldier immediately appeared at the doorway and, clearly anxious, asked:

"Did you hear noise from outside the walls, Inspector? I'm worried."

"It was probably just an owl or a fox, Corporal," said Eleni. "But we have back-up out there and they will deal with any problems. Just keep a sharp look-out."

The soldier saluted and reluctantly left the chapel.

*

He never heard the man who nearly garrotted him. Nor the second man who pulled a hood over his head and secured his arms behind his back. His attempts to call out were compressed into more of a groan and a final squeak.

Rough hands searched him thoroughly, removing his wallet and the pistol from his shoulder holster. Finally he was stripped of the knife he always carried strapped to his left leg and which he only ever removed on taking a bath.

His captors dragged him back into the undergrowth, made sure the gag was tight and tied him firmly to a tree. He felt a prick in his arm and the sound of a motor bike starting up. Finally there was silence and he was alone. Soon he began to shiver in the cooling air.

*

In the little room behind the arras, Eleni and Patrick began the search for the manuscript. Having a name to go by this time they were able to eliminate many of the piles of manuscripts much more quickly than before. Eleni carefully went through the shelves that had been sorted already by the caretaker monk and Patrick wandered round the room looking at the dusty piles. He suddenly had a fit of coughing as a cloud of dust rose from a pile which collapsed as he lifted off a parchment.

"*Eleni! Viens.*"

There in the middle of the heap was a leather bound codex. Some of the pages had broken off the spine binding and were hanging out of the covers. They could just make out the words *de Vinsauf* on the yellowing top parchment page. They knelt down to look more closely and carefully brushed away the dust of centuries to reveal more pages. Tracing the lines with her finger Eleni read out softly the opening lines:

"In the year of the incarnate word 1197, when Urban III ..."

She stopped in awe at what she had before her eyes.

"This really is it, Patrick – his manuscript! I hardly dare touch it. We've found it! I can hardly believe it. The ink had faded to a very faint brown, but the velum was still surprisingly strong.

They carefully gathered the pages up, resisting the temptation to read more of the text or to examine it any further for fear of causing damage. They slid the codex into the stout bag they had brought with them and made their way to the entrance to the library.

As they emerged from behind the arras and entered the nave, blinking in the stronger light of the candles, they were suddenly aware of a man sitting on one of the old chairs gazing at the frescoes above him. He was dressed for the cold night air in hunter's clothes, his face blacked up like that of a commando on night patrol. On his belt hung a large hunting knife. Patrick noted the slight bulge under his jacket and realised he was wearing a shoulder holster. Instinctively he pushed Eleni behind him.

The man smiled at Patrick's reaction and stood up, saying:

"Don't worry, Inspector." He addressed Eleni: "Your uncle sent me."

"So you are…?" replied Eleni, guardedly.

"Mr Constantine."

At the chair by his side was a bag identical to the one Eleni was carrying. She stared at it in amazement.

"How did you ..."

"Ours to know, yours to admire," he replied with a grin. "We have neutralised the opposition, but thought it better nonetheless, in case there are others out there, for us to take the manuscript back to the hotel for you."

"And so what is in your bag?"

"The copy."

They exchanged bags and the man slipped away silently.

"I hope we're doing the right thing, I'd hate to lose the manuscript now we have just found it," said Patrick, watching him go. "I wouldn't like to meet him in the dark."

"Don't worry. That was the password. And anyway the guard obviously had been briefed to let him in."

"My respect for Kóstas grows every day. How does he do it?"

The young soldier on guard let them out and made no mention of the extra visitor. Eleni and Patrick started off down the track to walk to the hotel, feeling elated at the success of their operation.

"It won't be difficult to look as if we are celebrating this evening," said Patrick, putting his arm around Eleni's shoulders as they walked along the track.

Feeling tired, but pleased with themselves, they approached the hotel and entered the reception area. Eleni made no secret of holding the brief case and waited while Patrick collected their key. The lift took them up to the fourth floor and they went into their room.

No longer able to resist, Patrick opened the case and pulled out the parcel inside. He unwrapped it carefully and they both stared at the facsimile in admiration.

"That's perfect. You'd think it was the original."

Turning the first page they gazed at the imitation of the old faded writing of the early scribes who took down the dictation.

"I wonder how many copies were made back then with the illuminations and where they are now," mused Eleni.

"That's something we'll never know," said Patrick as he rewrapped the copy and put it back in the case.

"Where would the best place be to hide it?"

Going over to where their empty suitcases were, he opened his and put the document case inside, locked the suitcase and put it back in the walk-in wardrobe.

"OK, that should do it."

There was a knock on the door and Patrick signalled to Eleni to open it after he had drawn his gun and taken up position so he would be behind the door when it opened.

Eleni found herself looking at a smartly dressed Mr Constantine who was holding out a document case. He merely nodded as she took hold of it and with an ironic salute turned and walked back down the corridor.

Both she and Patrick breathed a sigh of relief as they gingerly took the genuine manuscript out of the case and wrapped it in a cloth. Eleni placed it in her large shoulder bag, brought for the occasion.

Looking at his watch Patrick said:

"Just time for a quick shower and then down to meet Pierre for a late meal – I'm starving after all that walking and excitement and I bet he'll be hungry too."

The shower wasn't really big enough for two, but they managed.

*

When the drug wore off and he came to, he found his hands had been untied and he was no longer roped to the tree. Ripping off the hood and the pulling out the gag he looked around him. There was no sign of his attackers and darkness had fallen. He had no way of knowing how long he had been there as they had taken his watch.

Behind him he could just make out the monastery which was in total darkness. The woods were full only of the natural sounds of the night. He rose stiffly to his feet and walked unsteadily to where he had hidden his motor bike.

"What the hell! *Luridos bastardos*! They take my bike! I make them pay for this."

Angrily he picked his way back to the path and began walking slowly down the track feeling the stiffness in his joints. As he walked he considered the options left to him if he was to salvage the situation and avoid Lucca's final judgement.

Later, lying in a hot bath in the hotel soaking the soreness out of his body, he was still furious at having allowed himself to be taken so easily.

To save his skin he had to regain the advantage. He was sure this time they knew where to find the manuscript or why would they have gone back? Assuming they did discover it, there was no way they could have got the manuscript out of the hotel this late at night so it must still be there. He just had to find it. It was his only chance to stay alive.

He heaved himself out of the bath and stood dripping water everywhere. As he grabbed his towel he growled to himself:

"And I will find the bastards who jump me and steal my bike. They will die slowly."

*

Down in the bar Pierre checked his watch and ordered another *ouzo,* while he waited for Patrick and Eleni. The two of them entered the bar fifteen minutes later and greeted him warmly. A waiter showed them to their table. They took their seats and Eleni was careful to place her bag on the floor between her feet. They concentrated on choosing from the main menu as the *mezés* arrived. Pierre and Patrick went for the *scháras,* and Eleni, not being too good with fish, went for the *choirinó souvláki.*

"Will you leave the choice of wine to me?" asked Eleni suddenly smiling and trying hard not to look over their shoulders. The two men looked up from the menu and nodded.

"Good decision, gentlemen," said a voice. "Glad to see even Frenchmen can be new men."

The two of them rose to greet her and a waiter swiftly pulled up another chair for Antonia.

"I didn't see why you three should have all the fun, while I languished in the heat of Athens. This certainly is a beautiful place," she said looking round as she sat down.

"Tell me what you've all been doing with yourselves."

Eleni spoke to the waiter and ordered another *souvláki* for Antonia and two bottles from the Merkoúri estate on the western peninsular. Antonia nodded in agreement with her choice.

*

Marco watched the activity at their table via the mirror on the other side of the bar and noted the mood of the gathering. He slipped out of the dining room and made his way to the fourth floor not using the lift, knowing the lights would show. There was no-one about as he approached the door of their room. Fearful of falling into a trap, but having no time to waste he unlocked the door with a pass key he had persuaded one of the maids to let him borrow the night before.

He shut the door quietly behind him and locked it. Standing in the middle of the room he looked about him. This time he knew what he was looking for, having seen what the bag Eleni had carried out to the monastery looked like. He rubbed his wrists which were still sore from being tied up earlier. After checking the obvious places under the bed and in the drawers he headed towards the large wardrobe.

He froze abruptly, sweat gathering on his forehead when he heard a knock on the door. He just had time to make it inside the wardrobe as a key rattled in the lock and a maid came in to fuss around the bed and turn the covers back. He almost stopped breathing while she was there and released a long sigh of relief when she finally left and he heard the key turning. As he opened the door to step out his foot caught on a suitcase. A slow grin spread over his face as he grabbed the case to throw it on the bed. Not empty, he realised.

A quick flick with his knife broke the locks and revealed the bag inside. Two more flicks with his knife and he was looking at the manuscript. He quickly replaced the suitcase, picked up the bag and let himself out into the corridor. Back in his own room on the same floor, he transferred the manuscript to his own suitcase, covered it with clothes and went down to the reception to check out.

In the dining room the four of them were still enjoying their meal. Outside, two wiry looking men were restoring their energy with food from their backpacks after a long evening's work. They could see everything that was going on inside the hotel through the glowing windows. When Marco came out carrying a shoulder bag, they picked up their packs, and, still munching, set off in the footsteps of the Italian.

Chapter 18

Isabella and Katja sat outside on the terrace of the café on the corner of the *place Gambetta*. For Katja it was where she normally went after work to relax after a day at her desk in the architect's office; for Isabella it was a time for reflection as to what she should do next. Both women remained silent apparently lost in thought, enjoying the sun playing on their faces and idly watching the passers by. From time to time they leaned forward to pick up the cold drinks the waiter had brought them.

That evening though, Katja was not as relaxed in Isabella's company as she had been, since she was no longer innocent of what Isabella might be doing in Bordeaux. She was unsure of how to meet Rousseau's request for her to casually mention going to Sardinia to see an Italian dealer without raising Isabella's suspicions.

Nor was she quite clear why this news would interest Isabella. The police had not given her much information to go on. They had only said it was important she report back to them if Isabella either showed a particular interest or even offered to go with her the next time.

Despite having being very close to the wrong side of the law in the past, this role of police informant made her feel awkward. She just hoped it didn't show.

Isabella in her turn sat puzzling over what she should do next to find out where Lucca was. The only link she had had was via Deveau. So, the best chance seemed to be to break into his bookshop and to see if there was anything there which would provide a clue or even an address.

She knew the bookshop was under surveillance. That would make it much harder, though not impossible, to break in. She had eluded police security many times before, so that was not a problem if she was careful.

The gurgling sound of Katja reaching the bottom of the glass with her straw was enough to rouse her from her thoughts and she turned, smiling, towards Katja.

"Oh! I'm sorry, did I wake you," asked Katja. "You were day dreaming in the sun."

"That's OK – I was just enjoying the warmth ... and dozing a bit too I have to admit."

Katja laughed and confessed to having drifted off for few moments herself. She signalled to the waiter to bring a couple more drinks. Time to make an effort and to make conversation. The waiter arrived and set down the new glasses.

"So how do you propose to spend the rest of your stay in Bordeaux?" she asked.

"Well, there are plenty of bookshops in the old quarter you showed me to. That should keep me busy for a while."

She paused.

"There was one which had a police guard outside. I assume that was Deveau's?"

"Yes. I told you about how I was outside his door and he was lying dead inside? Well, the police thought the clue to why he died must be somewhere there in the shop."

"So they do think his death is suspicious?"

"Yes, I think so," Katja replied realising this was her chance. "The police already knew he dealt in stolen books and manuscripts, but could never pin anything on him. I assume they think his death has something to do with a deal that went wrong."

"Do you think so too?"

"Well I do know he was working with a rather scary Italian dealer, because he asked me to authenticate a manuscript he and this dealer were looking for."

"The one you mentioned earlier? What sort of manuscript?"

"It's an old Crusader chronicle."

"So that's why he contacted me to see if I knew anyone with expertise in that area? He never told me much, the sly old fox."

Katja sensed her next question and her mind was working furiously.

"So who is this Italian dealer and why is he scary?"

"His name's Giovanni Lucca."

Isabella carefully continued stirring her drink with the straw not trusting herself to look at Katja.

"I've been out to Sardinia to see him," Katja continued. "He's paying me well, but he frightens me a bit."

"Sardinia? That must be fun! What part?" said Isabella quickly, ignoring Katja's last remark.

"He lives in the north of the island. Beautiful house overlooking the sea. He invited me out for an interview and asked me to go to Greece to do some research into where the manuscript might be. Later I went out to Sardinia again to tell him what I had found out. He seemed pleased and said he would contact me when he has the manuscript."

Katja looked at her watch and picked up her drink to finish it.

"Look, it's already eight o'clock. I'm hungry and I mustn't be too late tonight – I have to be in the office tomorrow early. It's all very well for you people on holiday."

Isabella smiled but said nothing and they got up to leave the table. They made their way across to the *Porte Dijeaux* on the other side of the square and down the *rue des Remparts* to a Moroccan restaurant which by coincidence was not far from Deveau's flat.

A man sitting at the back of café reading the paper not far from where they had been sitting picked up his phone and tapped in a number.

"Commissaire? They have just left to go to eat – I'm not far behind. Looks like the Moroccan restaurant on the *rue des Remparts*."

"*Bien.* You can stand down and thank you. Someone else will take over."

"*Merci, Commissaire. Bonsoir.*"

*

When they left the restaurant later that evening, the two women returned to the apartment block in the *rue du Palais Gallien*. They said good night on the stairway and went to their respective flats.

Later that evening after midnight, Isabella, dressed in dark clothing, slipped out of the building and walked towards the old quarter. A pair of eyes followed her progress and a hand pressed a phone to an ear.

Chapter 19

Katja took particular care over her appearance as she got ready for the evening to come. Marcel Bouvier had invited her out again and she had to admit to herself she was attracted to him. Having a relationship with the boss where you work is fraught with pitfalls and in the past she had seen many tears shed when the almost inevitable break-up followed. She felt very uncertain how far she wanted to go. She had not been with her new firm long enough to know all the background and past history. Perhaps that didn't matter.

With a final look in the mirror and a twirl of her skirt to gage the total effect, she felt confident enough to pick up her bag and leave the flat. She walked slowly down the street and into the *place Gambetta* towards the flower stall on the corner, where Marcel was waiting for her. He presented her with a blue carnation – speciality of the stand – and a kiss on both cheeks.

She took his arm and they sauntered down through the arch of the *Porte Dijeaux,* down a side street and out into the cathedral square. She asked where they were going, but he just smiled and said to wait and see. They fell into a pleasant companionable silence, enjoying the warmth of the evening sun.

Out of the corner of her eye Katja admired the casual elegance of his appearance, jacket loosely hanging from both shoulders covering a silk shirt and light trousers. Rather classic and close to being dated perhaps, but carried off with style.

"Nothing 'cool' about this place," said Marcel looking at her as they stopped in front of the *Restaurant du musée des arts décoratifs*, "but the food is excellent."

They entered the building and went upstairs to the balcony with its view over the square and the cathedral. The evening sun shining on the golden statue high above them on the separate bell tower imparted a further magnificence to the view.

Already Katja was relaxing and looking forward to what she felt might become a perfect evening when from across the room there was a sudden screech like none other and a figure she recognised rose up from a table on the far side.

"Cooee! Kattie. Over here," beseeched the figure. There was nothing for it, but to approach the source of the sound. Katja's face told the whole story as Marcel gave her an inquiring look.

"*Bonsoir* Mira, George. What a happy coincidence."

"It sure is a happy one, my dear. We've only just got here and here you are to help us with the menu. You must join us as our guests. No, no, we insist, don't we George? And you must introduce me to this handsome young man with you."

Waiters appeared and the two of them found themselves sitting at a table transformed for four. Menus were placed before them and Mira was asking Katja what on earth a 'chicken screwer' could be as she read the English version of the menu. Marcel received a kick on the ankle for muttering *'coq au vin'* under his breath, as Katja consulted the French version and explained *'brochette de poulet'* to her mystified host.

The evening continued with George staying mostly silent and Mira flirting with the waiters and with Marcel, in between questioning Katja about her work and the link with Lucca. Katja remained on her guard during what she realised was an interrogation and revealed nothing more of her contact with Lucca.

Finally, after a replay of the 'cream brooly', followed by an extra ice cream, Mira got to her feet, jerked the dozing George back into life and handed his credit card to the waiter. After noisy goodbyes, and a gale of scraping chairs and tables the couple left the dining room. An unusual calm began to settle over the room as the other diners turned their attention back to their partners and the atmosphere returned to normal.

Marcel shook his head slightly as if to bring himself back to reality and called the waiter over. With a confirming glance to Katja he signaled to the waiter and ordered two coffees and two Armagnacs.

Turning back to Katja he said:

"Now I'm beginning to understand."

"You must admit they are good actors," replied Katja, relieved at his reaction. "They never let the mask slip in their roles."

"George was very good. He didn't let himself be drawn in at all."

"No need to really," she laughed. "Mira is more than enough on her own. She really worked hard to worm more details out of me. Something George said made me realise this is not the first time they've dealt with Lucca."

"I'm impressed by the way you gave nothing away," he said. "And I'm relieved you went to the police and told them all about this. You must feel a bit safer."

"Yes, I am thanks to you. I just didn't know what to do," she said putting her hand over his.

They chatted on for another hour before realising the time and getting up to leave. The waiter refused to let Marcel pay for the coffees and Armagnac saying the Americans had left more than enough over the bill to cover that.

"Playing the part to the very last," said Marcel appreciatively. "Real professionals."

They strolled arm in arm back to the *place Gambetta* and Katja prepared herself to keep the initiative. When they reached the spot where he had given her the carnation, she kissed him lightly on the cheek and thanked him for the evening.

"Well, it wasn't quite what I had planned," he said, "but in fact it was quite instructive after what you told me the other night. I have more of an idea of what you are involved in. If all the others in this business are as clever as those two Americans then I have to admit I'm still worried for your safety, Katja."

"I'll be fine, but thanks for caring, Marcel. Don't worry. I will tell you if I'm asked to go out to Sardinia again."

She kissed him again on the cheek and, before he could react, started to move away, her arm pulled almost directly behind her as he reluctantly released her hand. As she turned the corner she looked back and saw he had watched her all the way. Perhaps next time, she thought as she covered the final few metres with a spring in her step.

*

Isabella left the bookshop after a fruitless two hours searching and started back to her flat in a bad mood. She had found nothing to add to

what Katja had told her about what Lucca was engaged in. She knew
her best chance of locating him was to follow the clues Katja had given
her to where he was living. Nearing her flat she turned the final corner
and she caught a glimpse of Katja saying good night to a man she did
not recognise and heading back to her flat. Isabella watched from the
dark shadows of a doorway for a few moments before entering the
building.

Chapter 20

In the dining room of the hotel in Dimitsána a discreet celebration dinner was taking place. Soon after Antonia's unexpected arrival another visitor approached the table. Eleni saw him first, jumped up and threw her arms around him.

"Thank you, Uncle," she whispered into his ear.

Kóstas joined them at the table and they leaned forward as he recounted quietly how his men had dealt with Marco on the trail. The mood quickly changed as the food arrived and he regaled them with stories about what happened in the valley during their resistance to the Colonels. He found it hard to tone down his natural exuberance and the others had to hush him from time to time, as diners at the other tables were glancing in their direction to see what the noise was all about.

After the meal they all went up to Antonia's room where she could hardly contain herself when Eleni produced the genuine manuscript from her bag. Her hands trembled as she touched this original manuscript written centuries before. The priceless document would be in the hands of the Athens museum within hours.

"The next stage will be to somehow persuade the Greek Orthodox Church to allow all the documents you saw in the library to be properly catalogued and preserved," said Antonia.

"Now they know one of their monks has been murdered it will be easier to convince them it is impossible to assure the security of the monastery," said Kóstas.

"And the fact that Patrick and Eleni didn't have any difficulty in finding the library, shows others may discover it too," added Pierre.

"The question now is whether Platini will go with the copy to Lucca in Sardinia or hang on to it himself."

"My men are following him as we speak and we will soon know. But I think he is too frightened of Lucca to try any tricks."

Kóstas' expression betrayed what he considered would be his preferred next move. Eleni correctly interpreted what he was thinking and quickly and firmly said:

"No, Uncle. You have helped us enormously so far, but the rest you must leave to us. We want Lucca as much, if not more, than you do. But he has to be caught red-handed and according to the correct procedure which will have to be handled by the Italian police. Even we can only advise them and hope for the best."

"The Italians have first claim on him for murder on Italian soil remember. The manuscript will be a very much lesser affair in their eyes compared with that," added Antonia , with a nod to Eleni.

Patrick was looking uncomfortable with the way the conversation was going and looked as if he was about to speak. Pierre spotted his discomfort and asked:

"What's on your mind, Patrick?"

"We seem to have forgotten Lucca will want the manuscript to be authenticated by Kokoschka. He won't risk taking it to her in Bordeaux, so he'll summon her to Sardinia. Won't she be in danger? What happens when she sees it? Has she been warned it is a facsimile? She's bound to spot it."

Before anyone could reply, there was a knock on the door. One of Kóstas' men entered the room and reported quietly to him. At the same time the sound of a helicopter could be heard coming in to land in front of the hotel.

They all got to their feet and prepared to leave. Antonia clasped Eleni's bag containing the manuscript close to her and went out first to the aircraft. Pierre and Patrick went to fetch their cases and followed, leaving Eleni with her uncle.

"Remember what I said, Uncle. Leave this to us and the Italians, please. I don't want to have to visit you in prison somewhere or, worse, in a morgue. You have done enough and must admit we have given you some extra fun."

Kóstas looked carefully at her and with a sigh gave her a reply she was not really expecting.

"I promised your father I would look after you after he died. That is more important than the rest. As you say you have given us lots of fun and excitement. My men and I will stay here a few days longer to replay old memories and remember old friends. We will say a mass at the monastery. We owe that to the monks who risked their lives to hide us.

Then I promise you we will return to Athens, but I can tell you already that Platini is on his way out of Greece and will very soon be in Sardinia."

Eleni hugged him and whispered in his ear. He laughed and as she departed to join the others on the helicopter he called:

"Messaged received. There will be a party the like of which you have never seen!"

*

In the helicopter Antonia turned to Eleni.

"I know it's late, but I want you to take the manuscript straight to the museum tonight. They are expecting you."

"Of course."

"Pierre and I need to work out the next move and to contact the Italian police. They will have to work fast, if they want to get their hands on Lucca."

"And I'll need to contact Kokoschka and brief her before the call from Lucca to go to Sardinia comes through," said Pierre. "A lot depends on her and how she will handle the pressure."

"Have I missed something here? Brief her?" asked Patrick.

"Are you going to go with Eleni to the museum, Patrick? You deserve that."

There he goes again – answering a question by asking another, sighed Patrick. When will I learn?

"I'd like to go if you don't need me for the moment."

"You'll be busy soon enough. Go and enjoy your moment of fame at the Museum."

The helicopter pilot spoke to them over the intercom:

"Sorry to interrupt, but we are preparing to land."

Two cars were waiting for them on the runway and Eleni and Patrick were taken with police escort straight to the Museum. Pierre and Antonia were driven back to her flat. Once inside they both breathed a sigh of relief.

"All going according to plan so far," said Antonia, kicking off her shoes and flopping down onto the sofa.

"You do tease poor Patrick mercilessly, don't you? What are you going to tell Kokoschka?"

"I'll make some calls while you relax," Pierre said by way of reply. Antonia acknowledged the jibe with a toss of her head.

*

Marcel Bouvier arrived at the office early, to find Katja alone and already working at her desk. He went over and stood behind her studying her design projection. She turned and smiled at him.

"You're here early," he said. "Are you still worried about the manuscript and Lucca?"

"Working takes my mind off it. But yes, I am worried. Now's crunch time. I've had a message from Lucca. He wants me to go to Sardinia to look at a manuscript. He thinks it might be the real one. The Americans will be there too."

"In a way that's exciting if it really is the real thing. I know it's illegal, but nonetheless, how exciting is that to hold a genuine Crusader's chronicle in your hands?"

"It would be very exciting, except that it's part of a crooked deal and may disappear from view, instead of being displayed for everyone to see and enjoy."

She looked up at him, sharply this time.

"This is not a game, Marcel. A monk has already lost his life over this."

"You're right, I'm sorry …"

"No, no, please don't apologise, that was wrong of me. You've already been wonderful about all this and I'll have to ask you to let me go to Sardinia one last time to finish the job. I got myself into this mess so I'll have to see it through to the end myself."

She paused and swivelled round on her stool to face him.

"I'd rather come with you; I don't like the idea of you going there on your own at this stage."

"Lucca would immediately realise I had told others about the whole affair and we would both be in danger. Commissaire Rousseau has already spoken to me. He says the Italian police will be there to protect me – if I need protecting that is. Anyway as I said the Americans will be there too."

"So you will just check the manuscript and all leave together?"

"Yes. I'll be quite safe."

"You're right of course, as usual."

She looked up at him gratefully and he made to raise her chin to kiss her when they both heard other staff arriving and pulled away like guilty children.

Marcel greeted the newcomers and spent the next half hour talking to each one. After he left the room, all eyes turned towards Katja; no-one had been fooled by the diversion. Katja could feel herself blushing, but said nothing.

They had the answer they wanted.

*

Marco relaxed into the comfortable back seat of the car, the parcel containing the precious manuscript resting on his lap. He was enjoying the exceptional treatment already. He had contacted Lucca from Athens to give him the good news.

Then he had had to concentrate on working out how to leave Greece without attracting attention. He had considered going overland via Macedonia, but decided it would be too slow and dangerous.

He also knew eyes other than those of the police were watching him constantly. Perhaps he was imagining it, but after what had happened on the way to the monastery, he knew he could take no chances. The Greek police would definitely be searching for him, but he knew how to avoid them. As for the bastards who had caught him in the woods, that was more worrying.

Leaving by air would be difficult with all the searches and the X-ray checks, so it had to be by boat from Patrás to Bari. From there it would be easy to cross to the other side of Italy and to take another boat from Civitatavecchio to Olbia on the island.

When he reached Athens after leaving Dimitsána, he left the manuscript in his hotel and visited a new bookshop where he purchased a large coffee table book on Greek myths and legends. The cost shocked him, but what were a few euros, against the prize waiting for him? Back in his room, trying to forget what he had paid for the book he was ruining, he separated the covers from the text and placed them carefully round the manuscript. They fitted round perfectly and the dust jacket completed the effect. He was pleased with himself, safe in the knowledge the same device had worked well for him once before.

He rewrapped the book in the special way the assistant in the shop had done when he asked for it to be gift wrapped and added as a final touch a birthday card to his dear mother, which he carefully stuck on the outside. He knew his mother, who had died many years before, but was surely looking down at him, would appreciate the thought.

Leaving Greece went without a hitch and he had quite enjoyed the boat trip to Bari, which was something he normally avoided. The train journey across Italy had been long and boring, but he caught the ferry to cross over to Sardinia according to plan and now here he was settled comfortably in Lucca's chauffeur-driven car on his way to a warm reception. Perhaps Lucca would trust him at last and he would become his right hand man.

He was so lost in thought it came as surprise when the chauffeur opened the door and he realised he was at Lucca's villa. For a moment his nerve almost failed him and he sat frozen in the seat unable to move. With an effort he shook himself and stepped out of the car.

As he went up the steps to the house Lucca was standing in the doorway looking down at him. Without a word he took the parcel out of his hands and went back inside leaving Marco to follow hesitantly.

Lucca ripped off the wrapping paper and throwing the birthday card onto the floor. He opened the covers of the book and removed the manuscript. As he watched, Marco started telling Lucca the risks he had run to acquire the manuscript. He nearly told him he had been kidnapped, but something in the way Lucca was looking at him made him fall silent.

Lucca turned abruptly and left the room. Marco looked round and wondered whether he should sit down or remain standing. He decided to stay on his feet and went across to the window to look out over the sea.

After what seemed a lifetime, Lucca returned carrying the manuscript, followed by a young woman he quickly recognised as the one he had chatted up and failed to get into bed during the first trip to Dimitsána – Katja something. Lucca led her to the table and ordered her to examine the manuscript. It was not long before she straightened up, looked at Lucca and shook her head.

Instantly Lucca grabbed Marco round the throat, throwing him off balance and sending him crashing to the floor.

"*Cretino!* This is fake! So how many people know who you are and what you look for?"

"No-one I swear … Giovanni …"

"To make fake as good as this, it must be experts in Athens. You know what that means. You were set up. You lead the police straight to me, *imbecille*."

Lucca kicked Marco hard in the ribs and he gasped in pain before managing to gulp out:

"But if it is as good as you say it will be good enough to convince the *Americanos* … if the bitch will say it is real."

Lucca paused before delivering another vicious kick.

"That idea may well have saved your life, Marco."

He turned to Katja who was standing stock still watching the scene being played out before her. She could feel the panic rising and sweat forming on her forehead. She felt Lucca take her arm and start to lead her to the other side of the room.

"Come, my dear. We have things to talk about you and I," he said drawing her to one side near the window.

Lucca's men Carlo and Angelo suddenly entered the room answering a signal from Lucca which neither of the others had seen.

"Take that *sacco di merda* to the cellar and lock him in."

Marco felt himself being lifted effortlessly into the air.

*

Outside the house, lying flat on the ground in the cover of the scrub vegetation, Isabella could see Lucca and Katja standing in the window.

It was obvious something was wrong. Lucca was gripping her arm tightly and Katja was trying to pull away.

"Typical man," she thought. "She has done what he wants and now he wants more."

Earlier that day she had met Katja coming out of her flat carrying a suitcase.

"Not going to work today?" she had asked casually.

"Not in the way you mean, Isabella! Lucca has asked me to go to Sardinia again. I think he must have the manuscript I told you about. He sounded really excited."

"Be careful, Katja – from what you told me he's not a nice man."

"I'll be there and back before you notice," she had replied.

Isabella had quickly returned to her flat and took the *navette* out to the airport at Mérignac. She was in time to see Katja at the check-in desk, but couldn't risk taking the same flight. Luckily there was a second flight later that morning to Alghero in the south of the island and from there she could hire a car. Finally arriving in Olbia she had asked around and easily found out where 'Signor Lucca' lived. And now she was watching the scene taking place inside his house with some puzzlement.

She heard the sound only at the last minute as an arm grabbed her round the neck and a hand on her forehead forced her head back. The pain was sharp and intense.

"Do not move, or you break your neck and save me job," said a voice.

She was dragged to her feet and almost carried into the house and into the main room.

"Look what I found in the garden, Signore. I thought you would want to know," Carlo said, pushing Isabella roughly to the floor.

Lucca looked down at her.

"*Oddio! Isabella Marquessa!* Welcome to my house! Why didn't you just knock on the front door, *cara mia*? You know you are always welcome."

He turned to Angelo.

"So many guests tonight. Take them both away and lock them in the bedroom."

Lucca watched the two women being bundled roughly out of the room. He began to pace up and down in front of the window. Too many people obviously knew what he was involved in and where he lived. It was just possible he might be able to pass the fake off on the Americans, but he knew they were not the fools they presented to the outside world. A lot depended on how much they trusted Katja to tell them the truth and how convincing she would make her authentication.

The problem was he had no real hold over her; no way of forcing her to lie. Offering her a larger cut of the proceeds would not work. He didn't think she could be bought in that way. He threw himself into the nearest armchair and stared up at the ceiling for inspiration.

The light had faded completely. Outside the stars were appearing and the moon was reflected across the sea. Lucca had fallen into a half sleep, when there was a tap on the door. Carlo reappeared, this time leading a man in front of him, his arms pinned behind his back. The guard forced him to his knees and looked at Lucca.

"It's a busy night, Signore. I found this wandering round the garden."

He jerked the man to his feet.

Feigning a confidence he did not feel, Marcel brushed himself down angrily.

"*Signor Lucca, buonasera*. I was just checking I had the right house when I was assaulted by your guard. Silly of me not to have just knocked on the door. Let me introduce myself. I am a friend of Katja Kokoschka, Marcel Bouvier, and I was worried when she did not return to work, so I decided to come out here myself to see if I could contact her."

"I am sorry for your rough welcome, Signor Bouvier, but Sardinia is not like *Francia*. There are bad people here who do not love me and I must make my house safe. I cannot be too careful in this isolated place."

"*Grazie, Carlo*," he said dismissing him.

"Please, come and sit, Signor Bouvier. Can I offer you a drink?"

Lucca's mood had changed as he realised fate had sent a solution to some at least of his problems.

"Thank you, Signore," said Marcel as he settled gratefully in the armchair and accepted the glass of wine set before him.

"So, my dear Katja works for you, Signor Bouvier? *Una bella signorina* and so clever. You are a remarkable man, to come out all the way here to look for an employee who take a few days away from her work. Maybe she is more to you than just an employee, no?"

Lucca smiled.

Marcel shifted uncomfortably in his chair, unable to think quickly of a response and knowing a denial would sound hollow.

"Yes, she was here as you know," he went on. "I needed her to authenticate a manuscript I have. But she left and I not see her after."

"Yes, she told me about the work she was doing for you. She must have been delayed somehow on the way back to Bordeaux."

"I am sorry I cannot help you more, Signor Bouvier. It is late – I could order the car to take you back to Olbia but I doubt you find room easily. Why don't you stay here? I have plenty rooms and I like company."

"That is very kind of you, Signor Lucca …"

"… then it is agreed."

Lucca pressed a bell and Carlo appeared.

"We are two for dinner tonight. Prepare room for my guest in west wing."

Turning back to Marcel, he said:

"So, Signor Bouvier, tell me more about the work you and Katja do. We have both interest in the talents of this beautiful woman."

Chapter 21

Pierre was listening to the messages on his phone when Antonia entered the living room changed and ready to go out to eat. Pierre gestured his approval of her appearance, but remaining listening, his face betraying his concern.

"What is it, Pierre?"

"Bouvier left a message to say he's worried because of what Kokoschka told him about Lucca. He's gone out to Sardinia on his own to look for her."

"That wasn't wise …"

"And there's more. Marquessa has left Bordeaux. Mérignac airport police have confirmed she boarded a different flight for Sardinia the same morning as Kokoschka. They have only just thought to let us know."

"We had best let the Italians know."

"Patrick already has that in hand. He and Eleni are watching Lucca's house as we speak. We should go out there immediately too."

"I agree. Bouvier shouldn't have gone out there. That wasn't part of the plan."

"And there's no news yet of the whereabouts of the Americans. Let's hope Kokoschka follows the script when they arrive at Lucca's as they surely will."

"What do you mean, Pierre? What have you told her to do?"

"I'll tell you later. Right now we should be on our way to the airport. May I call for a car? Sorry about the meal."

Antonia went into the bedroom to change while Pierre picked up the phone and pressed in the numbers.

*

"So, cards on the table Katja. What are you doing here and why are you locked in too?"

Isabella was leaning against the wall in the bedroom and looking at Katja sitting on the edge of the bed. Katja looked up angrily and wiped away the tears in her eyes.

"Only as long as you tell me what you are doing here first and why you have been thrown in here with me. You didn't tell me you knew Lucca, so why have you followed me here and why were you spying on me? I thought we were friends."

"OK, calm down. I wasn't really spying on you. It was just the only way I could find out where he was hiding out."

She moved across to sit on the bed by Katja and put her arm round her shoulder.

"Lucca and I go back a long way and he owes me. He's a nutcase, as you know now. It was just unfortunate he had guards in the grounds and one of them spotted me. I should have been more careful. Now it's your turn."

"I did wonder about you and him. He flew into a rage once when I mentioned your name on my first visit here."

"Why did you do that?"

"I just said you had recommended me to Deveau and he got really angry. I was scared at first, but it seemed like an easy way to earn some good money and to see a rare manuscript. That's all I had to do – just check the manuscript to see if it was genuine."

She shifted her position and looked directly at Isabella.

"Then when he showed me what they had found I had to tell him it was a very good copy – a facsimile in fact – he flew into a rage and laid into Marco. It was horrible."

"Marco!" said Isabella, straightening up and almost shouting. "Marco Platini? What's he got to do with all this?"

"He works for Lucca. He was on the same tour as I was to the Lousiós Gorge. Lucca told me I was not to let on I knew he was working for him too."

"Marco! That little snake!"

"You know him?"

"Oh yes! Nasty piece of work. I suppose he tried to get you into bed."

"Yes, but I fended him off easily. He didn't know who I was, though he certainly does now. Another of Lucca's little games. Anyway, when I told Lucca the manuscript was a fake he ordered the guards to throw Marco into the cellar and lock him in."

"So what happens now?"

"Lucca is pressuring me to tell the American buyers the manuscript is genuine. He's still going to try to pass it off on them. I refused at first but I'll have to agree in the end. Otherwise I don't think he'll let me go. He wants me to meet them again. I think they are coming here."

"We'll be lucky if he lets either of us go," Isabella replied.

"But if it works and the Americans accept it as genuine, surely Lucca will know I'll never admit what I have done," said Katja.

"Why?"

"If anyone finds out I've given a false authentication I'll never be given another assignment like this."

"I'm not so sure anyone will find out. The Americans will never admit they bought a dud – that is when they realise later of course. They'll keep quiet to save their own reputations. After all, look at all the great museums around the world which are full of fake Picassos and Monets and so on."

They both fell silent for a minute.

"Does anyone else know where you are?" asked Isabella.

"Yes, I told my boss I was coming here, but he won't be concerned yet."

Katja was about to go on to tell her the French police were also aware she was in Sardinia when Isabella interrupted her.

"So, why don't you just give in? Do what he wants. The Americans don't deserve the truth, they are just as crooked as Lucca What's the harm – it may just save your skin."

Realising she had jumped in too quickly, she added: "Sorry I cut you off. What were you going to say."

"Oh! It was nothing. Perhaps you're right, maybe I should agree to do it. What a nightmare! So, what do we do now?"

"We wait."

They both fell silent thinking their own thoughts. Katja realised that Isabella still hadn't told her the real reason for her being there.

Chapter 22

Patrick and Eleni were lying flat on the ground observing from the top of the hill overlooking Lucca's house. Their night vision binoculars allowed them to see most of what was going on. Beside them the Italian police chief was speaking quietly into his phone.

"We wait until the Americans arrive. Probably tomorrow," said Capitano Frisoni with a sigh at the thought of staying there all night.

"Shouldn't we go in before that, Capitano? It's a really explosive situation now that Marquessa is there. Kokoschka may in danger. Lucca won't like it at all when she tells him the manuscript is a fake," said Eleni.

"He will be more angry with Platini I think. He's not stupid. He will know the fake was made by an expert. So he know it is us behind it. But I think still he try to make the Americans buy it. It is his only hope to have his money."

Frisoni paused and looked at Patrick who did not react. Eleni thought she caught a gleam in his eye in the half-light.

"I think he force the French woman to say it is genuine," he went on thoughtfully to no-one in particular and picked up his binoculars to check the house again.

"*Attenzionne!* Someone else is out there. You know who this is?"

Patrick and Eleni quickly raised their binoculars.

"No idea," said Eleni.

"*Merde!* That's Kokoschka's employer – Marcel Bouvier," said Patrick. "I'm sure he doesn't really know much of what is going on, but Kokoschka did confide in him and he was the one who advised her to contact us."

"So, he ride in like the knight in shiny armour to rescue his damsel," said Frisoni with a sigh. "You Frenchmen are worse than we Italians over the women."

"You may be right, Capitano, but let's hope he doesn't try anything too heroic and complicate the whole operation," said Patrick.

*

When Antonia reappeared, changed and ready to go, Pierre was looking far from pleased.

"What's happened?"

"Eleni and Patrick have just seen Bouvier enter Lucca's house in the company of a gorilla who was patrolling the grounds. He hasn't come out."

"That's all we need. This could really complicate things."

"It gets worse. Marquessa was caught in the grounds too and is somewhere in the house – that is if she's still alive."

"You look worried Pierre. What were you going to tell me about Kokoschka?"

"When I saw her the second time, she agreed to help us. I was worried that when the facsimile finally reached Lucca via Platini, he would summon Kokoschka and she would of course have to tell him it's a fake. Lucca will work out the rest for himself."

"You mean he'll realise Platini has led the Italian police straight to him?"

"Exactly. But I think he will make one more attempt to get his money. I warned her he might insist that she must say the manuscript is genuine when the Americans arrive. I told her to do what he wanted."

"So he takes the money and the Leontarakis leave with the facsimile?" said Antonia. "But will he let Kokoschka go? Won't she know too much?"

"That's what I'm worried about."

"What about the Americans? We still won't be able to arrest them. They aren't breaking any laws taking a copy out of the country."

"Don't worry! I've got that covered. They won't get away this time with smuggling out works of art. In fact they won't ever again be able to hold their heads up or sell an other piece of art in the U.S.A."

"And how do you plan to do that?" asked Antonia.

There was the sound of a horn outside and Pierre picked up his bag.

"Time we went out to the airport, that's the car."

*

After the meal, Marcel was escorted by Angelo to a bedroom on the first floor. The conversation had remained on amicable terms throughout the rest of the evening during the meal of excellent local fish and fruit. The way he had been received had wrong-footed Marcel who had not expected such courtesy. Lucca had behaved like a perfect gentleman. Marcel even wondered whether Katja was imagining things. What was she so afraid of? He seemed a reasonable man.

It had been a long and tiring day and he lay back on the bed trying to think it all through. He was considering going to bed, when he caught the sound of talking coming from across the corridor.

Two women were talking, quietly at first, but then there was a short outburst and Marcel was sure he recognised Katja's voice. Going across to the door of his bedroom, he opened it slightly and listened again. The voices continued and he was more and more sure one of them was Katja's.

There was no one in the corridor so he crossed over to the door of the room opposite. To his surprise there was a key in the lock on the outside. He knocked gently on the door and the voices immediately stopped. He knocked again and heard someone approach the door on the other side.

"Who's there?"

It was Katja, he was sure.

"It's me, Marcel. What's happening ? Why are you locked in?"

"Marcel! Thank god! Can you get us out of here?"

He turned the key in the lock and opened the door. Katja flung her arms around him.

"Am I pleased to see you!"

She turned round to introduce him to Isabella Marquessa, but she was too late. Isabella had made for the door as soon as it opened, pushed passed her and Marcel and was out of the room in a flash.

"Isabella! Where …?"

She stared in amazement for a moment and then quickly pulled Marcel inside and closed the door.

"Sit down, Marcel. I need to tell you what has been happening. I really am in trouble and that man Lucca frightens me."

"I don't see …"

"Please, Marcel, just listen. We may not have much time."

*

Isabella crept quietly down the stairs. There were no guards about and she made her way to the ground floor without being spotted. The next part would be more difficult as outside she knew there were movement sensors and guards in the grounds. She was about to try a small window at the back of the house when she noticed a stairway leading down to a cellar. She felt her way down not risking switching the light on. At bottom there was a narrow landing strewn with old boxes and a stout wooden door with old fashioned metal studs. It was locked, but there was just enough light for her to spot a large key hanging on a rusty nail to one side.

Quietly she took the key down and unlocked the door. Warily she felt for the first step and pulled the door to behind her. The steps led down to the cellar proper. A little light filtered through from a small window at outside ground level so she was able to feel her way down keeping close to the inside wall as there was no barrier or railing on the open side.

On reaching the bottom she was suddenly pushed off her feet as someone grabbed her from behind and knocked her down. She managed to cry out, as she put her hands up to protect her face from the attack:

"Friend not foe, stop for shit's sake!"

Marco paused for a second and peered down at her face.

"Isabella! What are you doing here, you bitch!"

"Thanks for the nice welcome, Marco, you little bastard. Here to rescue you by the looks of it, so be very grateful."

He pulled her roughly to her feet.

"OK, so tell me."

"Let's get out of here first and then we can talk," she replied.

"That window is no good," said Marco. "I can't shift it and it looks out onto the front of the house anyway. They'll see us immediately."

"Up the steps! Come on, move!"

They reached the top of the steps and froze for an instant as they saw that the door to the cellar was shut. Then Isabella remembered and pushed it open. Above them there was still the narrow flight of steps up to the corridor.

As they neared the top a figure cut off the light in the doorway. Angelo was blocking their way. Isabella reacted first and the judo techniques she had so long practised finally paid off. She grabbed him by the wrists, pulled him forward off balance and bent her knees. Gravity did the rest as the guard flew over her head and, taking Marco with him, crashed headlong down the steps.

Isabella peered down into the stairwell, rubbing her shoulder which had immediately begun to ache as the old injury flared up, and called softly:

"Marco."

There was a low groan in reply. She went back down the steps to find Marco trying to free himself from under the body of the guard. Angelo lay in crumpled heap, his head against the studded door of the cellar and a pool of blood forming around him.

Marco heaved himself up, wiping the blood off himself, and stood up unsteadily.

"You nearly killed me, you bitch."

"Pity I didn't. Stop being such a wimp and give me a hand. We must put him in the cellar and quickly in case anyone heard the noise."

They dragged Angelo away from the door and pushed him down the steps to the cellar.

"Take his shirt off. Quickly!"

"But it's covered in blood…"

"Exactly. Put yours on him. We must prop him up against the wall there where the light from the window isn't too strong. Anyone opening the door from the top must think it's you when they look in."

They heaved Angelo into a sitting position and Isabella pulled his gun free of his shoulder holster and went back up the steps. She made Marco mop up some of the blood by the door with Angelo's shirt, which he then threw in disgust behind the boxes. She locked the door and replaced the key on the nail.

"What now?" asked Marco, still shaken from his fall.

"We get the hell out of here."

"I'm freezing," he said rubbing his arms.

"That's the least of our worries. *Basta!* Someone's coming. Over there, quick in the corner!"

A voice from the top of the stairs called out.

"Angelo. Is that you?"

Then there was the sound of someone coming down the steps, blocking out the light; just a silhouetted shape.

One of Lucca's men they did not recognise reached up for the key and opened the door to the cellar. In the semi-darkness he could make out the figure sitting with his back to the wall in the corner. Then he felt himself flying through the air off the top of the steps and after his head hit the stone floor below, he knew no more.

Isabella relocked the cellar door, put the key in her pocket and began to climb the steps to the ground floor. Marco followed, still trying to rub some life back into his frozen body. Isabella looked at him when they reached the light at the top. He was covered in blood and there was a large bruise forming over his left eye.

"You'd better get cleaned up. I'll be outside."

With that she slipped quietly out of the front door, leaving Marco standing in the hallway.

Chapter 23

Capitano Frisoni briefed his surveillance team to keep a sharp watch and to report any developments to him immediately. He, Patrick and Eleni were taken by car to a small hotel in the next village.

"The privilege of rank," chuckled the Italian as he bade the other two good night and went off to his room.

"No way we'll sleep," said Eleni. "Pierre and Antonia will arrive in Olbia soon and come straight here."

"There's not really a lot we can tell them. Almost all the main players are inside Lucca's house and we have no idea of what's going on. The next move is up to Frisoni."

"I did ask him if he could get a man inside under cover, but he said Lucca was too shrewd to fall for that."

"This is becoming like a game of chess with the only the opposition moving the pieces about. How will Lucca use Bouvier I wonder? And when will the Americans arrive?" Patrick mused not expecting a reply.

"We might as well go into the lounge and have a drink while we're waiting ..." was Eleni's response.

They walked into the small bar area and were immediately aware of English being spoken in guarded tones by a couple in the corner. The furniture of the hotel was arranged with comfortable high backed chairs rather like a old English pub. Patrick and Eleni chose chairs near the voices. The accents of the couple were clearly American and they had no doubt who they were listening to. It was unlikely they would be recognised from their previous brief encounter at the customs in the summer, but they were nonetheless careful to remain out of the Americans' line of sight.

"So, how do we know we can trust Lucca this time?" Mira was saying. "He was ripped off same as we were over the icon on the last deal and he'll be sure not to want a repeat."

"We look at the manuscript, ask the girl to tell us if it's real or not and only then do we tell him where the money is," said George.

"You have got the key with you, haven't you?" asked Mira in a sudden panic.

"Sure," he replied patting his top pocket. "Lucca'll send one of his men to the airport to open the locker and bring back the money."

"Then we just walk on out and everything is fine and dandy – is that it? That's the plan?" said Mira.

"Yeah. Lucca won't double-cross us," replied George. "He wants the money, not the manuscript. Despite the foul up last time, he's a smooth operator and we can use him again."

"Gee. I hope you're right, George. I'm none too happy about this."

They got up to go to their room and passed right by where Eleni and Patrick were sitting heads down.

"That was close, but very useful," breathed Eleni.

Patrick's phone went and he opened it with a sigh. Eleni watched as he listened and a smile spread across his face.

"That was Pierre. They have only just arrived and will stay down in Olbia tonight. They'll be with us tomorrow early unless something dramatic happens."

They finished their drinks, stood up and went to the reception desk. The receptionist connected them through to Capitano Frisoni's room and handed the receiver to Patrick. After a few words he put the phone down and nodded to Eleni. Back in their room, they undressed and fell into bed. They both were asleep the moment their heads touched the pillow.

*

At the house early the next morning Lucca knew he was losing control of events. Carlo had just informed him Angelo had disappeared and Tonio was nowhere to be found.

"Then go and find them, you fool! *No! Aspetta!* Come with me first."

With Carlo following, Lucca went to the room where the two women had been locked in. Seeing it was no longer locked he flung the door open.

Katja looked up in terror when she saw his reaction on seeing that just her and Marcel were in the room. He strode across and grabbed her by the throat.

"Where's that bitch, Marquessa? How did she get out?"

Katja struggled against him but shook her head. Lucca let her go and whirled round on Marcel who was standing unable to move as Carlo pinned his arms behind his back.

"So, the white knight think he can make a fool of me," he said, striking him hard across the mouth.

"Now, *cara mia*, you see what trouble you cause your boss. Will I ask Carlo to continue to punish him a little more or will you do what I ask when the *Americanos* arrive?"

He raised his hand again. Katja looked at Marcel's face, blood running out of the corner of his mouth and nodded with tears in her eyes. Lucca smiled and said:

"You make good choice, Signorina. No need for Signor Bouvier to be hurt at all. I hope he forgive you and not fire you."

They could hear his laughter as he went down the corridor. Then his bark to Carlo:

"Find the bitch Marquessa!"

Katja went over to Marcel and flung her arms round him.

"I'm so sorry, Marcel," she said. "… I had to make it look convincing."

"What do you mean, you had to make it look convincing?"

"You didn't know? I thought the police had sent you and that …"

"Nobody sent me. I came because I was worried when you didn't return to work as you said …"

"Oh! Marcel, I'm so sorry …"

The door burst open and Carlo stabbed his finger at Katja.

"You. Come . You. Stay here."

He grabbed Katja roughly by the arm and pulled her to him. Marcel started towards them, but stopped when he saw Carlo's gun pointing at his chest.

"The *Americanos* arrive soon and boss want you ready," he growled at her.

She shook herself free and faced him.

"Wait while I tidy myself up. I won't be able to do what your boss wants and convince the Americans if I go in looking like this."

"Be very quick," said Carlo.

She picked up some clothes and went towards the bathroom.

"You want I 'elp?"

"Don't even think about it."

Carlo waited, his gun never wavering from Marcel's chest.

*

The phone in their room rang at five o'clock. The receptionist apologised and said there were visitors waiting to see them. They quickly dressed and went down stairs to where Pierre and Antonia were waiting in the lounge. They had already persuaded the hotel to provide coffee and Patrick poured himself a cup before sitting down.

"Good you arrived at this ungodly hour," he said after he had drained his cup. "The Americans are staying here too, so we need to leave as soon as possible before they wake up."

"Does Frisoni know?" asked Pierre.

Before Patrick could reply Capitano Frisoni walked into the room and greeted Pierre and Antonia.

"Yes, Inspector Bruni informed me last night. So we must leave *pronto* to be in position before they arrive at Lucca's."

In the car outside on the way to the observation point, Patrick briefed them about what they had overheard the previous evening.

"One of my men, he succeed in setting up a microphone opposite the main window of the house as you suggested Inspector Tsikas. My men, they are ready to act when it is the right moment."

"What is your plan, Capitano?" asked Pierre.

"We let the Americans do the dealing first and leave the house. They are of no interest to us. I do not want them to get in the way. We can stop them later. Then my men, they go in and arrest Lucca."

"If you can arrest Platini as well, we would be grateful. We want him for the probable murder of a book dealer in Bordeaux," added Pierre.

"We shall see what we shall see, Commissaire," replied Frisoni. "But I assure you we do our best."

They arrived at the high point on the hill overlooking the house and Frisoni left them to speak to his men. Pierre and Antonia studied the house through their binoculars, but there was no movement they could see.

It wasn't until after nine o'clock that they were alerted to the sound of a car drawing up in front of the house. They watched as the Leontarakis opened the doors and stepped out of the car. They could see Lucca waiting at the top of the steps to welcome them.

"These European cars are so small," complained Mira, straightening her dress as she stood on the drive.

"How nice to meet you both in person," said Lucca. "I fear we missed each other last time."

Georges Leontarakis ignored him completely. Losing half a million dollars over the icon deal the previous summer still rankled and he was not about to forgive anyone. Pushing past Lucca he went into the house, leaving Mira to struggle up the steps.

"Just show us the manuscript and we can wrap up this business as fast as possible," he muttered.

Lucca didn't wait for Mira either, but followed George Leontarakis into the main room.

"I like a man who go straight to the point," replied Lucca. "The manuscript is here on the table. Take your time, but be careful, it is very delicate."

"Just fetch the girl. I want to hear from her own lips whether it's genuine or not."

"I can assure you, Signor Leontarakis, it is genuine…"

"Fetch the girl," repeated George. Lucca flicked his fingers and Carlo left the room to fetch Katja as Mira finally made it to the living room looking flushed in the face.

"Ooh! This room is awesome, Signor Lucca. Such a great view."

Lucca bowed briefly in acknowledgement and watched Mira carefully as she studied the manuscript without a word. He knew it had to pass her inspection too, or the deal would be off, whatever Katja said.

"What a beautiful piece of work," said Mira softly, as she gently turned the pages and studied the script and the outlines of unfinished illustrations roughly sketched in centuries ago.

There was a stir as Katja entered the room and was warmly greeted by Lucca.

"Do come in, Signorina Kokoschka. I hope you were comfortable last night. Our American guests were just admiring the manuscript."

Mira hurried over to her and gave her a hug.

"Great to see you again, Kattie dear. How is that nice young man of yours? I hope he's looking after you."

She looked at Lucca.

"Kattie has such a nice boy – a real sweetie."

George Leontarakis decided it was time to take over.

"So, Katja, what do you reckon on the manuscript? Is it genuine?"

Katja crossed over to the table, putting on the white cotton gloves of her trade as she did. She picked up the manuscript, turned it over and showed them the back, which was slightly darker than the front.

"This where the manuscript is showing signs of wear from being handled. See, there are even a few dark patches which I think are ink stains, possibly from the scribe's desk. Also if you look at different pages you can see the writing differs. That's because there would have been more than one scribe working on this. They would take over from one another every two or three hours."

They peered over her shoulder to see what she was pointing at.

"We can work out from this how many hours it took to dictate the story of the Crusade. Look here too. You can see the scribes made outlines of where they wanted later copies to have full illustrations."

"So, it is genuine?" asked George.

"As far as I can tell, and comparing it with other documents of the period I would say the chances of it being a later copy are minimal."

"I'll take that as a yes," he said. "OK. just pack it in the box and we'll take it from here."

Lucca was shrewd enough to leave it to George Leontarakis to convince himself of the authenticity of the manuscript. He could see there was already an established relationship between them and Kokoschka which was helping the Americans to believe that what they were seeing was what they wanted to see.

He walked across to the table where Katja was carefully repacking the manuscript. Her attention to such detail in the charade was impeccable. He invited George and Mira to take a seat.

"So, to business. I think you are ready to make the deal, no?"

"Sure. The money is in a locker at the airport. I have the key here," replied Leontarakis.

"I send my man down to pick it up. I can see you are a careful man, Signor Leontarakis. I like that."

Carlo came into the room. Lucca handed him the key with his instructions.

"Signorina Kokoschka will write a signed statement of how do you say ... "

"... authenticity and provenance ..." supplied Katja.

"Thank you, my dear ... for you," said Lucca. "And another one which says the manuscript is just a facsimile. Be careful to show the right one to the custom man!"

Lucca laughed at his own joke.

*

Up on the hill the team were listening in and had been able to follow most of the scene in the house. They saw Carlo leave the house in the car.

"Kokoschka has done a good job. No sign of Bouvier though," said Pierre.

"Nor of Marquessa," added Patrick.

"This Isabella Marquessa," asked Frisoni, "What do we do with her?"

"We want her for possible murder and burglary too, and she is a French citizen," replied Pierre. "So, when you round them all up, please hold her for us. If you agree, I think it would be best to keep to the plan and let the Americans leave the house before your men go in, Capitano."

"We see what happens when the money arrive and they make the exchange."

While the others were studying the scene below through their binoculars watching for signs of activity, Pierre took Frisoni aside and they stood talking quietly for a moment.

"What about Kokoschka? Do you think Lucca will let her go? She is of no more use to him, but she knows too much," asked Antonia looking in the direction of the two men.

"I think he might want to keep her until he knows the Leontarakis have left Sardinia. He won't want to risk sending her away with them," Pierre replied moving back to look down at the house.

"And there's Bouvier. Has he been caught or is he there waiting for a chance to rescue Kokoschka?" asked Patrick.

"No doubt we'll find out soon enough."

There were no signs of activity at the house and the microphone was picking up mere chit-chat from Mira as they all awaited the return of Carlo with the money.

*

Thirty minutes later they could see the car returning in the distance along the narrow winding road. It entered the driveway and stopped in front of the house. Carlo got out carrying a black attaché case and began to mount the steps to the front door. What happened next was like a scene unrolling before them in a silent film. Carlo suddenly staggered, dropped the case and fell to the ground.

The front door opened and Lucca appeared in the doorway having heard the car arrive. He paused for a moment taking in the scene before him. Carlo was half way down the steps, a pool of blood forming beneath him and starting to trickle in a thin rivulet down the steps to the drive. Lucca's eyes flashed round to see where the shot had come from, but there was no sign of the attacker.

Carlo managed to raise an arm slowly as if to signal to Lucca where the danger lay or in a bid for help. If Lucca saw the gesture he gave no sign of it. Without a glance at the wounded Carlo he darted forward and grabbed the case. Carlo made another weak movement in his direction, but Lucca was already back in the safety of the doorway. He paused to gesture to the driver, who was still taking cover on the floor of the car afraid to move, to see to Carlo and clear up the mess.

"Where the hell is Angelo?" he shouted.

Back in the living room no-one had heard anything suspicious and Lucca composed himself before going in carrying the attaché case with the money. The business was transacted with little ceremony and an almost complete economy of words. George operated the code to open the case and counted out the $500,000. Lucca picked up $50,000 which he handed to Katja.

"Just so you see I honour my word," he said to her, but with a sideways glance at the Americans. "My driver, he take you back to the airport."

"Why don't you come back with us, Kattie my dear. Your job is done here and we are very grateful," said Mira.

"She has some unfinished business here, Signora," said Lucca quickly before Katja could reply.

"Well, we must meet again in Bordeaux before we fly home," said Mira giving her a kiss. "Be sure to contact us at the hotel when you come back."

Lucca preceded them and took a precautionary look outside before opening the door wide. To his relief the driver had done his job and there was no sign anything unusual had happened. With the briefest of handshakes and a final hug for Katja, the two Americans went down the steps to the waiting car.

From the hill they had watched the gunning down of Carlo and Lucca's dash for the money. His complete disregard for his lieutenant had not come as a surprise to any of them.

"He took a hell of a risk running out like that," said Patrick. "The gunman could easily have shot him too."

"I think, Inspector," replied Frisoni, "the gunman is wanting to eliminate as many of the opposition as possible before confronting Lucca."

"Shouldn't we go ..."

"I think we let them kill each other first. It make less work for us!" chuckled Frisoni before Patrick could finish his sentence.

A movement below attracted Frisoni's attention.

"There look! The kitchen staff, they run out of the back of the building as fast as they can. I think the deck is nearly clear for the action."

"So, who's shooting?" asked Antonia.

"It must be Marquessa. She wants Lucca badly. It's the only reason she's here," said Patrick.

"But it could be Platini. He's disappeared and wasn't there when the deal was done. I'd guess he has no love for Lucca either."

Then they saw the door open and the Americans saying goodbye.

"Kokoschka is not with them," said Eleni. "Lucca's not letting her go."

After Isabella left him, Marco had managed to find his way out of the house by heading for the noise coming from the kitchen. Once through the back door into the garden he had heard the shot and seen Carlo fall. He ran quickly back into the kitchen and ordered the staff to leave immediately.

Outside he watched the driver drag Carlo's body away. Looking round, he saw a movement among the trees at the far side of the lawn.

He whistled softly to Isabella and crept across to where she was lying observing the house from the safety of the shadows of a large tree. The breeze from the sea was moving the branches and casting shapes onto the ground in front of them and the smell of the pines and the maquis would have made it a romantic moment in other circumstances. But this was not one of them.

"Why you not shoot Lucca when he was on the steps? The money was there for you to take."

"This was never about money, Marco. This is about revenge. I want him to know it is me before he dies and to beg."

"*Oddio!* You really hate him I think. But as for me," he said, "I just want to strangle the bastard and take the money."

"Don't worry. You'll have your chance maybe to do just that."

"OK. How is the plan?"

"There are no staff left in the house. Angelo and Carlo are out of action. Kokoschka and Bouvier are still in there somewhere, but they're not going to help Lucca. So, I'll go in to the house through the kitchen and up to the hallway. You stay out here and in five minutes you start throwing stones at the window to attract his attention."

"He'll just shoot me…"

"No he won't, you idiot. You're quite safe. Bullet proof glass works in both directions. The only way he can get to you would be to leave the room and go outside."

"You'd better be right."

"I am right. As soon as you make him angry enough he'll have to go into the hall to reach the front door. I'll be waiting and that's when I shoot him down."

"*Dio!*" he exclaimed making the sigh of the cross. "OK, it a deal, but I have half the money when the *bastardo* is dead."

"*Trente percento.*"

"*Quaranta!*"

"*D'accordo.*"

Lucca held Katja firmly by the arm and led her back to the bedroom. Pushing her roughly inside, he said:

"Oh! And you give me the money back. You did a good job, but ..."

"You bastard! I did what you wanted, so why can't you just let us go?"

Marcel rose to his feet as Lucca snatched the money off Katja and pushed her backwards.

"Stay out of this, Signore. This is not the time to play hero unless you want bullet in the stomach."

Lucca covered them both with his gun as he backed out of the room and shut the door. They heard the sound of the lock turning.

The two of them looked at each other and Marcel caught her in his arms as Katja's legs began to give way. Then they heard the sound of gunfire.

Up on the high ground the watchers heard the shots and the crash as the window of the living room shattered.

Frisoni spoke quickly into his radio.

"*Avanti! Avanti!*"

The armed police squad quickly fanned out across the grounds and converged at a run on the house. Their shouts could be heard up on the hill and like a Napoleonic general Frisoni gave orders guiding his troops below.

Marco had ducked just in time as Lucca fired at him through the window on hearing the stones hit the glass.

"*La puttana*! She lie to me," Marco shouted as he threw himself on the ground. "Some bullet proof glass!"

The police were firing stun grenades over his head into the room and he rolled away fast. The noise and the smoke disorientated Lucca but he regained his presence of mind in time to make it out of the room with the money into the hallway before the police burst in through the window.

In the hall Isabella was waiting for him. He reacted instinctively and dived for the floor. Her first shot hit him in the shoulder and whirled him round. As he fell he reached for his own gun, but Isabella shot it out of his hand. As he lay on the floor looking up at her and screaming in pain, she coolly took aim for his head but at the last moment turned the gun to his stomach and fired a third time.

Hearing the shots the armed police hesitated before entering the hallway from the living room. Isabella grabbed the case with the money, ran through the front door and leapt down the steps. Outside, she just had time to go round the side of the house and out of sight before the police came out onto the front steps. Looking back to see if they were following she crashed into Marco who had managed to reach the back of the house from the other side.

They picked themselves up and ran for Lucca's car parked on the far side of the driveway. She threw the money into the back, while Marco turned the key the chauffeur had left in the ignition and gunned the engine. In a squeal of tyres and a shower of gravel he wheeled the car round just as the police squad swarmed down the steps. Frisoni frantically shouted instructions and a hail of bullets followed the speeding car as it shunted aside the police car stationed across the gateway and roared out of the main gates.

They watched helplessly as the tail lights disappeared round the first bend.

Back at the house the Italian police reported to Frisoni as he and the others came down towards the house.

"One badly injured male in the hallway; one dead male apparently dumped at the back of the house; two dead males in the cellar. One male and one female locked in a bedroom; frightened but otherwise unharmed."

"Thank god for that," said Pierre, when Frisoni relayed the information to the others. "That will be Kokoschka and Bouvier. Neither deserved to die in this mess."

"Marquessa has nine lives – she's escaped again," remarked Antonia.

"Maybe not for long this time. We'll catch her in France," added Patrick.

They reached the house and watched as the paramedics attempted to stem the flow from Lucca's wounds. He had lost a lot of blood but would probably survive.

Pierre and Patrick moved on to look for Kokoschka and Bouvier. They were both still in the bedroom, looking shocked but relieved.

More police cars and ambulances began to arrive and fill the driveway. Frisoni walked around the site with his phone pressed to his ear giving instructions for road blocks and for high security at the airport. He waited impatiently for results, but there was no sign of Isabella and Marco. They appeared to have vanished.

"*Impossibile*!" barked Frisoni. "Get everyone out there looking for them and bring them in. Move!"

In answer to Pierre's question, Frisoni replied:

"Yes! I do what you ask. The Americans were waved through at the check-out just in time to catch their flight. But no-one has seen this Marquessa and Platini. We will catch them. Do not worry."

At the airport itself, the news of the shootings had gone round like wildfire. The crowded check-in hall was full of shouting journalists wanting pictures and details from the police about what had happened up at Signor Lucca's house.

Since none of the *carabinieri* at the airport had any real idea themselves and had only been acting on Frisoni's orders to secure the building, they simply forced the mass of journalists back out of the hall, knocking a few cameras out of the hands of the photographers in the process, and stood impassively behind the glass doors facing a kaleidoscope of flashlights from the outside.

Realising there was nothing more to be gained by staying there the press pack rushed to their cars to race up the hill to Lucca's house. Half way up they reached the first road block and were allowed no further on Frisoni's orders. The more intrepid reporters abandoned their cars and struck out on foot across the maquis towards the house.

Back at Lucca's Katja and Marcel described what had happened, but could not add much to what Pierre and Patrick already knew. There was little the visiting detectives could do and, with Katja and Marcel, they prepared to take their leave.

"So, *molte grazie*, *Capitano*. Not a bad result really. A couple of villains off the scene and you have the big prize. I hope he lives to stand trial and is put away for a long time."

"*Certo, Commissario*. Perhaps this will help us stop such smuggling out of our countries."

"Let us hope so. We will stop the Americans too, never fear."

"I am sure of it. I like your little plan."

Antonia and Eleni looked puzzled as they shook Capitano Frisoni's hand and prepared to leave with the others for the airport. They stood aside for a moment as Lucca was carried out on a stretcher to a waiting ambulance. At the gate a group of out of breath reporters appeared just in time to take pictures of the departing ambulance as it passed them by.

Chapter 24

In the little port of Sant'Antioco in the far south of the island, Marco and Isabella sat at a table by the harbour in the late day sun. The fishing boats lay at anchor or stern on to the dock and the wind had died after the earlier blustery weather. Coming along the quay a fisherman was approaching them. His rolling gait would have told any observant watcher he was a man more used to standing on a deck than walking on dry land. He joined them at the table without a word and accepted the glass of grappa Marco pushed across the table towards him.

Heads down close together the three of them became immediately involved in negotiations. After a good ten minutes haggling the glasses were refilled and raised. The fisherman pushed back his chair and got to his feet.

He pocketed half the agreed fee and went to prepare his boat for the crossing.

"He'll take us as far as Marsala and there we split up."

"*D'accordo.*"

"It's too dangerous for me in France at the moment, so I will fly from Palermo to Roma."

"Won't they recognise you at the airport?"

"Not after I've changed my name and appearance to match my other passport."

"As always, you have all the tricks, Isabella. Maybe one day we make good team the two of us, no?"

He looked thoughtful as he gazed with unseeing eyes across the little harbour. The movement of the boats seemed to mesmerise him for a moment.

"I've an old friend in Sicily who owe me," he said slowly. "He will make me passport. I take ferry to Napoli. After I not sure. Perhaps I just do nothing for a little while. I will think."

They both fell silent, thinking over the past events and on the future.

"What makes me cross," said Isabella, "is that I didn't shoot the bastard in the head with my first shot. He went for the floor so fast I only hit him in the shoulder. But when he was lying on the floor I couldn't quite make myself blow his head off, so I shot him in the stomach."

"You get sentimental now?"

"Perhaps. He was at my mercy and I almost felt sorry for him. But a shot in the stomach is the most painful way to die, so …"

She hesitated a moment and looked at Marco as if for the first time.

"Now it's all over, Marco, it feels like an anti-climax. I've wanted revenge on the bastard for so long. It's as if part of my life has gone."

"I hope he survive and go to the trial. Then he go to prison and die very slow," he replied.

"You've changed your tune, Marco. You used to idolise Lucca."

"I served him well, but he treat me all the time like a dog. I make just one mistake and he beat me and throw me in the cellar. He would have killed me for sure after the deal with the *Americanos*."

They got up and headed towards the trawler which was to take them to Sicily. The crossing would not be comfortable, but it would be discreet.

*

The plane coasted to a halt on the tarmac beside the terminal Merignac airport. They stood up to collect their luggage from the overhead lockers and shuffled their way to the exit. Carrying their hand luggage, they passed quickly through customs and out into the warm sunshine. Marcel steered Katja towards the taxi rank and they got into a waiting cab. Marcel gave the driver instructions and they were soon heading down the ring road towards his flat in the suburb of Cauderan.

"Ouf! It's good to be back," Katja said relaxing into the seat. "That was all too close to the bone for my liking. I promise I won't get involved in any more deals like that."

His response was not what she had been expecting.

"That won't last. You were really on a high there and I have to admit it was frightening and exciting at the same time. Just what I needed to bounce me back to life, thanks to you."

"Do you really mean that?" she said.

"Of course!" he replied, touching his bruised cheek.

At first he had been far from appreciative of his unwitting role in the plot. His face was still sore from the beating he had taken. But, he reflected, the upside was he knew there was much more between him and Katja after their shared adventure. The danger had brought them closer.

They arrived at his flat half an hour later. Marcel showed her into the living room.

"Make yourself at home. I take it you are as hungry as I am. I couldn't eat the stuff they gave us on the plane."

Without waiting for a reply he went into the kitchen. It was the first time Katja had been in his flat and she looked around her taking in the books and the pictures on the walls. It betrayed no signs of female influence but then again it was not exactly what she had been expecting.

Predictably, the shelves contained a number of books about famous architects and the built environment. There were also several works of modern poets and a section of crime novels. The most intriguing section to her was made up of old volumes beautifully illustrated with engravings of towns and people as they were in the eighteenth and nineteenth centuries.

"I'm rather proud of those," he said coming back into the room. "The details are so fascinating and I like to try to imagine what life was like for those people without all the modern gadgets we have now."

"But you would not want to return to those days would you?"

"Not at all. I certainly wouldn't like to live without modern medicine."

He returned to the kitchen and Katja began to look at the pictures and photographs on the walls. The bright colours of the photographs and paintings on one wall were balanced by large black and white images on another. Faced with this carefully arranged décor in the main room, she found herself wondering what his bedroom would be like.

The smell of cooking made her realise how tired and hungry she was. She hovered in the kitchen doorway and watched him at work.

"Do I have time for a quick shower and change of clothes," she asked, suddenly aware of her appearance amongst all the order and neatness of the flat.

"Sorry, I should have asked you before. Go ahead. Do you have everything you need? There are spare towels in the bathroom. It's between the two bedrooms."

She picked up her bag and opened the first door to reveal what was clearly his room. Still neat and modern. The guest room was similar and she emptied her case onto the bed, realising she had nothing very presentable after the last few days of living out of her suitcase. Glancing over her shoulder, she went into his room and opened the wardrobe. She picked out a sweatshirt and hurried back into the bathroom.

Ten minutes later he heard her call out she was on her way. She came out of the bedroom wearing her last pair of clean jeans and his sweatshirt. The table in the alcove was laid and Marcel came into the living room carrying the plates. Seeing her standing there, looking slightly nervous, he said:

"You look great – I like the sweatshirt."

"Sorry, I …"

"I'm teasing! Have a seat. We both need this. Only a salad I'm afraid."

"Don't apologise, Marcel, it's perfect."

For a while they said nothing, simply enjoying the calm and the food and wine. Marcel finished before her and pushed back his chair. Katja looked up as he rose from the table.

"Don't move. I just thought I would put some music on. Any favourites?"

"No, you choose."

"Zaz, OK?"

She had expected jazz, but was pleasantly surprised at his choice. He went back to the table and poured her more wine, saying:

"I'll just go and change."

Marcel returned to find Katja carrying two cups of coffee over to the table. He went across to the sideboard and took out a couple of glasses and a bottle of Armagnac.

They sat talking over what had happened in Sardinia.

"Well, I suppose that will be the last time I will be involved in authenticating works of art," Katja said.

"I don't see why," he replied. "You have a gift for it."

"I'm not sure I would have survived if you had not come out to rescue me, Marcel. Lucca is a vicious man."

She shuddered at the memory.

"I wasn't very good at the rescuing bit. Lucca took me in all too easily. He certainly could turn on the charm when it was needed. I can quite see why you agreed to work for him."

"That was kind, Marcel. I feel such a fool."

Outside the light had begun to fade and darkness had fallen when their conversation came to a natural end. There was a brief moment of hesitation as they stood up. Then Katja took his hand. In the bedroom, she kicked off her jeans and crawled between the cool sheets. Marcel drew the curtains and went across to her. He sat on the edge of the bed looking down at her and she reached up softly to touch the bruise on his face.

*

Back in Athens, the four of them sat around the table in Antonia's flat. The first bottle of wine was soon replaced by another as they analysed the consequences of what had happened on Sardinia.

"So, we have finally delivered Lucca up to Italian justice, thanks to Marquessa. Though I think she would far rather have finished him off herself on the spot," said Pierre.

Before anyone could respond he added cryptically: "And of course we have seen the last of the Americans."

"How do you know they won't try again?" responded Patrick, deliberately taking the bait. "You haven't told us why you asked Frisoni to let them leave the house before sending his men in."

"He's right. Why didn't Frisoni have their car followed? And why weren't they stopped at the airport …?" added Antonia. "The Italians would have loved that."

"And what did he mean when he said he liked your little plan?" added Eleni.

Pierre smiled as he looked round the table and saw the frustration on their faces. Instead of continuing, he changed tack:

"… but we are still left with question of how Deveau died," he said ignoring their reactions. "Was it just from natural causes, or at the hands of Platini or even Marquessa? Both of them had been in his flat at various times as we now know."

"That's true," said Patrick, "but the post mortem was inconclusive."

"So we may never know," Pierre replied,effectively ending the conversation. They were going to get nothing more out of him that evening.

With a sigh Eleni got to her feet and, glancing at Antonia, indicated it was time for her and Patrick to leave.

As they were preparing to go, Pierre looked at Patrick and said:

"Yes, that's enough for now. I suggest we all meet at the Commissariat here in the morning. We need to restore communications with Bordeaux and to organise our return. There is nothing more we can do here in Athens."

"But you can't go before tomorrow evening. Kóstas is organising a celebration at his restaurant which promises to be quite an event," said Antonia quickly.

"*Pas de problème!* We can't miss that. I'll let Bordeaux know we'll be having an important debriefing here tomorrow evening and they can expect our return the following day."

"Till tomorrow then," said Patrick as Eleni steered him towards the door.

Pierre saw that Antonia was gathering up the plates and glasses and was about to take them into the small kitchen. He went over to help.

"Are you still hungry, Pierre?" she asked. "I can do us some pork *souvlákia* with *tzatzíki?*"

He nodded his agreement.

"We'll need another bottle then."

He went to the cupboard and picked one out. He looked at the label and let out a gentle sigh.

"Sorry it's not like the wines of Bordeaux, but I thought I would try to educate you in genuine Greek wines," she said, rescuing the bottle from his doubtful hands.

"Oh! I'm sure it's great. I was just looking to see where it came from."

"Liar!"

They sat down and Pierre realised he was hungrier than he had thought. They ate without saying much, both still engrossed in mulling over what had happened over the last couple of days and trying to make sense of it.

"It still annoys me the Americans will walk away from this scot free," she said.

"Don't worry, they won't get away with it this time and they have paid dearly for the manuscript."

"What do you mean? What are you not telling me, Pierre? You can be the most annoying person, I've ever known!"

"*C'est bizarre*, Patrick sometimes thinks the same. All will be revealed at Kóstas' little party for us tomorrow evening."

Later, as she looked down at him and saw the grin on his face, she pummelled his bare chest in exasperation.

"Are you going to tell me now? I have you at my mercy, Commissaire."

"I am aware of that, Chief Inspector, but I have no problem with it."

*

The small fishing boat was approaching Marsala on the island of Sicily. Down below in the only shelter where they could talk discreetly out of the sight and hearing of the captain, Isabella and Marco were splitting the money 60/40 as agreed.

Unmarked used American dollars are a bonus, thought Isabella with a grateful nod to the Leontarakis.

"So, what will you do now, Marco?"

"I've been thinking more about that. I will go back to Tuscany and train up my own *tombaroli* – this time I will be the *capo*. There will be no Lucca."

"Well, be very careful, Marco. Do not show the money around. Someone will tell the police for sure. That could give both of us away."

"And you, Isabella? What will you do?"

"Me to know and you to only guess."

*

They converged on Kóstas' restaurant. As usual he greeted them with huge bear hugs and showed them to a table. The other customers were all smiling as the four of them sat down and everyone began to shout and clap.

"Uncle, you old fox, what have you done? What have you told them?" said Eleni.

"Nothing really. Only that we celebrate tonight and the drinks are on the house."

"If you've done anything else and Lýtras hears of it, I will personally arrest you, Kóstas," said Antonia.

"No worries. My men will rescue me, I am sure of it."

Suddenly turning on his heel and heading for the kitchen he called over his shoulder:

"Stay. I have a little surprise for you."

He went through into the kitchen and reappeared shortly after with Chief Superintendent Lýtras, who was carrying a small case. Antonia and Eleni did not know whether to look embarrassed, worried or pleased to see him in the restaurant. Pierre rose to greet the Athens Chief of Police and they spoke quietly together before Lýtras turned towards Antonia.

"Do not look so surprised, Chief Inspector. Kóstas and I go back a long way. He always keeps me informed of his activities."

"You mean …"

"Yes, of course,! I know everything. Or at least I think I do," he added with a sideways glance at his old friend.

Both Eleni and Antonia remained speechless, staring accusingly at Kóstas who had assumed an air of innocence ignoring Eleni's wagging finger.

Lýtras looked pleased with the effect he had had and resumed:

"My congratulations, Chief Inspector. A good result – the Italian police are delighted to be able to get their hands on Lucca at last. They sought my permission to present you with a small appreciation, which I readily agreed to. They would like it to be displayed in the Museum for all see, but it is nonetheless a personal gift for you."

He put the case carefully down on the table. The others stood up to look over Antonia's shoulder as she snapped the catches open and pulled back the packing to discover a magnificent Etruscan bowl.

"Capitano Frisoni asked me to say he would always be happy to welcome you back to Sardinia, should you have occasion to go over there. And of course you too, Commissaire."

"But just not at the same time, I think, Ioànnis" said Kóstas with a twinkle his eye. "I don't often raise my glass to an Italian, but I make an exception this time."

They raised their glasses and Lýtras turned to Antonia.

"I have another surprise for you, Chief Inspector," he said. "The Patriarch is so impressed with what you discovered in the monastery library he has asked the Museum to send in experts to catalogue the manuscripts properly. In return the Orthodox Church will allow the whole collection to be displayed in the National Library of Athens."

"That is fantastic news."

"The Patriarch knows they do not have the resources or expertise to research the manuscripts properly and to preserve them, so the arrangement will ultimately benefit them too."

Glasses were raised. The atmosphere in the restaurant was beginning to warm up and the **balalaikas** were speeding up the rhythm. The main course arrived and Kóstas refilled everyone's glasses.Lýtras turned out to be a very amusing raconteur telling stories that had never reached the press. Antonia and Eleni remained overcome with amazement at this side of Chief Superintendent IoànnisLýtras' character which he had never revealed to them before.

Eleni looked quietly aside at Patrick who had been eyeing Pierre more and more as the meal continued.

"Are you thinking what I'm thinking?" she whispered.

Noticing their lowered heads and complicity Kóstas broke in:

"Be careful, or the other guests in the restaurant will think you are about to make an announcement!"

Eleni made a face at him and turned towards Pierre.

"Well Pierre, are you finally going to tell us what you have done about the Americans? You have kept us in the dark long enough."

"Yes, Commissaire, you really should tell them," Lýtras said. "For once I am not the last to know what is going on; but everyone else is mystified. You must tell me how you do it – I can't keep anything a secret it sometimes seems to me."

All eyes were on Pierre. Kóstas topped up his glass and Lýtras leaned forward the better to catch what he was going to say over the sound of the music.

Pierre sat back and took a folded newspaper cutting out of his pocket, straightened out the creases on the table for dramatic effect and looked round at his expectant audience.

"You will remember I had a second interview with Katja Kokoschka? She knew Lucca was no fool and she couldn't lie to him without him catching her out."

He paused and glanced down again at the cutting, smoothing out imaginary creases. Kóstas laughed as he watched him.

"This is as good a performance as I have ever seen on stage. Your have missed your vocation, my friend."

With a smile Pierre looked up and continued.

"We decided she would tell Lucca the truth, that is, that the manuscript Platini had brought him was a fake. The next step was for her to agree to tell the Americans it was genuine. In fact we now know it was Platini who suggested exactly that, which made it all the more convincing."

He took a sip of his wine.

"Things nearly went wrong when first Marquessa and then Bouvier turned up. However it made Kokoschka's capitulation seem more genuine when Bouvier was threatened."

He paused for effect increasing the frustration of his listeners.

"So go on," said Antonia, poking him in the ribs.

"As we saw, the Americans paid up and left the house with the manuscript. Kokoschka had agreed to make out two documents. One authenticated the manuscript as genuine and the other stated it was a facsimile. We heard Lucca even make a joke of it to the Americans reminding them to show the right one to the customs officials."

While he had been speakingLýtras **had been peering over Pierre's**
shoulder looking at the cutting spread out in front of him. Again
Pierre came to a stop.

A strange silence had fallen throughout the restaurant as
conversations on the other tables gradually dried up sensing something
was going on.

"So, finish it Pierre! You still haven't told us anything we don't
already know. Why did you and Frisoni let the Americans leave? We
could have charged them at least with attempting to smuggle out works
of art, perhaps even with complicity to murder."

Antonia looked ready to snatch the cutting from him. Ioànnis looked
at Pierre.

"Will you permit me, Pierre," he asked with exaggerated politeness,
enjoying the game, "to read out the cutting from the New York Times
which you have brought with you. It isn't often I get the last word in.
Twice in one evening would be very special," he added, looking
amusedly at Antonia and Eleni.

"With pleasure, Ioànnis."

Pierre passed the cutting across to him and he began to read under
the stunned glances of Antonia and Eleni at this familiarity between the
two men which they had never guessed at.

"This is a report from the New York Times of two days ago," he
said, looking round over his glasses. The headline reads:

WELL-KNOWN ART DEALERS ARRESTED AT JFK FOR
SMUGGLING STOLEN WORKS OF ART.

"It goes on:

"Well known American art collectors and museum benefactors George (54) and
Mira (52) Leontarakis, of Greek origin, were taken into custody at JFK airport
late yesterday afternoon by officers of the FBI art crime squad. They had in their
possession what they were convinced was a genuine rare eleventh century manuscript,
but presented a certificate signed by a well respected French art expert attesting the
manuscript was a copy.

"But following a tip-off from the Greek Fine Art Fraud Squad, the customs officials found another certificate hidden in one of their suitcases clearly confirming that the manuscript was in fact a genuine chronicle from the European Crusades.

"Certain they had the genuine article, the Leontarakis had intended to sell the Crusader's Chronicle on to the highest bidder, possibly a museum which would not ask too many questions about how they had obtained the rare document.

"However they had been victims of an ingenious sting organised by the Greek Art Fraud Squad, who had planted a facsimile on them. The provenance expert was working with the Greek police and had assured the Leontarakis that the facsimile was in fact a genuine manuscript. They asked her to provide them with a second certificate, which is the one they would present to the American customs officers, stating the document was merely a facsimile, not realising it stated the truth about the document."

"So the Leontarakis will never be able to deal in the art market again. They'll be a laughing stock, falling for such a trick," said Antonia.

"No museum or auction house will touch them either," continued Lýtras, "that was Pierre's plan, to destroy their reputation. One more illegal dealer put out of business, at least for while, for which we and the Italian Art Fraud Squad are extremely grateful."

Kóstas slapped Pierre on the back:

"Once more we are indebted to you, my friend. You know you will always be welcome here in Greece."

Lýtras looked at Kóstas and nodded. Kóstas turned to the waiter and appeared to call for more wine.

Moments later the waiter returned carrying a large carefully wrapped package which he placed in the middle of the table for all to examine.

"This is for you, Pierre," the Chief of the Athens police said, pushing the package towards him. "I think you may guess what it is. The American authorities were reluctant at first but finally agreed it could be returned to us. The Director of the Museum wishes me to present it to you in recognition of what you have done for the heritage of Greece. The facsimile is rightfully yours, as, thanks to you and Patrick, we still have the original."

"Let's hope the Museum hasn't muddled the two up," laughed Kóstas pouring more wine. "I wouldn't be that surprised. I think you'd better ask Katja to check it, Antonia. We don't want to turn the Commissaire into an art thief! "

*

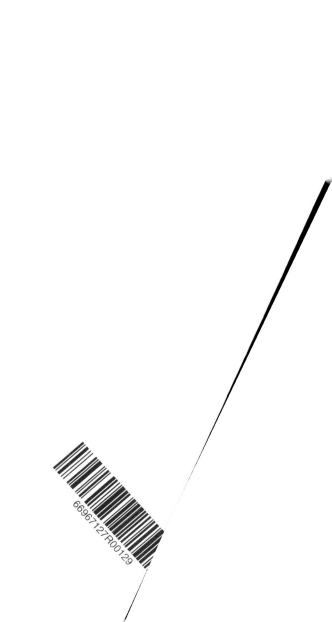

Printed in Great Britain
by Amazon